SINGLE IN THE FIELD

Newly-qualified, cautious and a little shy, Rachel Bellamy arrives in the small Cotswold town of Milchester to begin her veterinary career, assisting Malcolm Halliday, the respected local man. Halliday is kind and protective, but still, Rachel is a woman, scarcely five feet tall and inexperienced. She knows there will be trials ahead. Rachel is right; she is to meet diffident farmers with amorous sons, problem animals and awkward owners.

SINGLE
IN THE FIELD

by
ANNE KNOWLES

MAGNA PRINT BOOKS
Long Preston, North Yorkshire,
England.

British Library Cataloguing in Publication Data.

Knowles, Anne
  Single in the field.—Large print ed.
  I. Title
  823'.914(F)   PR6061.N547

  ISBN 0-86009-894-X
  ISBN 0-86009-895-8 Pbk

First Published in Great Britain by Methuen London Ltd, 1983

Copyright © 1983 by Anne Knowles.

Published in Large Print 1986 by arrangement with Methuen
London Ltd, London, St. Martin's Press Inc, New York.

Photoset in Great Britain by
Dermar Phototypesetting Co, Long Preston, North Yorkshire.

Printed and bound in Great Britain by
Redwood Burn Limited, Trowbridge, Wiltshire.

she wanted to work with the larger animals. She had said as much, and had got the reaction she knew she must expect, as her gender and small size were set in the balance against her qualifications, her reports from the Shropshire vet with whom she had seen practice, and her sheer determination that the Milchester job was the one she wanted.

'I am afraid even nowadays you may find that in our profession being a woman does in itself put you at a disadvantage; and in a farming practice, physical strength is often a necessity,' Malcolm Halliday had told her. Halliday was the man with whom she had made up her mind she was going to work. He was tall and thin, grey and fifty: a man of excellent reputation as a vet and very little reputation for humour, but he seemed to find something to amuse him as he made this remark. Rachel was, after all, small even for a woman, and with very little bodily weight behind her. She had learnt to live with jokes about her size. Her grandfather had been a great one for teasing her about it when she was a kid, saying she ought to stand on the muck heap and grow a bit. Then at college she had scarcely been able to reach the bony cranium of the skeleton horse they used in lectures, and Mark Ames, the horse man, had advised her

11

to stick to Shetland ponies, as he solemnly fetched a stool for her to stand on. There had been a good deal of laughter from a tutorial group that had been, to a man, male except for her, and although she had tried to ignore their amusement, inside herself she had felt as cross as a wet cat.

With the experience of two failed interviews behind her—one for a job she had been turned down for, and one she had herself decided against—she had gone to this one prepared to defend her ability as a creature its young, and had quite pounced upon Malcolm Halliday's expected remarks when he uttered them.

'We all have to live with our handicaps,' she told him. 'I should like the chance to show you that mine don't make any difference, either to me or to my work.'

So she had got the job. To her amazement, he had looked at her, very grave and serious, for a long silent moment, and then had stretched out a thin grey hand for her and said, 'Start in three weeks then?' without more than a colouring of doubt in his voice, and with a solemn assurance that she would get no more than her fair share of the small animal work and no less then her due of the surrounding farming practice.

And now, in a day or so, she would start

work, and the thought brought a keen and nervous excitement with it; an itch to be started, an anxiety to prove herself. She still had not grown accustomed to the fact that she was now a proper, qualified vet, fledged of all her feathers, capable of diagnosis, decision, treatment, care and, above all, responsibility, where the animals of the practice were concerned. It seemed to her, if she thought too hard about it, that her long years of training had launched her on a vast sea of theory upon which the tiny amount of practical work she had done might prove a rather frail craft. She could envisage waves and whirlpools of an alarming sort, and sometimes she felt plain scared, but hell, no one should know it. She was on her way now, to something she had set her sights on many long years ago. She had got this far, where many had failed.

She tried to relax in her seat, to adjust her short back to a shape designed for giants, and after a while the clacking rhythm of the train began to lull her as it had done her nodding companions. She closed her eyes, and let her thoughts drift into dreams.

At first inconsequential, the pictures in her sleeping brain began to show her familiar things. She was in a building like an aircraft hangar, huge, lofty and cold. It had a well-known smell about it. She thought hard and recalled what it was. The whole huge place stank pungently and inescapably of sheep. In small pens on either side of passageways that transected it the great modern barn was full of ewes; some vastly pregnant, some with lambs, some bleating, some vacantly chewing, others regarding their limited world with the stolid gloom that so often seems to creep over animals that are too much in the grip of man. The little party of students, like a small flock themselves under the shepherding of Colin Ross who had come to lecture to them, had spent the morning restraining sheep, up-ending them, injecting them, learning how to hold small slippery lambs correctly, and how to ring their tails and castrate the ram-lambs with the least possible discomfort to them.

Rachel drifted about in her dream, perform-ing these tasks alongside her shadowy compa-nions, and then, half-waking, recalled the reality of that day. She was seeing practice with Colin Ross in a very rural area of Shropshire, not far from Gobowen, and he had taken her along with him on a lambing course that he was running for the local Agricultural Ad-visory Service. She had learned a great deal from Colin Ross, and on that particular day she felt she had gained more knowledge alongside those trainee shepherds and flockmasters than in many a long hour in the lecture hall. Ross made no caustic comments about her size, nor did he allow her any concessions to it, except to point out to her, as to the others, that knack and skill outwit sheer strength every time.

'Watch old Joe there,' he had said, pointing out the farm's under-shepherd, a frail-built old man who looked to have no strength in him at all. 'He's no size, but he can turn a ram as clever as a judo expert.'

Rachel had watched: had seen the old man's dexterity as he caught and up-turned a disgruntled creature that must certainly have out-weighed him.

'I'll never do that,' one of the students commented.

'Just give it fifty years,' was Joe's reply.

Then Colin Ross had announced that he intended to introduce them to Cynthia.

Cynthia was a plastic ewe. Curled up in a most unlikely position in her hard and inhospitable womb was a cold, dead lamb, real and pathetic in this hollow pretence of maternity.

For the rest of that bleak, draughty February afternoon Rachel had both watched and assisted as the lamb was delivered from every possible position until the poor dead creature looked like a limp rag. There were several women in the group of trainees. In all this manipulation Rachel was interested to see how their smaller hands made the task easier for them. One or two kept their own flocks already and were there out of interest, to increase their knowledge, and they spoke to Rachel with pleasure and enthusiasm of the stock they owned, their lambing totals, their plans for the future. She had felt enormously encouraged by them, even on such a cold and exhausting day. She recalled her weariness, the stiff ache of her bones, the effort of replying briskly to Colin Ross's 'Tired, Miss Bellamy?'

'No, not a bit,' she had told him. 'It's been a really useful day.'

'Good. I'll take you to Parsonage Farm tomorrow. Cattle. You'll need a good breakfast. Even with a little know-how, cattle are heavy work.'

'Yes, Mr Ross.'

'Have you had experience with cattle?' he asked.

Had she felt any need to be defensive with him she would already have declared it, but there had been no need.

'We have a Jersey herd at home. Eighty head. I've helped with them since I could

16

walk.'

She could not help a glint of triumph in her voice, and he smiled, aware of it.

He looked at her. 'Bellamy,' he said, reflectively. 'Goodness me, are you one of those Bellamys? Parkwood Sweetbriar, Champion at the Royal?'

As she nodded, he said, 'Well, well, so those are your father's cattle.'

She smiled and said, 'No, my mother's. Father died five years ago.'

Colin Ross took his sheep-stained hat off and swept it dramatically before her, with the respect due to one who is associated with the finest Jersey herd in England.

'I bow to the Bellamy women then,' he said. 'A force to be reckoned with.'

His voice seemed to go on sounding in her head and her limbs ached more and more from the efforts of the long day in the lambing shed, which looked for a moment just like Paddington station with its platforms a-jostle with sheep. She shook herself to unstiffen her bones, and awoke fully and suddenly in the train again with one of her unheeded companions, the fierce-faced woman with the documents, asking if the next station would be Reading. Rachel had dozed away almost a third of the journey.

17

It was Reading. The Metal Box Company to their left and the brick and glass tower of the Thames River Authority ushered them in to the grubby station and the echoing garbled announcement of where their train had come from and whither it was bound. Doors clattered and slammed, and the sun came out and peered at them through cracks in the dusty awning. A paper cup rolled gently along the platform, until the pink-haired boy—who had left the train to be replaced by a dapper little man in a tweed suit—kicked it in passing, down on to the line. Posters advised, go here, buy this, life is not complete without----. People shuffled past with heavy cases, not sparing a glance to either side, ignoring these messages, and once pink-hair had completed his cocky progress down the platform and vanished through the exit only a bunch of school children on an outing, and a young couple holding hands by the bookstall, showed any animation at all.

Watching the people on the platform, glancing again at the other occupants of the carriage, Rachel was glad that she would have animals under her care, not humans. The communication of animals, without the intermediary of language, was direct, honest, unshifty, their motives uncomplicated. Still, as Malcolm

Halliday had pointed out to her at the interview, ninety per cent of the animals she would treat would belong to somebody, and the treatment she gave would be influenced by, modified by, even at times made useless by the attitude of the owner. 'You have to think of the owners as your patients too,' he told her. 'Like it or not. For myself, misanthropy is a luxury I have had to force myself to forgo. You are young enough to be more tolerant by nature, but there will be moments when you may be tempted into disliking the human race.' Halliday was a strange man, there was no doubting it. There seemed to be no warmth in him, except for the odd illuminating flash of wit, yet she was looking forward to working with him, and had heard nothing but praise for his work, even at the local pub where she had stayed overnight for her interview, and had had him described to her as 'a funny old bird, but the best there is.'

The publican, Bill Saunders, hard put to conceal his amazement that here was a woman after a job as a vet, had told Rachel it seemed odd to him that Mr Halliday should want to take anyone else on at all, when he had worked alone for so many years and shown no inclination for company. 'And not a man, I must say, to suffer fools gladly,' Bill had announced, with it plainly readable in his expression that female fools would be even less easily tolerated. Well, they would all be waiting to see if she was going to be a fool or not: the local farmers, the hunt kennels, the stud at Ashton Wick, the indulgent parents of pony-mad daughters, the owners of the countless dogs and cats and small furred creatures that populated the market town and the surrounding villages, these would be her examiners, and more searching than any she had faced yet.

The train drew now into Swindon, sighed and fell silent. A smaller train would take Rachel on its single track towards her destination. She allowed the carriage to empty, saw her temporary companions scuttle away to whatever awaited them, then took her suit-case down from the rack and braced herself for the next step.

'I'm a vet,' she told herself, firmly. Somehow, it did not seem likely at all. She could not convince herself. Perhaps that conviction would come the first time the telephone summoned her out to a case, or when the door opened on her first surgery morning. She climbed down from the train and joined the stragglers on the platform. Someone smiled at her.

'Nice day. Come far?' It was a pleasant

greeting; the voice broad Gloucester, the face plain and open. An elderly woman, round-faced and brawny, was staggering towards the local train weighed down by the spoils of a day's shopping in the town.

'I'll be glad to get off my feet,' she said. 'Coming my way are you?'

'Yes,' said Rachel.

'On holiday, is that it? Left it a bit late in the year, haven't you?

'I'm going to live in Milchester,' Rachel said. 'I'm a vet.' It sounded better this time.

'Well now. Just fancy that.' The idea seemed to please Rachel's companion. She hitched up her shopping bags and trundled along towards the train by Rachel's side, chirpy and interrogative. They found a carriage door ajar, and climbed aboard, both encumbered with luggage, and the older woman sat down with a great sagging of springs and a sigh like a tyre deflating. Her friendliness lightened Rachel's heart. She felt, like a physical lifting, relief from that anxious determination that had pressed on her throughout the journey. She felt she could live among people like this old dear, and be happy.

Now the second train of her day moved away from the platform with a fussy, self-important foot, leaving the complexity of lines around the station, until ahead of her, through the driver's window, Rachel could see the long perspective of the single track. On either side the September countryside looked prosperous: rich land that had yeilded well, and lay moist and brown under the plough, ready to start the year again. Pastures were still lush and green, with cattle grazing in them quite unworried by the passing of the train.

In one enclosure of paler sward, nibbled down close to its roots, roamed a small flock of Jacob's sheep, straked and spotted, and with fantastic horns. In some far fields, horses stood under a cluster of trees as if posed for a Stubbs' painting: a couple of them with necks interarched were grooming each other with their teeth, the muscles tensing under the brightness of their skin. Rachel regarded all these creatures with a farmer's as well as a vet's appraisal, and the horses with that particular pleasure that she always felt in watching them. She was glad there would be horses. This was hunting country, of course, and a centre for polo and show-jumping and gymkhanas and all such gatherings as a horsy community will indulge in, so she was bound to be involved with them to some extent at least. Of course it did not do to let it be known that horses were your real interest, that you hoped above all to be able to work with them. Rachel knew she must show herself content with the bread and butter of her trade, the commercial animals that were the livelihood of the district. It was good bread, excellent butter. Horses would have to be cake, to be enjoyed when available but not expected. With looking out at the view, and half listening to the elderly woman's recounting of her day's adventures in Swindon, this short second journey was soon over, and at the next small station Rachel collected her luggage and got down from the train, to be waved away by her new acquaintance, who wished her well and, with enthusiastic gestures through the window-glass called out that she hoped they might meet again and to be sure and look out for her if she was ever in Swindon of a Friday.

The train left, the station settled back to quietness. Rachel watched the retreating shape for a moment, then picked up all her stuff again and walked through the gap marked 'Way Out', relishing the freshness of the air, the smells of a mild autumn evening. Outside the station, in a small dusty square surrounded by picket fencing, Malcolm Halliday was waiting for her, to drive her to Milchester. There was no railway in Milchester now. It had been 'rationalised' in that fit of reformimg zeal that removed so many miles from the chain of railways that bound communities together. Now the station at Milchester was a Social Centre, its railway bridge had been pulled down, and the community was still squabbling over what should happen to the old permanent way. Small industries had sprung up like desert flowers in the old goods yards and sidings. Some flourished still and had been incorporated with a modern industrial estate where plastiglass buildings tried to be unobtrusive among their careful shrubberies, others had withered in the recession and faded away, leaving their boarded-up premises to the demolition men.

Rachel saw Malcolm's car at once, and walked towards it. It had surprised her that he owned a new Peugeot estate: it seemed totally unlike the kind of vehicle one would have expected of the man. She could envisage him in a dusty black Humber, at least two decades old, or a Riley of an even earlier vintage, kept not out of enthusiasm but because of having no desire for change. Such a car she had imagined he would drive when she first met him. Then he had taken her out to see some local farms in the gleaming vehicle towards which she now walked with her cases, and, out of character or not, it was obvious that this reliable, efficient machine was essential.

She could see Malcolm Halliday now, climbing out of the car. He set out towards her; formal, cool, if possible even greyer than she remembered him. It was a greyness not only of hair and eyes, and the pallor of his face, it was his whole atmosphere; an air about him, that she found, oddly, not at all displeasing.

He shook her hand, took her cases, asked her pardon for not having met her on the platform, but as he had arrived just as the train was pulling out it had seemed more sensible to wait where he was. All this he said in a tone which was, in the proper sense, dispassionate. Rachel found herself replying with equal gravity, and catching herself at it, smiled inwardly. She regarded him, covertly, as they got into the car, and decided with relief that she liked him every bit as much as she remembered doing at the interview. Since that occasion she had discovered quite by chance that two other applicants had elected not to take up the post as they had not felt they could work with him. She could see that it would be possible to find him unlikable, even forbidding, but was very glad that she had not been deterred. As they drove, Halliday would occasionally point out some house or farm, identifying each not so often by its name or the name of its occupants, as by what case he had most recently treated there. Apart from these comments, they drove without conversation, and not to have to make small-talk was a relief to Rachel. It had been a long day, and it was not over yet. She settled back and let the landscape slide past.

It was not long before they came into Milchester, approaching through that new small industrial estate where the station had been. The inevitable rows of brash new housing clung to its edges and spilled down into the surrounding fields where old timber fencing had sprouted high barbed wire to keep out the trespassing young. The wide road that led through this area then swept on round a roundabout and away towards Oxford, but the car took the local road, which narrowed between grey houses, becoming a plain, sober street of stone walls and slated roofs, with occasional little dark shop-fronts: a bakery, antiques, books, a pet shop with rabbits in the window. Then from this little canyon of houses it opened itself out again into the town's central square: pleasant, wide and cobbled, which was the site, as Rachel had already been told, of the Monday market, the annual Mop Fair, and any other such junketings that the town saw fit to put on. At one side of the square the huge parish church towered up, sunlit and beautiful, built as much to the glory of the wool-trade as to the glory of God, or at least to salve the consciences, even to save the souls, of the merchants who grew fat on the fleeces of the Cotswold long-wool sheep. Whatever the motives of the purses that funded it, the masons had put their skill into it, to give it a singing, airy quality that caught Rachel's breath. From somewhere in the high tower a bell spoke, and all the grey walls seemed to catch the sound of it.

'It's such a pleasant town,' Rachel said. 'There seems no sense of hurry to it.'

Malcolm Halliday considered this in silence for a while.

'Familiar things are seldom sufficiently appreciated,' he said at last. 'I have lived in Milchester all my life, except for my university years. Apart from minor changes it has remained very much the same, and I somehow assume it always will. It is pleasant enough, I suppose. Now, if you remember, we take this turning here, just past the saddler's shop, and we shall soon be home.'

After only a few more streets, just as the fields began again, and the landscape was opening up to the blueness of far woods and the huddled shapes of distant villages, they came to Stapleton House, where the surgery

27

was, where she was now to live.

'I shan't put the car away,' Halliday said. 'I shall be going out again later.'

It was a formal, stone house, symmetrical as a dolls' house, with a central, panelled oak door, windows set about in precise order, and a small flagged forecourt surrounded by a wall. The wall was low in front, and curved up at each side to meet the frontage of the house at the level of the tops of the ground-floor windows. Vertical iron railways sprung from the lower part of the wall, and a railed gate to match stood ajar immediately opposite the front door. There was something almost French in the severity of its design. There was a sombre quality about it despite the warmth of evening sunlight that washed the stone, which was dressed and smooth, unlike some of the smaller cottages they had passed that day, their rough walls built with the same dry-stone technique as those at the field edges, enduring but unsophisticated, their appearance belying the skill with which they were built.

Rachel looked up at Stapleton House, and liked it every bit as much as she had at first sight, at her first nervous approach on the day of her interview. Now the gate stood open for her. Halliday was sortng out equipment at the back of the car.

'Please, do go in,' he said.

Rachel picked up her suit-cases and walked down the warm flagstones to the door.

CHAPTER 2

It had been a family joke, and was part of Bellamy family history, that Rachel's father had had nothing to offer her mother in marriage but a pocket-sized farm in north Oxfordshire, and his few beautiful Jersey cattle, yet to him these had been like some ancient tribesman's gift of riches, which she had accepted in a similar spirit. She would have taken him without them, and he knew it, but it had been the greatest satisfaction to both of them to have this corner-stone to their marriage. Surrounded by rich farmers whose acreages stretched to the horizon, they never managed to become rich themselves. Their economy limped under the perpetual assaults of incoming bills and outgoing capital, yet under her father's skilful stockmanship the cows bloomed into prize-winning condition, and he became known and very much respected on every major show-ground as his golden girls paraded their splendid shapes and fruitful udders, time and again to carry away whatever prizes there were. Brought up on this small farm, her whole life involved with it, it did not occur to Rachel that things might be different; that there might be holidays, new clothes, bicycles, tape recorders. Once in the village shop she had overheard herself discussed by two old biddies over a quarter of tea. 'Poor little mite, never a new dress to her back. That Bellamy thinks more of his cows than he does of his own flesh and blood.' They had not seen her standing there behind them, but they had heard her all right when she had shouted at them, and stormed out of the shop, slamming the door so hard that the jangling of its bell had sounded on in her head all the breathless, tear-choked way home.

Her father had hugged her, and laughed, and said what did it matter, that she knew it wasn't true. Then they had gone off together to the barn to name the new calves, and he had let her name the best of the heifer-calves. She had decided on Parkwood Fuchsia, and neither of them were sure if they had the spelling right so they had to look it up to be sure, and he had made a stupid pun about there being 'no future in it' that had made Rachel's mother groan. Rachel knew now how lucky she had been having such parents. Even in her awkward years, kicking against the world and everything in it, when everything that was long-established seemed suddenly oppressive, she had been rock-sure of their affection.

The high peaks of her life as a small child had been the outings to cattle shows: the culmination of all the extra feeding and grooming and spit-and-polish, the teaching of young calves to lead on a halter, the holding of the breath in case some great hope should suddenly become ill or lose condition. She had felt, like electricity, the tingling excitement of these occasions, and was filled with enormous pride at the sight of the great plushy championship rosettes with which her father so often left the ring. These victories were not the only pleasure Rachel felt at the show-ground. She was about five when she first found her loyalties being drawn away from the familiar cattle to the ring where the glossy ponies pranced and snorted. She found she loved the smell of them, the polish on their hides, the exuberance of their movement over the bright green grass. She began to watch out for horses and ponies in the fields and lanes at home, and would take any opportunity that arose to speak to them; occasionally, and with bated breath, to sit on one. Never did she entertain any thought of ownership. That was for dreams. Then, when she was nine years old, a neighbouring farmer—whose five children had all learned to ride on an ancient shaggy creature who had taught them enough for them to venture on to mounts that were larger and more demanding—came to the Bellamys' farmyard one morning with a Landrover and trailer, its rear doors enclosing a mystery. Rachel herself had been lifted up to unfasten the stiff metal pegs of the top doors of the ramp: had stared large-eyed and dumbfounded as the opening of the trailer had revealed an unlooked for but most passionately desired gift. Nero, the black, hairy, out-grown pony was elderly, lugubrious, with a tendency to aches, pains and minor ailments for which, as they revealed themselves, Rachel searched assiduously in every book she could find for alleviation or cure. To keep him well enough to ride, she learned patience, care and skill. She also found that to see him eased, where he had been hopping with lameness, was a satisfaction in itself: it rewarded her. She had always helped when the cattle were ill or injured, watched them calving, helped pen them for tests and injections: that was all part of the normal run of life, but this cantankerous Nero was her own responsibility, had his own quirks and conditions entirely unlike those of the cows, and as she searched books in pursuit of his care she learned how hugely complex is the system of any animal, and how enormously varied the diseases that may attack it, the accidents that may befall it.

When Miss Blanchard, the local vet, came to the farm for any purpose, Rachel would follow her, hound her with questions, watch everything she did. Miss Blanchard encouraged her. She told Peter Bellamy that his daughter had a real interest, a genuine gift: that she should be encouraged to use it.

'Make sure she works at school. Keep her at it. Otherwise she won't get in.'

'Get in?' Peter Bellamy had enquired.

'College, of course,' Miss Blanchard had snapped, exasperated, as if he were being deliberately obtuse. 'She'll have to go to college, if she's to be a vet.'

'A vet?'

'It'll be a damned waste if she isn't,' was the answering comment.

Mary Blanchard was of the generation of women who snatched their qualifications from a wasps' nest of ridicule, prejudice and physical abuse. She had, in her time, had stones thrown at her, her instrument case filled with cow-shit. Her early years in practice had been a long hard struggle, and she had gone hungry many times while she persuaded the local people of her ability and her skill. Now,

34

many years later, her weather-worn appearance and fierce manner were familiar to the whole country, and Peter Bellamy, among many, would have no other vet. She ran her own practice, was one of the bigger chiefs at the local veterinary hospital, and was consulted with considerable deference by the ministry vets at the Animal Health department. Most people had forgotten she was a woman at all, she admitted on one occasion to Peter Bellamy, and she had cackled with pleasure, as if that were in some way a compliment. She had heard some young lad with his ears still soapy say something of the kind at a conference she was attending, and she had snorted at him like the old war-horse she was, so that he had cowered in his seat.

'It wouldn't be easy, you know,' she went on. 'You mustn't let her think it will be. It's still hard for women, even now. You don't get rid of stupid prejudices by passing laws against 'em. Besides all that, it's a thankless enough job in itself, a good deal of the time. Your patients are a pretty ungrateful lot on the whole, and all the thanks you get for your efforts are some great beast treading on your foot, and the knowledge that its owner will stick your account behind the clock and forget about it for as long as possible. Still, someone's got to do it. It might as well be someone who'll make a good job of it.'

The Bellamy's had taken it all as something of a joke, to begin with. Rachel, perhaps, most of all. Yet as she continued to help with the cattle, to practice her doctoring on Nero, that sparked-off interest kindled. Once or twice she went out on rounds with Mary Blanchard, acting as unpaid nurse and animal attendant; holding syringes, marking sheep after their injections so that they did not get done twice over, soothing nervous creatures, helping to hold refractory ones. In his decreasing patches of soundness she learned to ride about the farm on Nero, and found herself watching the cattle as they grazed with a different and keener eye. She learned at last, and harshly, how to lose a well-loved friend when she could find no more remedies for Nero's ills.

She worked like a demon at school, to the amusement of her friends, and the amazement of the staff, who had seen her as a dreamy child, anxious only to be out of the classroom.

Her mind was made up now, and it was of her own making. Miss Blanchard had only made it clear to her. She would have found her own way to it in the end, there was no doubting that. Her whole thought became concentrated, channelled. She struggled to over-

36

come a natural disinclination for maths, which she knew would stand like a tank-trap between her and any chance of a university place. Amazingly, after agonies and efforts, it resolved itself, and left her way clear. As, with her contemporaries, she grew older, she saw how many of her friends drifted and dreamed, wafting their newly acquired curves into endless romantic situations with shadowy lovers, or in some cases, with a spottier and harder hearted reality. She appeared to listen to their sagas of conquest or defeat, whilst mapping out in her mind the bone structure of the dog. She pushed to one side the glamour mags which were the bible to them, and which they lent to her in hopes of reformation. She could dress up as gaudy as any of them when she felt in the mood, shatter the quiet farmhouse with the shuddering beat of the Stones records that Martin Tanner from the Glebe brought over to play to her. She went out with him once or twice, with a handful of others, but never for long. Instead she pored over anatomy books, and drew precise diagrams of the genitalia of the larger mammals. Her friends gave up and said there must be something wrong with her. One or two even edged away from friendship with her in case she was queer. There was nothing odd about any of *them*, after all. Once she was at college, she found to her relief that she was not alone in feeling this driving force, this compulsion towards a goal. Here friendships were easier because motives, interests, were of a like kind. She grew, too, out of the intolerances of her teens, all her unnecessary rebellions. She grew up.

Now, when her parents came to visit her, or when she went home to them, she saw them as people, loved and special, but people in their own right, no longer mere adjuncts to her own life, and certainly no longer an enemy against whom it was necessary to assert herself. She saw, ruefully, that they were as relieved as she was by this new relationship. Her mother urged her not to overwork, her father, to take advantage of the time, to widen her horizons. Her blossomed self saw the wisdom of this, and she did so: went to concerts, joined the dramatic society, ate meals in smoky basements with the young men who were her colleagues, set the world to rights with the handful of women who shared the course with her. In all the disciplines there were still more men than women, and Rachel, being both intelligent and presentable, was amused to find herself very much in demand. The young men took her to muddy rugger matches and expected her to cheer them on. It was all a great game and she enjoyed it, but always she was aware of where she wished her life to lead, and this was no real part of it. By treading lightly she kept these friendships as she wanted them, easy, uninvolved. 'Frigid,' said those who had asked more and got short shrift. She laughed inwardly, knowing she was nothing of the kind. A clock doesn't have to shout 'cuckoo' all the time to prove it works. She knew that within her was more than one kind of passion. Sometimes they merged in her to create an almost frightening energy; but always the urge to achieve what she had set out to achieve was strongest in her. To be herself, she needed to achieve it.

So when there was work to be done, she drove herself fiercely, never allowing herself second best. She would work into the night on black coffee and biscuits, fall on to her bed sometimes still in her clothes, and wake at first light, aching and cold; but she was resilient and young and it did her no harm.

After one particularly demanding session of work, spring sunshine had tempted her out with some friends to a favourite pub in a nearby village. It was a thatched, pink-washed house by a stream, with wooden benches out under willows in their first brilliant green, and ducks with a passion for crisps, that brought them waddling web-footed out of the water to any hand that would feed them. The sunshine was cool and bright. It flashed in brilliant shapes off the broken planes of the swiftly running stream, and threw their reflections on to the stone arc of the road bridge that spanned it nearby. It was a day to think in deeply: more intoxicating than the tall glasses that quenched the thirst of the group that laughed and talked together under the trees.

When Rachel came back to her rooms she was so full of the sparkling elation of the day that she almost danced the last few paces to the door. She went in, singing, her face bright. There, in the armchair by the window, her mother sat like a stone, and when Rachel saw her expression, laughter died in her that would take many months to resurrect. Mary Bellamy came towards her daughter, reached out to her.

'I had to come,' she said. 'I couldn't have told you on the 'phone. I couldn't have said the words into a 'phone.'

Her arms went round Rachel and there was a silence, a taking of breath.

'Darling, your father died this morning: just suddenly: there was very little pain.'

Rachel felt the world shift on its foundations. Her mother held her as she swayed, led her gently to the chair, sat her down, and knelt beside her, holding her hands fiercely, as if the small pain of that might help the terrible ache that gripped her.

'It was angina,' her mother said. 'He'd had attacks before. He would never let me tell you.'

Why had he not said? Why had he not given her the chance to savour every moment of him, to make every effort to see him, to let him know she loved him? Too late now. It was the old, sad cry, too late. Her grief verged almost on anger that he had not told her, but what use was it to be angry? He was dead.

Slowly, in her misery, she came to realise that her mother, who was comforting her, must be even more desolate. The marriage had been so unfashionably close and enduring. For over twenty years they had completed each other, complemented each other. Now they were wrenched apart by some pointless, useless whim of fate.

Rachel and her mother held each other tightly; two desperately sad women in the sunny, light-filled room, weeping until all their tears were done.

At home in Parkwood a week went by, leaden, unreal, as in a terrible dazedness they went through all the necessary ordeals. It occurred to Rachel that she should offer to give up her studies and stay home until her mother had had time to recover and decide the future of the farm. It was the last thing she wanted to do, but it had to be volunteered, so, ashamed of her own reluctance, of a scarcely admitted longing to escape from the sadness of the house, she made the offer.

'Don't be silly, dear,' her mother said, smiling gently at her as if Rachel were a child again, and had spoken some mild nonsense.

'But how are you going to manage?'

'Rachel, my love, when people have to manage, they manage.'

'But what will you do?'

'Do?'

'About the farm—and everything.'

'I shall run the farm, of course. I shall keep on the herd: do the shows your father had entries for.'

There was no doubt in Mary Bellamy's voice. She spoke as if this were the only possible thing. Rachel, in her whole hearted pursuit of her own chosen profession, had had little time to spare to consider her mother's abilities. Father had been the stockman: mother, quietly, his assistant, groom, nurse, second-in-command. It seemed to Rachel, as she looked perceptively at her mother, that maybe she might not make a bad job of it, at that.

All that she had set herself to do, and more, Mary Bellamy had accomplished over the next years: had slowly increased and improved the herd: had ploughed her grief into the soil of the farm, enriching it with the love whose original object she had now lost. The oppressive sadness in the house that had weighed Rachel down in those days after the funeral vanished from it, and Rachel was glad, always, to come home to it. Her father was remembered everywhere, yet it was not a memorial to a dead man, but flourishing and vigorous. Mary Bellamy developed a financial flair, greater than her husband's; revealed a genius for when to buy and when to sell. She invested well and expanded wisely; applied for grants, put in new equipment. Rosettes and silver cups still came home to Parkwood, and good sweet milk filled the cooling tanks every day when the cows came in from the field.

Rachel, waking early in a strange bed on her first morning at Stapleton House, imagined how her mother would be standing now in the milking parlour, dungareed and booted in this first grey light. She would call out to Sam the cowman, 'Let 'em in,' and through would come Dulcie and Coral, Bella and Daisy, to their known places, dark-eyed, smelling of the wet grass and the coolness of morning. Rachel felt a childish, inward lurch of homesickness; only for a moment, only because she was not yet truly awake. She sniffed, stretched her feet down into the bed, glad of an hour more in which to assemble her thoughts, to arm herself for the day.

Her rooms at Stapleton House took up one half of the first floor: there was the room in which she now lay and another smaller one connected to it; a box-bedroom, which had been converted into a bathroom; or not so much converted as declared a bathroom within the meaning of the act. In recognition of this an ornate bath with clawed feet rested itself upon a peninsular platform. There was also a basin on a moulded plinth and an impressive lavatory with a mahogany seat. Pipework rambled here and there upon the walls like a climbing plant, and had proved itself to be, as Rachel had suspected, the kind of plumbing that sings to itself at midnight.

Rachel surveyed her present, immediate surroundings as the growing light revealed them. The furniture was dark and carved, and although it had not yet reached antiquity, it would arrive soon. The bed was complete with heavily decorated headboard and footboard. There was a large wardrobe, a tallboy, a dressing-table and two plump upholstered chairs set each side of a gas-fire in the wall. The walls and woodwork had been freshly papered and painted some twenty years ago, and the room little used since, for the creamness of the paint and the brownnes of the wallpaper had no marks or scars on them. They were not so much worn as weathered to the various shades of parchment colour that they had not attained. Rachel had not been surprised to learn from Malcolm Halliday that this had been his mother's house.

'I have the use of it for my lifetime,' he had told her. 'I have cousins abroad, in Australia. It goes to them eventually.'

Halliday had approached with some diffidence, at Rachel's interview—once the decision had been made to appoint her—the question of where she should live. It was evident that a man would have been expected to live 'over the shop', and there seemed to Rachel no good reason for her not to do so. It was a large enough place to give privacy to them both.

Now that she was established, her first day about to begin, she did wonder whether he really minded her presence in the house: he gave away so little of what he felt. His morning greeting, when she went downstairs at

45

what she hoped was an acceptable time, was meticulously courteous and correct as usual.

Breakfast was surprisingly good: orange juice, wholemeal rolls that tasted home-made: good coffee, out of a pot, not out of a jar. Halliday ate very little, but pressed her to do so.

'At midday it is a moveable feast,' he said, 'to be seized if you're in a position to do so. In the evenings, however, Mrs Partridge cooks a meal for us. She keeps the house clean, and so on. I do not expect you to be domestic unless you wish.'

He made his excuses, and left her to finish her breakfast. She was glad of the respite: glad to have time alone, to give up the pretence of good appetite and calm efficiency. Her nerves were plucking at her as she realised how the time was drawing on towards morning surgery. Soon he would be introducing her to their customers. He would not call them 'clients'. 'It makes us sound like hairdressers,' he had said to her.

When Rachel had looked around the private rooms at Stapleton House she had wondered why Malcolm Halliday had not put more of himself into the place. It had obviously remained the same for years. Then when she had seen the surgery she had realised that this was probably the only room that mattered to him. The surgery and the waiting-room were large, pleasant and airy, overlooking the lawn and vegetable garden at the back of the house. The approach to the waiting-room was by way of the car park at the side of the house, so that there need be no invasion of the privacy of the other rooms. The surgery itself, as Rachel had already seen, was gleaming—clean and with new paint, well stocked with modern equipment, orderly and efficient.

On the turn of the passageway that led to the surgery, a long mirror hung against the wall, and as she passed it Rachel could not help but glance at herself in it. It showed a small, slender competent young woman, dark-eyed and pleasant faced, her dark hair drawn neatly back. She felt that her appearance successfully hid every doubt and uncertainty that trembled in her, but she paused, for all that, and stared harder at her reflected self, to be sure.

Outwardly she did indeed look spruce, attentive, like a newly preened bird, in the white overall that had only just come out of its wrappings.

Inwardly she felt like the first day of school. She entered the surgery, and the session began at once. Halliday did not ask how she felt, made no concession to her newness. She was to find that he never did. Having assessed her competence, he expected it to be consistent.

The waiting-room was full, mostly of elderly men and women with dogs or cats. There was also a harassed young girl with a toddler, a baby, a pregnant bulge and some pigeons in a basket.

'Come in,' Malcolm Halliday said to the first in the queue. Rachel felt as if she were on trial, as one after another the people came in with their pets, and eyed her curiously. She wondered if, despite her lack of inches, she measured up, and to what expectations.

To her relief, the cases that morning were all quite simple: there was nothing to baffle her, to stretch her beyond her capabilities. She began to relax a little, enjoying being busy.

Halliday, occupied with plastering the broken forepaw of a small brown dog, indicated that she should deal with the next patient.

'It's me cat,' the next in the queue informed Rachel, quite unnecessarily, for the creature clasped in the arms of his owner was enormous, furry and undeniably feline. 'I wants 'im neutralised.'

At the sound of this voice, and hearing its request, Halliday looked up from his plastering and called across the surgery: 'Mrs Allerton, you know I only operate on Tuesdays and Thursdays, except in an emergency. You should have made an appointment to bring Tiger in on one of those days.'

The cat's owner looked at the two vets with a heavily patient expression and explained carefully that they'd took off the Tuesday bus, hadn't they?

'Well, we'll make it Thursday then, shall we, Mrs Allerton?'

Mrs Allerton's expression shifted to mild exasperation. 'You know there's no bus on Thursday, Mr Halliday.'

'All right then, leave Tiger with us. We'll operate, and bring him back to you. I've got to come out your way to see Mrs Holder's goat. Would you put Tiger in one of the cages in the recovery room, please, Miss Bellamy?'

Rachel took the huge cat from his elderly owner. He was relaxed, purring, his claws sheathed. Mrs Allerton, on the contrary, was all a-bristle with agitation. She sidled up to Malcolm Halliday and whispered hoarsely that he would see to Tiger himself, wouldn't he, as 'it wouldn't be quite nice for a lady to do it, would it?'

'Please don't worry,' Halliday assured her. 'The proprieties shall be observed,' and he ushered her politely out of the surgery, his face grave. Over her shoulder he looked across to Rachel and allowed himself the glimmer of a smile.

'I think it's the pigeons next,' he said. 'They belong to the pregnant lady's husband. They've got a vitamin deficiency. So, I suspect, has the young woman, but we have to stick to treating the pigeons.'

The pigeons, who had had a week's treatment with Abidec, were looking pert and perky, their eyes bright, their beautiful subtle coloured plumage in good order, their feet like coral. Rachel prescribed another bottle of their cure and observed brightly that it was excellent stuff for people too. The young woman heaved the baby up so that it rested above the bulge, anchored the toddler's hand to her skirt with admonitions not to let go, and picked up the pigeon basket in the remaining hand.

'You having me on?' she said, looking dispiritedly at Rachel.

'No, really I'm not. Why don't you ask at the clinic? Now, can you manage all right?'

'Have to, won't I?'

Malcolm Halliday had been scrubbing the surgery table, and came up just as the door closed behind the little group.

'He's a real pigeon-fancier, her husband.'

'It seems to me he'd do her a favour if he'd stick to fancying pigeons,' Rachel said.

CHAPTER 3

By the end of the first week Rachel had tested cattle, castrated piglets, removed a damaged horn from a Jacob's ram that was all muscle and determination. Compared with the work into which she was plunged, her days with Colin Ross had been restful. It amazed her that Malcolm Halliday had, until now, coped with so much alone. Rachel had the additional drain on her energy of being uncertain how she would be received at each new house or farm at which she called. As Miss Blanchard had warned her, so long ago, the law might now say she was the equal of any man in her work, but around Milchester that was still a matter for persuasion, and she very soon grew accustomed to being greeted at farm doorways with, 'Where is 'ee then?'

'Who?'

'Mr Halliday, of course. The vet!'

For some it was simply a surprise to see her. With others she sensed a real hostility, a rudeness that made her angry, though she was careful not to show it. 'Womanish' bad temper was not likely to plead her cause well. So, against odds, she kept calm, did her work and closed her ears.

Only once, in that first week, did she run across real trouble, and that was when John Hamden, a farmer at Shipton Clive, refused to allow her to attend a cow with milk fever, and when she protested, had telephoned Malcolm Halliday long and loudly, voicing his opinion of 'bloody women'. There was nothing Rachel could do. She could not insist, but had to go on to the next call, knowing that now Halliday would have to make a special visit, and hoping he was not going to be given too much cause to regret having taken her on.

She had made her apology to him later, and he had seemed quite surprised she should find it necessary.

'But it's a long way for you to go. Your visits were all in the Stroud direction,' she said.

'I didn't go,' he told her. 'I said he could telephone you tomorrow for a visit.'

'What did he say?' Rachel enquired, dreading the reply.

'What he said is immaterial,' Halliday said, drily. 'I am the only vet locally who will attend his stock, because he has such a bad reputation for paying his bills, or rather, not paying them. If I will not go, then he must

53

call you, or lose his cow, and he knows it.'

Next day, to Rachel's amazement, John Hampden telephoned and asked, though with unconcealed annoyance, that she should call. When she arrived, the farmyard was empty, and a note had been pinned to the door of a shed saying, 'Cow in here. Will pay at end of month.' No-one came near while she saw to the beast, which was just as great a relief to Rachel as it obviously was to John Hampden.

The sensitive tendrils of local gossip soon picked up and passed on the news that the new vet was a female, even to the remotest holdings of the area, and gradually the utterances of surprise with which Rachel was so often greeted began to fade away, though she knew she faced a lifetime of seeing and hearing disbelief expressed that someone not only of her sex but of her size should undertake the jobs she set out to do. Sometimes she herself quailed, but she learned. Every day she found and practiced techniques of animal handling that were, as Colin Ross had suggested, a kind of veterinary judo. And when in spite of all she tried, she found some manoeuvre impossible, then she would command help from the nearest supply of muscle.

'Can't you manage then, miss?' one pigman was ill-adivsed enough to ask. They stood in an enclosure containing a huge old Gloster Spot sow, of imponderable weight and irritable temper. Her small eyes showed no enthusiasm for having the gash in her side sewn up by Rachel. The pigman stood with his hands in his pockets, all set to enjoy the proceedings, and Rachel felt small twitchings of panic beginning to stir in her. Then she took a quick, steadying breath and said, crisply: 'It's my brain you're paying me for: I suggest you hold the canvas, and I'll get on with the master-piece.'

He had looked at her for a long moment with his mouth open, as if about to counter this remark, but to her relief he did not. Instead he got the huge creature into a crush, with annoyingly little difficulty, and held her still while Rachel sewed her up.

As Rachel went farther afield, travelling about the narrow lanes around Milchester, she grew slowly familiar with the local country-side: the spare, stony fields of the Cotswold landscape, so different from Parkwood's lush pastures, its gentler undulations. Milchester itself stood on a slight downward sweep of the wolds, so that you could see the high church tower piercing the view from many miles' distance as you came down from the villages of the plateau. Then over towards Stroud the rounded wolds spilled over into little secret combes, and beyond them there lay the great valley, all gravel and clay, that was silvered along its length by the sea-bound Severn.

On these early, misty mornings of mid-autumn the smaller valleys were bowls over-flowing with mist, and distant clumps of trees looked flat and grey against the swirl of it. The whole landscape was in washes of grey like a Chinese painting.

On one such morning, Rachel, driving down from the high curved fields to the west of Milchester, slowed the car and looked across at the drift of the mist among the dark trees. Her destination lay in one of those deep valleys. It would be like dropping down into a cloud.

It was cold too, she discovered, as the lane twisted downward and hedges loomed on either side, hung with a million water-drops. There was more hedgerow here, and less wall: not easy to build walls on these steep-angled fields. It was new country to her and not part of their patch anyway, but Lady Bramwell, an old friend of Malcolm Halliday's mother, was insistent on having Malcolm to treat her animals, though the Stroud vets were a good deal closer, and Rachel wondered how it would be possible to arrive quickly in case of emergency.

'She's an autocratic old bird,' Halliday had warned Rachel. 'I don't think any creature of hers would dare to die without her permission. She used to sit on committees with my mother, though a good deal higher up the table, I suspect. She thinks I'm still in short trousers, and pays me as if she were tipping the paper boy. She'll be amazed to see you, I don't doubt.'

When she arrived at Fletcher's Mill House and climbed out of the car into the cold damp air, Rachel found her knees were shaking, and not only because of the chilling mist. As she walked to the steps that led to an imposing studded door, she chided herself, made up arguments in defence of her person, her presence, her right to practice her hard-won skills. It was all very stupid, for there was no need at all. Lady Bramwell could accept her, or do without. Still, within her head the thoughts ran about like agitated mice and would not be still.

A butler opened the door. He was tall, large-boned and impressive in his uniform, and well schooled in the aloofness of his calling. He led Rachel through the hall of the beautiful old Cotswold mill-house. The walls were unrendered stone, the floors of polished, golden oak.

Paintings in plain frames hung everywhere and their colours were fresh, brilliant; their subjects a reflection of Cotswold in all its seasons. This was not at all what Rachel had expected.

The butler opened a door at the far end of the hall, and announced to the room beyond that the veterinary surgeon had arrived. 'Malcolm, my dear boy!' A very old woman rose from a chair that had its back turned to the doorway, turned, held out her hand and stopped, with her mouth still open from the greeting.

'And who might you be?' The voice was sharp.

'I'm the—er—veterinary surgeon,' Rachel informed her. 'I believe you have a horse that wants vaccinating.'

Lady Bramwell came across to where Rachel was standing and inspected her thoroughly, walking all round her as one might when appraising a horse for sale.

'Small, aren't you?' she said. 'So'm I. Never found that a disadvantage though. Sit down. Sit, sit.' She propelled Rachel across to a chair by poking her in the small of the back with a bony finger tipped with a pointed nail.

'What's your name? Where are you from? Where did you train? What do you think of young Malcolm, then?'

58

It was a bullet-hail of questions. Rachel answered them, while the old woman leaned forward in her own chair and listened, and said, 'Yes. Well. Go on,' from time to time to encourage expansion.

At last she seemed satisfied: stood up, indicated that Rachel should do so too, and said abruptly, 'They'll show you where the horse is. Go through that door there.'

Rachel began her exit from the room. As she reached the door, the old woman spoke again. 'I'm a Pankhurst, you know. On my mother's side.' Across a passageway a door stood open into a lobby, and from there another one led out into a stable-yard, where a groom stood waiting with a bay horse.

At the door, still as an Easter Island statue, and with an expression just as unreadable, stood the butler. In his hand he carried a small silver tray of a kind once used for calling cards. Perhaps Lady Bramwell still used it for this purpose, but now it bore a small rectangular box with a cellophane cover, and towards this box the butler dipped his high-bridged nose and murmured, 'Madam would wish you to take these.'

They were Rachel's favourite sweets: chocolate peppermints of the most expensive kind. The sort one hoped for at Christmas and seldom received. She could smell the luxurious smell of them, and could taste their richness in anticipation. Perhaps this was a traditional 'perk' for the vet at Fletcher's Mill House. 'Thank you,' she said, allowing a dignified tone to disguise a childish delight in the gift.

She walked across and made herself known to the groom. She examined the bay horse to see that he was well. He was a grand sort with good limbs and a fine head. He looked in splendid health.

'No cough, no discharges?' she asked.

'No, miss.'

'Right. I'll inject him then, and give you the certificate. Then that'll be him safe against tetanus and 'flu. He's a nice fellow, this. Who rides him?'

'Her Ladyship.'

'But she must be ninety if she's a day!'

'Eighty-seven, miss. Have you got the chocolates?'

'Well—yes, I have,' Rachel said, wondering why he should ask. Was he hoping to be offered one?

'You'd better give them to him, then. He always has his chocolates after his injection.'

Rachel opened the box, her mouth watering.

'Here,' said the groom, grinning, 'you have one. He can't count.'

Rachel drove back towards Milchester by way of a goat with mastitis, a lame donkey, a goose belonging to the shopkeeper at Allington Ford, which had swallowed a fish-hook, and a Staffordshire bull-terrier belonging to a Mrs Randall at a remote farm, who dared not bring the brindle bitch into the surgery. 'For if there's another bitch there, her'll have it, quick as you like.' The dog was brimming over with affection, her lips stretched back to her eyes in a welcoming grin. She looked to Rachel the least aggressive creature in the world as she met her on the garden path and escorted her to the kitchen door, where Mrs Randall was waiting.

'Come in, then, Miss Bellamy. I'll have to trouble you to wait while I wash my hands. I'm all over flour.'

Mrs Randall had been making bread. Bowls of dough were stood to rise on a shelf above the stove. There was flour on the table, on the old woman's arms and all down the front of her apron. She busied herself, clearing up.

'I make it for my sons,' she said. 'Their wives don't seem to have the knack, somehow.'

'I'll look at Bess then, shall I?' Rachel sked, the kitchen table now being clear. 'What a friendly dog she is.'

'That's as may be,' Mrs Randall said, 'but

don't you let her fool you. We had a salesman up here last week. Span'll he had, in the back of the car, and the window left open. He got him by the ear-hole and dragged him out. The span'll I mean, not the salesman. Killed him. Stone dead.'

With new respect, Rachel stood the Staffordshire up on the kitchen table to inspect the wart on her foreleg that Malcolm Halliday had been treating.

'Is it improving?' she asked.

'Oh, a lot better. Mr Halliday said if it wan't, it would have to be cut out. I don't want that. Bess wouldn't like that, would you old bitch?'

Bess lashed at her plump, muscled thighs with her tail and grinned even wider. Her teeth were large and white and seemed to march forever back into her capacious jaws. She turned her head and clamped them gently on to Rachel's wrist as she examined the foreleg. The teeth only lightly touched her skin, but she could sense the terrible power of those jaws.

'Mr Halliday always ties her mouth up with tape. Can't see why: she wouldn't hurt him.' Rachel knew that in all commonsense she should have done the same. Bess was an engaging bitch, friendly, and to people at least soft-natured, but it was a risk, and Rachel knew

62

she was stupid to have taken it. Well, I'm learning, she told herself, as she left another bottle of dressing with Mrs Randall and walked down the garden path to where the car stood among the ruts and potholes of the farm track.

She had wondered what they would do about sharing the Peugeot. She had no car of her own. Halliday knew that; and having seen his gleaming vehicle she was alarmed at the prospect of being responsible for it. She drove well enough, she thought, but things could have happened to a car on lanes and tracks like these, and in farmyards milling with cattle and blundering machinery, that no-one could avoid. Then, parked in the gravelled square to the side of Stapleton House, he had shown her the bright yellow 2CV that squatted there, gaudy as some exotic bug.

'Yours,' he had told her. 'Goes with the job.'

'Oh!' she had exclamimed, delighted.

'Didn't I tell you? I must have forgotten.'

He was such a strange man: the coolness of him: the quality of being once removed from the people around him. Yet he seemed a little warmed by her pleasure in this unexpected thing: the provision of a car for her own use. Had she been more accustomed to applying for jobs and asserting her rights she might perhaps have asked for one: even demanded it.

She was glad that she had done no such thing. She was not yet hardened against the delights of a pleasant surprise, and she liked this little car with its determined engine and its bright cheerful livery. All right, so it was anthropomorphic nonsense, but she felt it would not let her down. She called it Jessica, after a canary an aunt of hers had once kept. 'Sit, Jessica, and let the sound of music...' and so on. The bird would not sing, but it loved to listen to Radio 3, its head cocked to the sweetness of flute and violin. Jessica, the yellow bug, sang her own songs, her engine gearing itself to the sharp pull up the escarpment gradients, chuntering throatily along the undulating stretches of Roman road that saw a skyline and headed straight for it.

Rachel sang too as she headed homeward. She thought about Colin Ross who had taught her so much of her practical craft: who had forgiven her occasional appalling mistakes and made sure they did not rebound on any of his patients. 'Learn to live with the fact that however good you are, you will sometimes make mistakes. I do,' he told her. 'The thing to do is to catch them quick, shoot them down and bury them. They expect us to be perfect, you know, the people we work for. Sometimes I long for the days when we were just horse-doctors: the barber-surgeons of the animal world. After that we became useful people: not very interesting, but handy enough when you needed a dog put down, or your cattle got something you couldn't cure with granny's remedies. Now we've got fashionable: on the telly and all that. We get invited to social functions. We're acceptable heroes for the women's magazines, along with architects and advertising executives: and so people expect too much of us. They want wizardry in a white coat at the surgery, and God in gumboots on the farm. It's a hell of a lot to live up to.'

Rachel smiled to herself, remembering this, but she had already begun to realise that he was probably right. Those people in Milchester whose job it was—or so they felt—to offer social acceptance to newcomers had made it their business to let her know she was accepted.

'A few friends to dinner...'

'Sherry after church.'

'Buffet lunch in aid of the RSPCA...'

'Do come and support our coffee morning. Of course your time is very valuable, we do realise that, but we'd be delighted if...'

Malcolm Halliday no longer experienced the grasping of these social tentacles. He had frozen them off long since.

'You go,' he said. 'It may amuse you. They'll make you feel like a piece of catnip in a pussycat house.'

When she arrived back at the surgery he was busy with a pekinese whose eyes were inflamed. Rachel went to fetch her white coat.

'It's all right,' Halliday told her. 'We aren't too busy today. I'll manage here.'

He tipped the little dog's head to insert some drops, and it wriggled and sneezed.

'This is what happens when humans try engineering animals,' he said. 'These bulgy little eyes just ask for trouble. A thousand-year-old mistake, these poor little devils are, and we're still doing the same sort of thing now.'

He had not raised his voice, but she could feel anger in him. She was beginning to understand that this grey man was not only an extremely good vet, but also a compassionate one: not by any means an inevitable quality, and not one she had suspected in him.

'How was Lady Bramwell?' he asked.

'Very splendid. You might have warned me.'

He carried the peke to its owner, the last in the waiting room, and began to clear up the surgery.

'Did you enjoy the chocolates?' he asked.

CHAPTER 4

It was a Jersey cow. In an area where she had
so far seen so few of them, that was probably
what had caught Rachel's eye, made her look
again over the fence into the small paddock
where the animal grazed. It would have been
a poor thing at its best, compared with the
Parkwood beasts, but in addition it was dark
with sweat, agonised by some distress or illness to a degree that was obvious to anyone.
It was Rachel's day off. She was in her best
clothes, and on her way to Gloucester to meet
an old school friend for tea and to hear a Bach
recital in the Cathedral. The school friend was
one with whom she had lost contact for years,
and whom she had met again quite fortuitously
in London, discovering in conversation that
she too now lived in Gloucestershire. The
Bach recital was a treat Rachel had promised
herself ever since she saw the first posters
advertising it. She had no wish at this moment
to be involved with a sick cow, and one that she
had not been asked to attend. Maybe another
vet was already on the way to see to it. Maybe.

There was a house not far away, down a short straight drive that ran past the cow's paddock: whoever lived there would most probably own the cow. Rachel sighed, swung the wheel and drove to the front door.

It was a small elegant house, harmoniously proportioned, set down in its own private landscape by someone who had lovingly known his job, some two hundred years ago. It had once been trim and cared for and faithfully tended by, at a guess, four indoor staff and a handful of gardeners, grooms and odd-job men. Now its paintwork was bleached, the gardens gone to wilderness. Upstairs, several windows were broken, and had that black look of an empty room beyond.

A woman came to the door, and her looks so echoed the looks of the house that it quite startled Rachel.

'Yes?'

'I'm sorry to disturb you. Is that your cow in the field by the road: the Jersey cow?'

'Yes.' The woman looked somehow defensive, as if expecting to be accused of something. Perhaps she knew the beast was ill, and had not bothered about it. Surely no-one would be so callous.

'I think there's something wrong with her. She doesn't look well,' Rachel said.

'Oh? I thought you were going to say she's got out again. She often gets out. The fences are weak. Then they complain, you see: the people at the farm next door.'

There was a silence. The women looked at each other, as if wondering what the next move would be. Rachel grew impatient: she had very little time to spare.

'Shall we go and look at her?'

'All right then.'

'Could you lend me some boots, do you think, and an overall of some kind? I'm not really dressed for it.'

'Oh. All right. You know about cows, do you?'

'A fair bit.'

Her best clothes covered in a borrowed overall that smelt strongly of some effluvious animal, and her feet in boots that were far too large, Rachel set off towards the field with the cow's owner, who had made no offer to identify herself. She could have been as young as thirty, from the shape of her figure, but her face was haggard, her fair hair scraped back into a straggly bunch. What energy she had, she seemed to have gone far to find. Her clothes did not seem to fit, and she appeared to be the kind of person who might well once have minded about such things. Hoping to encourage the minimum of acquaintance, Rachel said: 'By the way, I'm Rachel Bellamy.'

'Anne Fowler,' was the response, abruptly.

They arrived where the cow stood, looking worse than ever.

'God she does look bad. Bill will be furious.'

'Your husband?'

'Yes. What the hell's wrong with her, do you think?'

Rachel looked carefully at the cow. Without a thermometer it was impossible to tell for sure, but the sweat that darkened the animal's hide seemed to be more from distress than fever. The cow's udder looked normal, but her flanks heaved and her eyes were wide. There was froth around her mouth beginning to form into long pendulous strings of slime.

'Could she have eaten anything to upset her?' Rachel had glanced around swiftly, looking for yew-bushes, nightshade, ragwort, all the old enemies; but she could not immediately see any.

'She was in the orchard earlier. She might have got at some windfalls. She wasn't there long though because I chased her out. I wanted to hang the washing there and I didn't want her knocking the prop down.'

Washing was indeed blowing on a long line in the orchard next door. There was a laundry

70

basket too, still piled high with wet clothes.

'I've still got all that lot to hang out. Bill must have taken the other line down. I couldn't find it anywhere.'

Rachel puzzled over the cow, absorbed this last last remark without much attending to it. Then like a mild taste with a powerful after-tang it woke up her senses with a start.

'Hold her, will you, Mrs Fowler?'

The woman put a piece of baler twine around the cow's neck. Rachel looked about for a piece of wood to use as a makeshift gag. She found one that seemed smooth and un-splintered enough; then she pulled out the animal's tongue and began to explore the back of the throat with her fingers. The cow's mouth was full of slobber that ran down her arms, under the sleeve of the overall and on to her dress. She heaved up the sleeves of both garments and fished further down, the cow's flesh clammy against her skin. She found it at last: the small ring that completes a plastic-covered clothes line. Slowly and carefully she pulled, and like some amazing bovine conjuring trick, length after length of line appeared from the cow's throat and fell upon the grass.

'Dear God,' Anne Fowler said. It could have been a prayer, but Rachel doubted it. The cow looked greatly relieved.

'She'll probably be all right now, but it might be sensible to get your vet out to her, just to check her over,' Rachel suggested.

'We don't have a vet,' said Mrs Fowler. 'Bill says they're an unnecessary expense. Thank's very much for what you did. I'd never have known what was the matter. Are you in farming or something?'

Rachel smiled. 'I'm an unnecessary expense,' she said.

Mrs Fowler went very pale. 'You're a vet? Look, I shan't be able to pay you. Bill will be furious.'

It seemed to Rachel that it was fairly unreasonable of Bill to be furious if the cow was ill and equally furious if it was better, even if it did cost him a vet's fee, but she only said, 'Please don't worry. You didn't send for me. I invited myself, and there's no charge.'

She arrived too late for tea, had time for only the briefest of chats with her friend, and in the Cathedral she was quite sure that people on neighbouring seats were drawing themselves as far away from her as possible. She felt like apologising loudly and explaining that she was on night-shift in the sewers but their faces told her they were not the kind to take a joke lightly. She closed her eyes and ignored them and let the splendid organ notes soak through to her bones.

Malcolm Halliday knew all about the Fowlers, Rachel discovered when she recounted to him, much later that evening, her adventures with the cow.

'I trust you will not spend too much of your spare time giving free help and counsel,' he said. 'It might catch on. People will litter the roadside fields with their ailing creatures in the hope you might pass by. St Frances *en passant,* as it were.'

'I'm sorry,' Rachel said.

Halliday went on looking through a reference book that he had been consulting, and the conversation appeared to have closed. Then he said, unexpectedly, 'Don't be.' He slammed the book shut, and returned it to the bookshelf. 'That animal was lucky,' he continued. 'Bill Fowler would have seen she was ill eventually, I expect, and he would have tried every kind of home remedy, and she'd have died on him, all to save ten pounds or so.'

He came and sat down in his armchair, across the fireplace from where she sat. He had invited her to sit downstairs for an hour or so after supper if she wished. There was a fire of logs and small coal, which was pleasant in the chilliness of the autumn evenings, and it gave them a chance to discuss the day, as long as neither of them was summoned away by the telephone.

'I feel sorry for the Fowlers, though,' Halliday went on. 'He's self-sufficiency mad, and she hates it. They used to be quite comfortably off until he was made redundant. He couldn't find a job he liked, and he wasn't offered much choice. He's forty-five: not a good age to change the way you earn your living. She's not forty yet, though she looks a good deal older now. Did you see round the back of the house?'

'No. I went to the front door.'

'I haven't either, being a member of the unnecessary profession, but I'm told the old stable-yard's full of hens and pigs, and he's got a mushroom shed and greenhouses and heaven knows what else, on the principle that if there's enough diversity, one of your efforts at least may succeed. He's not very good at it, but he won't be told.'

'She looked sick and tired of it all.'

'I believe she is exactly that. She used to be a very pretty woman. You would see them together at all the big occasions. She used to hunt: he went weekend shooting on the Penhill Estate. None of these things are much of a loss, I suppose, but she must feel they are. Status and the loss of it is very important to people like Anne Fowler. It's like the Chinese losing face.' He got up from his chair and pushed it back from the fire.

'I'm going to bed now,' he said. 'I'll lock up, and perhaps you will put the guard across before you go to your rooms.'

'I will,' said Rachel.

'I'm glad you enjoyed the concert.' He went to the door. Even under the greyness, he looked pale. 'Would you take the surgery tomorrow? I have an appointment to keep.'

'Yes, of course. Goodnight.'

Next day was a Wednesday, when Mrs Partridge came to 'do into the corners' as well as her usual preparation of the evening meal. Mrs Partridge was thin, wrinkled and ageless, and spoke such broad Gloucester that Rachel had to listen carefully, as if to a foreign language. She was agitated that morning over an accident that had befallen her grand-daughter the previous day. Mandy Partridge, having skived off school, had gone up to the local riding centre where pony-crazy girls from every possible background gathered like a flock of birds whenever time allowed. She had told a successful lie about a half-holiday and had been given a free ride in return for hours of mucking-out.

'Poor little kid—fell off 'er 'arse,' Mrs Partridge cried.

Rachel was a little surprised to hear this word from good Baptist Mrs Partridge.

'Got 'er in the 'arspital,' Mrs Partridge said and shook her head over the unreliability of horses. Rachel commiserated with her, and offered a lift into Gloucester to visit Mandy if Mrs Partridge wanted to go in.

'That's nice of you dear, but I'm goin' with Mr 'alliday. 'E's takin' me when I've done me upstairs. I'll do the downstairs when I gets back, and you'll 'ave finished with them animals.'

There were a great many of them that morning. In boxes, baskets, cages, wrapped in blankets, tucked inside coats, a steady stream of minor injuries and ailments flowed through the surgery. Rachel dosed, dressed, injected, stitched. She was enjoying herself: pleased that so many people should care enough for their pets to bring them for treatment. The customers were beginning to accept her, too. The surprised and doubtful looks were far fewer. Now they expected her to know what to do and to do it, just as they did with Malcolm Halliday.

Right at the end of the morning came a man she had not seen before. He was a very ordinary looking middle-aged man in working clothes, but brushed and clean, and there was a careful polish to his boots, brown and glossy as horse-chestnuts.

He had a border collie dog on a lead.

'Put him down, if you please,' he said.

Rachel examined the dog. It was a young dog, clean-limbed, bright-eyed: a bit thin, but with a gleaming coat. He looked at Rachel with his head on one side, intelligent and keen.

'There's nothing wrong with this dog, is there?' she asked. Perhaps Malcolm had diagnosed some hidden complaint, though she doubted it. The dog was quivering with health.

'No.'

Suddenly she felt very angry: all the pleasant small rewards of the morning spoiled. To destroy a dog, a good healthy dog, on what seemed to be a whim, was appalling.

'If you don't want him, Mr...?'

'Hodges.'

'If you don't want him, Mr Hodges, perhaps Mr Halliday or I can find him a home. Or you could advertise.'

'Put him down. Damn it, I want him put down.' The voice was harsh and Mr Hodges' hands were unsteady. She wondered if he were drunk but there was nothing on his breath. Rachel wasn't having it. He seemed so adamant about killing the dog. Deliberately she used the phrase. Be damned to the usual euphemism.

'You want me to kill him?'

She took the dog by his collar, and looked hard at the owner. She could not fathom what it was in his expression that was somehow more than anger. Then he spoke, and every word was an effort.

'I've raised this dog from a pup. He means more to me than any woman could, or child, or friend. He's been going off on his own lately—after a bitch, I thought. He got out again last night. They found him first thing this morning. On the estate: with three dead sheep, and his teeth in another. Kill him.'

What she had seen in his face were tears of desolation. She could do nothing to help but what he had asked her to do. She could not comfort him.

'You go,' she said. 'I'll see to him. He won't feel anything.'

She did the job. It was a job, wasn't it? One she had been trained for. When it was over, and because there was no one there to see, she cradled the dog's body in her arms and wept. A fool: an unprofessional, over-emotional, stupid, female fool. She cleared up the surgery with leaden legs and a hammering head, and she was glad for once when the telephone rang almost immediately, calling her out to a distant farm, to a long drive through autumn lanes, with time and space to recover in.

The trees were losing their leaves to a gusty wind and patches of sky showed through the thinning foliage, altering the nature of light across the fields. It was an autumn light, no doubt of it, though without the richness of sunshine. October, when the sun was out, made for a landscape as satisfying as good music or good wine: now it was grey, with high-flying clouds and chilly enough to make you look for shelter out of the wind, but even so Rachel stopped the car on a high place, and walked to the most elevated point she could find, where the wind roared in a hanger of beeches. The case that she was driving towards was not urgent, and so she spared herself a moment to let the wind blow through her and to look down across the patchwork fields, which lay, not flat and neat, but shaped as if by living forms breathing quietly beneath them. An old sadness welled up in her: of autumn, or mortality, of leaves sent blowing and whirling by a heedless wind. She remembered her father, and found that even after so many years, she ached for him. So she stood until the wind began to blow away her melancholy and she was ready to go on again.

The interior of the little car was pleasantly warm after the buffeting air outside.

'Jessica, my good friend,' she said. 'It's time we were off,' and she patted the steering wheel affectionately. Then she laughed, because it was really so foolish, talking to a car: and then she laughed again and began to hum to herself and at last went 'Rolling down to Rio' at the top of her voice, until it was time to assemble more serious thought and put on a professional face.

That evening as they sat reading after supper, Malcolm said: 'Sorry to hear about Ernie Hodges' dog.'

She was able to call Halliday 'Malcolm' now, though it had seemed difficult at first: he was not a man you first-named easily, and he was, after all, a good twenty years her senior, but he had invited the informality, except of course when they worked together in the surgery—and she was growing accustomed to it.

'Yes,' she said. 'I got it all wrong, you know. I thought he was one of those people that just want rid of their dog. I made things so much worse for the poor man. And do you know it sounds ridiculous, but I kept seeing how shiny his boots were, and thinking how could he set about polishing his boots, to come and bring a dog to be killed.'

'That's just Ernie,' Malcolm said. 'He's a man of habit. Other people might have a drink to give them courage to face a situation like that, or they might swallow sedatives. Ernie will polish his boots. When he's in his right mind, he'll give you proper credit for your reluctance to destroy his dog.'

He went back to his book then, closing the subject. He drew back into himself and became so involved with what he was reading that she might not have been there. On one occasion he had become so abstracted that later on he apologised and said, 'I am used to being alone, you see.'

She felt oddly honoured that he had accepted her into his solitary life: and it was a solitary one, despite the numbers of people with whom he came into contact during the day. It was not contact in the proper sense. Somehow they did not touch him. Only when he was dealing with his patients did he show real animation, real involvement, and in watching him at work Rachel was able to realise why such a man should be so much in demand, almost in spite of himself. She was learning from him, daily. He made no effort to teach her: indeed she felt it would not occur to him that she stood in need of it: he merely assumed that her interest in each case was as consuming as his own. He stretched her, taught her to keep her wits about her and her knowledge at her fingertips. Domestically, the distance remained. His courtesy to both the women of the household, to Rachel and Mrs Partridge, was impeccable. Whoever had taught him his manners had made a lasting job of it, but the aloofness remained.

Rachel had been surprised that he should make apology for his abstraction. She had grown used to this habit in him, and it neither annoyed nor offended her. It was his house: he was entitled to whatever privacy he wished, including the privacy of his own thoughts, even when they sat together in a room. She told him as much, and he looked at her with an expression of mild perplexity, that slowly resolved itself as if something previously unknown had been revealed. Almost, he smiled.

'How refreshing you are,' he remarked. 'That attitude is so unusual.' She had expected '...in a woman', but he did not say so. Once again he returned to his book, the conversation over, and she was left to her own thoughts, to watching the fire shifting and settling in the hearth. For a long while there was silence between them, and then it occurred to Rachel that within herself at least, she *was* making a minor invasion of his privacy: found herself studying the lines of his face in the firelight. It was a thin, long face, the bones prominent in it, with shadows like bruises under the eyes. He had a habit of compressing his mouth when he concentrated so that the lips barely showed. He was doing this now. She noticed, too, that absorbed though he was, his hands would sometimes clench for a moment or so and she wondered if he could be in pain. Eventually, when he closed the book and rose from the chair, she said: 'Did you go to the hospital today?'

'What?' his voice was very sharp.

'I thought you took Mrs Partridge to see Mandy.'

'Ah. Yes. Yes indeed. The child is very much better. She's drawn horses all over her sheets, in biro, and keeps asking when she'll be able to ride.'

When he had gone up to bed, Rachel went to the surgery. It was clean and orderly under the hard bright light. The table was scrubbed, the instruments gleaming in their glass cases; the drugs locked away in their cupboards. They had no overnight patients, and the recovery room was just as empty and clean.

Tired though she was, Rachel found her fingers itching to begin work again. She switched off the lights and went upstairs to bed.

CHAPTER 5

Amy Gunter's mission in life, or so it seemed, was to find out what people around her were doing, and if they were taking the least degree of pleasure in it, making sure they stopped, or that someone else stopped them. All the relatively harmless misdemeanours of humanity she would seize upon like a dog after fleas. She was a fat woman, but in no way jolly. Her face was lardy and she had eyes as black as a ferret's. They lit up only at the discovery of something that could be complained about. Scandal alone animated her. Gossip was good bread to her.

'I saw your Peter up the orchard after them apples,' she would inform some mother waiting at the school gates: or 'D'you know your girl's in the pub with that Albert?' Of someone's new fiancée she would mutter that anyone knew the girl was no better than she should be. She reported mild amorous adventures she stumbled across in the woods, spoiled boys' safaris among the bushes and hillocks of the common by holding forth on all the things they were doing that they shouldn't be doing.

To Mrs Partridge, whose opinion Rachel was growing to respect, Mrs Gunter was anathema. Mrs Partridge believed in letting people go their own way. She was indulgent to a fault towards human frailty, despite her straight upbringing and her own severe morality, which she applied to herself alone. The human race she loved with all its warts, with the exception of Amy Gunter, who was all wart in Mrs Partridge's opinion.

'More sinful than any of them poor folks 'er goes on about,' Mrs Partridge declared.

Rachel had come across the old grundy already. She had come into the surgery one morning, bringing her cat to be treated for canker, just as another patient, a young labrador, was leaving with its owner.

'Got no licence for that, you know.'

Rachel had pretended not to hear.

'Had her last dog twelve year,' Amy Gunter went on relentlessly. 'Never got no licence for it. I can tell you that for a fact. Never no licence. Not in twelve year. It's disgraceful.'

It occurred to Rachel to wonder how such a fact had become known, but she only murmured, as politely as she could, that the labrador was a puppy, not yet six months old.

Amy was not fooled for long.

'That's as maybe,' she said. 'Won't get no licence for it. You mark my words.'

Rachel had bitten back what she would have liked the old biddy to do with her words, and had contented herself with saying quietly that it was possibly none of Mrs Gunter's business.

Some days later, when Rachel went into the Stapleton House kitchen to fetch water for the plants in the waiting-room, she sensed a kind of hovering attention in Mrs Partridge. Rachel was beginning to know Malcolm's house-keeper quite well: had heard how she came to work at Stapleton House ten years ago: 'Since the day after I lost Partridge,' she had informed Rachel, sounding as if he had got mislaid somehow, like the unfortunate Ernest Worthing on the Brighton line. She did not speak of him otherwise: gave no indication whether the marriage had been happy or not and Rachel did not enquire, respecting her privacy as she did Malcolm's. Mrs Partridge had, after all, been entrenched in the household long enough to seem like part of the fabric, and having spent her decade of widowhood caring for Stapleton House and its owner she might well have resented Rachel's presence: indeed Rachel had been quite prepared for this, but far from it. Rachel, too, had been taken under the Partridge wing with great cheerfulness. They had many conversations together in the big kitchen, Mrs Partridge skilfully drawing from Rachel all the short history of her life, so that she soon knew about Parkwood and how Rachel's mother still ran the farm, and about the Shropshire practice, over which she exclaimed with a 'well-I-never' that Partridge's brother-in-law had once had a place in Shropshire and wasn't the world small when you came to think about it.

Rachel enjoyed being sounded out in this way. Coming to live, as she had, in a place where she was not known, but had no past connections, it was a kind of comfort.

On this particular morning, however, something was agitating Mrs Partridge. It was as if she wished to say something to Rachel but whatever it was was making her anxious and had creased up her face in a frown.

She would clatter dishes noisily for a moment or so, and then fall silent: move rapidly across the kitchen and as suddenly pause in flight as if uncertain what to do next. She looked very funny, Rachel thought, but not to be laughed at: she was so evidently worried.

'What's wrong, Mrs Partridge?' Rachel asked, after some minutes. 'Can I help?'

Mrs Partridge, having arrived in mid-flight at the kitchen table, sat down and leaned heavily on her thin arms. 'Oh dear,' she said. 'Oh dear now, something must be said, and I suppose I've got the saying of it, but how I'm to tell you I don't know.' She shook her head as if to rattle some sense into it. 'It's awkward, and that's a fact, but still: got to be told, haven't you?'

Rachel sat down opposite Mrs Partridge. 'Told what?' she asked, encouragingly.

Whatever it was, it was taking a great effort, but at last the matter emerged.

'Well, 'ere's the trouble; and I know you won't think I'm saying this in the way of gossip, but if I don't tell you, someone else may. These things get around in a place like Milchester. Or anywhere else, I suppose. What I 'ave to tell you is about that Amy Gunter. What that old Gunter monster's been putting around the town with 'er nasty evil tongue.'

Mrs Partridge paused here to reinforce her breath, and Rachel waited to be told what it was that was so provoking. The kitchen was bright and sunny. The clock ticked. Mrs Partridge, taking breath, sounded like a little old terrier working up to a fight. Her wrinkled face seemed more than usually wrinkled. Her mouth was pursed as if she were swallowing

89

something distasteful. At last, with an effort, she was able to go on.

' 'Er's been saying—been saying...' There was a sudden rush of words, 'that there's goings-on in this house between you and Mr 'alliday.'

Rachel let out such a hoot of laughter at this amazing and quite unexpected revelation that Mrs Partridge nearly knocked a cup off the table. This time Mrs Gunter had really outdone herself. Ridiculous, malicious old woman.

Her laughter seemed to cheer Mrs Partridge a little, but beneath her amusement Rachel began to feel a growing sickness. She and Malcolm were colleagues, and within the limits that Malcolm would allow, she hoped they were becoming friends. They lived beneath the same roof, because it was the obvious place for them both to live, to be on hand for their work, to be on instant call in emergency. Had Malcolm taken on a man instead of Rachel, would Mrs Gunter now be spreading rumours of homosexuality?

Rachel kept her voice cheerful, glad to see the anxiety fading from Mrs Partridge's face. Rachel took her hand and gave it a little shake.

'Well,' she asked smiling. 'Do you think people take her seriously? Do you honestly think it likely that Mr Halliday or I would risk our careers for the sake of some fun and games? Everyone knows Mr Halliday. Could they really imagine him chasing me round the bedroom with an evil leer?'

Something of the idiotic unlikelihood of this situation tickled Mrs Partridge, made her laugh away the last of her distress. She looked at Rachel, and the laughter burst out into a cackle of amusement. Wherever Amy Gunter may have been at that moment, she may perhaps have been aware of a mental boot in the backside.

Having so successfully cheered Mrs Partridge, Rachel was surprised to what extent the flavour of Amy Gunter's nastiness made the rest of the day taste sour. She wished almost that she could mention the incident to Malcolm. His cool astringency would dispell its unpleasantness at once. However, she and Mrs Partridge had agreed that they would not tell him, and the local people had long since given up trying to regale *him* with gossip.

Even next morning, when Rachel woke early, thoughts of the previous day's conversation in the kitchen had not entirely left her. Her mind, refusing to reason, harped irritatingly upon it, would not let it go, so that eventually, exasperated with herself, she tried

quite calmly and positively to assess her attitude to Malcolm.

She had felt strongly drawn to him as someone with whom she wanted to work, and that
despite his odd remoteness. His disapproval—
which he had made clear to her from the outset
—of eager enthusiasm as a substitute for detailed knowledge and considerd skill, she saw
reflected daily in his own work, and supported
wholeheartedly, even though within herself she
was aware of the effort it took to channel the
former into the latter. Fire—new knowledge
is mercurial: it has a tendency to rush hither
and yon, eluding the grasp; all there, but not
necessarily in the right place at the right time.
Rachel admired Malcolm's detachment, relish-
ed his rare praise, and as they worked together,
felt a growing, though unstated affection for
him. That was hardly sufficient for Amy
Gunter to hang her hat on though, and as for
any qualifications Rachel might have as a
femme fatale, they were equally insubstantial.
She was woman enough to be glad she was
pleasant to look at. She was not so prim that
she didn't enjoy being whistled at in the street.
She enjoyed the cheerful banter of the men
behind the stalls at the Monday market: it
boosted her morale, lifted her spirits. Unlike
Miss Blanchard, being female was important

to her, and female she was proud to be, disadvantages or no.

She turned over in bed and peered at her dim reflection in the mirror on the wardrobe. She could not see her face. It was still almost dark, and all that was visible was a pale blur. Still, she knew she was not unattractive. Her job might come a long way first with her, but for God's sake, she was only human. Had Malcolm been a very different kind of person, perhaps she might have been drawn to him in a way that might justify Mrs Gunter's nastiness, if such nastiness can ever be justified. As it was, her feelings for him were of professional respect, tinged with a mild pleasure in knowing that he accepted her presence in his life without apparent resentment. That was the most she would ask of him.

It was scarcely light when he knocked on her bedroom door and came in. For a second the poison made her see crooked. Then she noticed his ashen face and shaking hands. It was illness, not sudden unlikely passion that had brought him, and it made Rachel ashamed. 'There's been a call from Haylane Farm,' he said. 'Twin calves, badly presented. I'm just not fit, I'm afraid. Can you manage? I can send for Tom Adams if you like.'

Tom Adams was in practice on the other side of Milchester, the area that Rachel had come through when she had first arrived. There were four partners, of whom Tom Adams was the junior one. It was a younger practice than Malcolm Halliday's: a little more go-ahead, perhaps, but that did not detract from the reputation of Stapleton House.

When Malcolm had first set up in practice twenty years previously, Milchester had been a much smaller place, but now, with its light industries, its outlying radio station, the Air Force base not far away, it had been a larger, more complex and widespread community that demanded far more of its servants, its doctors, dentists, priests and vets, than it had done in those older and more self-contained days, when people were in any case more likely to cope with their own problems than to toss them to the experts. Now, Parker, Wilmott, Stratton and Adams carried their share of the veterinary work of the town and Malcolm was glad of it.

Alan Parker was the senior man: an expert on parasitology, a learned writer of articles on his subject: yet he looked like a jolly farmer, and behaved like one too, dividing his spare time between the hunting field and the Three Crowns Inn during the winter, and in the summer angling to be asked to officiate at

94

agricultural shows, where again he could be found either at the ringside or in the beer tent. He was never drunk, but was a great man for company and a good yarn, and would sing, with very little need of encouragement, in a pleasant, fruity baritone, the songs of his youth: the sort of songs that now languish yellow and mildew-spotted in a thousand piano-stools in a thousand forgotten parlours. He would beg Thora to come to him, Maud to enter the garden, Genevieve to be the darling of his heart.

Peter Wilmott was the man who most earned the partnership its reputation for being modern and go-ahead. He was keen to try out all the latest methods, the newest drugs. He had no patience with the old ways, and fiercely rooted out from the dispensary nostrums that had cured—or at least appeared to cure—the diseases of a decade ago. He was not the most popular of the vets, particularly among the older farmers, for he would shout with outrage and horror at some of their home-grown treatments. 'Useless nonsense,' he would say, and they would watch him at work with his syringes, and wonder secretly if their old remedies would not have worked just as well and cost them a good deal less. But then you had to move with the times, didn't you, and with beasts at the price they were you couldn't afford to lose one by being stubborn. Anyway, all vets had you by the short hairs when you came to consider it. If they said your cow had some tongue-twister of a disease that could only be cured by some unpronounceable drug, how could you argue with that? You learned a good deal about livestock when you'd worked with them all your life, but you couldn't know everything, or even think you did, like some of the young cockers out of the Royal Ag.

David Stratton was of an age with Tom Adams, and a great mate of his. They kept each other sane amidst the quirks of the two older men. David's interest lay more in the surgery than in the farmyard; and he was known—without intentional insult—as 'the pet vet'. He was a pleasant, reassuring young man, and something of a heart-throb among the younger women who queued up with their ailing dogs and cats, their long-beaked budgies, or their children's overfed hamsters at the surgeries he took.

They watched his skilful hands, the handsome face that was giving so much attention to the animal under his care, and they would sigh, and think him every bit as good as that doctor chap on the telly, and then go back to a disgruntled husband or nagging father, and sigh again at the unfairness of life.

Tom Adams himself Rachel had seen more of than the other three. He was a big, wildish man with a beard, who came sometimes to call on Malcolm, and at whose coming Mrs Partridge would bring out cakes and tea as if their visitor never ate except at Stapleton House. His voice would fill the kitchen, and Mrs Partridge would laugh as Rachel had never known her to do otherwise, happy as a young girl. Rachel had only heard these tea-parties at a distance while she worked in the surgery, but she had come across Tom Adams in Milchester once or twice as he strode along among the shoppers, looking as out of place as a friendly bear at a Sunday school outing.

Rachel knew that he had taken emergency calls for Malcolm before her coming to the practice, and there was no doubt he would do so now if asked, but 'I'll manage,' she said. 'You go back to bed. Can I get anything for you?'

'No, nothing. I must apologise for this.' He coughed and turned away. He looked a great deal older and very tired. Rachel felt that necessary surge of energy that had rescued her many times before when there seemed too little of her to spread across the amount of work to be done, and thanked heaven for it. She dressed, swallowed a cup of tea and went out to the car, clutching a thick sandwich of bread and marmalade. She would do little good at Haylane Farm if she keeled over from hunger.

It was a glorious morning. Rain in the night had washed the landscape clean, sharpened up the wintry outlines of trees. Puddles among the brown furrows of ploughland reflected silver-blue as the sky brightened to stronger daylight. The car beetled busily along and Rachel began to be alert, sharply awake, her mind ready for the job to be done. Then, suddenly there she was, back to that old problem again. Haylane Farm meant Steve Armitage, the young son of the place, large, big-handed, handsome in a slab-sided fashion, idolised too much for his own good by the giggling young girls of the village, and as randy a young lad as you could meet. Rachel had already found him a thorough nuisance. She was reminded whenever he came near her of the sort of ill-trained pup that rides the legs of visitors and won't leave them alone. Whenever she went to Haylane he would appear from nowhere, and stand unnecessarily close, finding any poor excuse to touch her, giving her looks that she imagined he hoped were masterful and passionate, but came across plain crude. He would be even more of a pain in the neck if he were going to be hanging around this morning, with a difficult labour needing her assistance. Maybe seeing her up to her armpit in a cow might douse his ardour. She grinned to herself. If she was not careful she would be watching every male customer as carefully for signs of lasciviousness, and she might end up like some nervous maiden lady looking assiduously for burglars under the bed, and very disappointed at not finding one.

She drove into Nether Leybourne, through the still sleeping grey stone houses. Many of the owners worked in Milchester and need not keep countrymen's hours. There was no-one about but an old man tidying his wintry garden, with its frost-blackened chrysanthemums and stiff stalks of golden rod. On a wall a cat sat with its fur fluffed against the chill of the morning. The curtains were drawn back in the old man's cottage and someone was frying bacon. For a second Rachel was back at home, watching her mother cooking breakfast on the Aga, talking to her in their brief time together between milking and school. How odd time was, and the passing of it. The scene seemed closer than any she remembered from college, from her time seeing practice, from the earliest days in her working life.

Haylane Farm lay a mile beyond Leybourne.

It was a neat, well-tended place with a good sound house and buildings. Peter Armitage's Friesian herd was well fed and well fenced and he liked the best for them. He would be anxious not to lose these calves.

He was waiting for her. His expression stated quite clearly that they might have sent a man to do a man's job, but he answered her questions about the cow with a reasonable grace while she put on boots and an overall before taking her equipment over to the stall from which she could hear the cow bawling. She made ready, examined the animal briefly, and saw she was in good fettle, and the right shape for breeding, as far as her outside showed. Now perhaps, Rachel would sort out the inner problems. Immediately inside the cow was a Chinese puzzle of assorted feet. Rachel took a steadying breath, aware of pairs of eyes upon her. She fixed her attention firmly on the job.

'Come on, little chaps,' she said. 'There's more room further back.' She began, carefully, to explore the shapes she could feel, trying to identify them: to map them in her mind.

It was hard work, sorting them out. Physical, mucky, sweating work, and the cow would strain and push the calves down again, just as she was getting them untangled. It was one of the worst presentations she had yet had to

100

cope with. After some time she began to feel panicky and ashamed of being panicky, all at once. She checked her face to assure herself that it registered only a professional concentration on the job, and hoped that it was convincing Peter Armitage, and his cowman and, God help us Steven, who had appeared right on cue.

She felt that her arm had been in the cow for days. She lost count of legs and began to feel there was a whole herd of calves in there. She wished Malcolm were with her. Hell, no she didn't: now she had, at last, two forelegs that matched, and a head that belonged. She roped the forelegs and gave an end to the cowman. She roped the head, gently over the ears and through the mouth. Who needs a calf with a broken jaw? She passed that one to the senior Armitage. The younger one was breathing irritatingly down her neck, his lust apparently quite undampened by the presence of his father and the somewhat dramatic *accouchement* of the cow. Rachel tried hard to ignore him and instructed the other two men to pull when the cow strained. 'Gently,' she admonished them. They were beefy fellows, in the village tug o' war team. She didn't want calves by halves.

Gently they pulled, and the cow, seeming

to realise that matters had improved, bore down and pushed, and the first calf came slithering down on to the straw, blatting and sneezing as the membrane was pulled from its nose. The cowman got to work on it while Rachel went back for the other one. It was sitting on its haunches like a dog, with its hindlegs so far forward, that pulled in that position it was bound to damage the cow. It was, thank God, only a small calf. Again she roped the forelegs, so that they could not get themselves displaced, and worked the hindlimbs gently into a better position. It took her all her strength. She knew exactly how the cow must be feeling. It was a triumph to Rachel when the second calf could at last be pulled free. She felt a fierce pride in it as she rubbed its wet body with hay and saw breath inflate its lungs.

'Nice little pair, them,' the cowman said; and it was sufficient praise.

After a while the afterbirth came away, and Rachel checked that all was well before having it taken away. 'And bring some water for the cow to drink please,' she said. 'Bring a couple of buckets.'

She waited to see that the calves could stand and would suckle. The cowman went to fetch the water she had requested. Peter Armitage, satisfied that his cow had produced successfully, nodded briefly to Rachel and went off to see to his other beasts.

The calves were struggling to stand. Steven, as if trying to take a closer look at them, came nearer to Rachel, leaned upon her shoulder.

'Proper good job you did,' he said, breathing close to her ear, his fingers digging into her shoulder blade. He was a strong lad and there was no way she could politely break away from him. She could elbow his ribs, or worse, but that seemed a little excessive, unless he made any further moves. The cowman returned and Steven stepped away from her. The cow drank the water thirstily. Rachel took the other bucket, as if to swill down the place where the cow's cleansings had fallen, but somehow her foot slipped, and the water slooshed out in a silver arc and caught Steven Armitage full in the stomach.

'My goodness, Mr Armitage, how careless of me. I'm so sorry,' Rachel said. Steven was doubled up against the sting of the icy water. His clothes were sodden: his trousers dripped pools on the floor: his teeth chattered. Over Steven's bowed head the cowman looked across at Rachel and shuttered one eye in a slow, delighted wink.

CHAPTER 6

Suddenly there were horses. Since her visit to Lady Bramwell Rachel had had no equine patients, though she had been far too busy to notice the lack. There were plenty to be seen, of course, as she drove about the countryside, clattering past her on hunting mornings, snorting frosty breath on early exercise, drumming along the grass verges, urged on by eager children. Out in the fields, polo ponies wintered in the bright green rugs, nursing the knocks and cuts of a hard season, their respite beginning just as the hunters were being hardened off grass. That was a time for all kinds of aches and ills: this exchange of one routine for another, in an animal for whom routine is security and good health.

Horses worked too suddenly or too soon while they were still fat and soft and out of condition were prone to sprains and strains and galls, and Malcolm grew quite irritable about the constant calls for treatment, when with care and patience the owners could so easily have avoided them. Rachel suspected he went out to these cases as much to deliver a severe lecture on the proper hardening off of horses in training, for whatever purpose, as to attend to the ills that stupidity had already caused.

Then one morning Malcolm announced that there was a horse for her to see, before lunch if possible. They had just finished a very busy surgery and her list of visits was long already, but she had heard him answer the 'phone only a few minutes previously and had suspected it might be another case for her.

She felt pleased to put a horse on her list. It was all pretty dull, routine stuff she had lined up for the rest of the day. A horse would make a pleasant change.

'Where is it?' she asked.

'At Hamden's.'

That was odd. John Hamden was known not to like horses. He had grown no fonder of Rachel, either.

'His wife's sister's staying with them,' Malcolm explained. 'Brought her horse up from Kent; apparently she wants to hunt with the Cotswold. I saw Mrs Hamden in the Abbey grounds the other day and she said her husband wasn't best pleased. I think horses, hunting and his wife's sister are equal in Hamden's dislike of them.'

I don't come much further down the list,

Rachel thought, but she only said: 'And you want me to visit?'

'Yes, please.'

'Very well, then,' said Rachel, but she thought, why the heck couldn't he go himself, knowing as he did how little Hamden approved of her.

'Unless of course, you would prefer not,' Halliday said, as if he sensed this unexpressed and small rebellion. She looked at him sharply, listened attentively for the least tinge of malice in his voice, but his face was serious, his expression bland.

To Rachel's surprise, John Hamden himself was about in the farmyard when she called there later. She had expected to be met by his wife's infamous sister, and had been comforted by the fact that that lady could scarcely give her less welcome than she would get from John Hamden.

'I've come to look at the horse,' Rachel told him.

'I know that,' he said. 'I've a couple of calves you may as well have a look at now you're here.'

Rachel went with him to see to the calves. They were scouring, but only mildly.

'I don't think you need to be too concerned,' she said. 'They seem very healthy. A little powdered nutmeg will help the scouring.'

'Is that all?' he asked, disgruntled.

Rachel felt she really could not win. If she suggested some expensive course of drugs he would have complained it was a waste of money. Now, when a simple household remedy was sufficient, he was equally dissatisfied.

'Yes, nutmeg should do the trick,' she said, carefully patient. 'I expect your wife will have some in the kitchen. Let me know if they don't improve. Now, will you show me the horse, please?' She felt irritated by his deflection of her from the proper purpose of her visit. She had a very full day's work to do.

He stumped off ahead of her then, muttering about bloody horses and unmentionable women, and she followed him to where, in the middle of a huge field, a very large horse was standing.

'Is the owner here?' Rachel asked.

Hamden intimated that she'd gone shoping.

'What seems wrong with the horse?' Rachel enquired.

'God only knows.' From Hamden's expression, God could keep the information to Himself, and welcome.

'Is there a stable nearby?' Rachel asked. Examining any creature in the middle of a field is not the easiest matter, and when the trouble has not been even sketchily indicated by the owner, diagnosis under such conditions is decidedly difficult.

Hamden was pointing across the vast expanse of field to a distant building.

'Stable's up there,' he said.

It looked like miles. It was so far distant that Rachel said, 'Perhaps I might put the horse in the cowshed while I look at him?'

Hamden made it clear that no horse was going to set foot in his cowshed, and try as Rachel might to assure him that there was no kind of equine disease that could be transferred to cattle, he would not budge. Rachel felt suddenly very weary, and the distance to the stable seemed daunting. The horse, however, did not. He stood placidly, head lowered, ears flickering gently, occasionally swishing his tail. There was no immediately evident sign of injury or disease. He was, Rachel noticed, wearing a head-collar. That, at least, would be a help. She would examine him where he was.

As she approached him she was greatly impressed by his size. She judged he must have some big-boned breed in him: Cleveland Bay, or something very like. He made no move away from her, nor did he protest when she took hold of him, but allowed her to feel all his limbs, inspect his feet, even take his temperature without any objection whatsoever. She could find nothing wrong. She trotted him up, and he was sound. Then she looked in his mouth. There was at least one of his troubles. There were sharp edges to his grinder teeth, and one or two sore places on the inside of his cheeks.

'You're a good boy. What a fine fellow,' she flannelled at him. 'A bit of a rasp and you'll feel a lot better.' She took a rasp out of her bag. This was a job some horses hated, but with such a placid creature it should all be easy enough. She reached up and took hold of the head-collar. 'There's a good lad.'

Some help would have been welcome, even from John Hamden, but he was standing right over by the gate and she was damned if she'd ask him.

The horse saw the rasp. His eyes widened and he snorted loudly through his nostrils; a sudden eruption of sound. Up went his head, and up went Rachel hanging on to the head-collar like an unwary ringer on a bell-rope. He ran backwards so fast, with his head so high in the air that she could not, and dared not, let go. She knew she looked a fool. She knew she was a fool. She felt scared, stupid, and furiously angry with herself and fate and

Hamden. She knew she had no justification for being angry with the horse, but she would have wrung his neck too if her present circumstances had allowed it.

He seemed to carry her around the field dangling from his head-collar for a very long time. When she could at last get her feet to the ground again her legs were shaking. Chastened, she began the long trudge to the stable, and the horse, back in his right mind again, went quite peaceably with her. She refused to look in Hamden's direction. She would not give him that satisfaction.

A voice called her from the direction of the house. A woman had emerged from the front door and was making her way to the field gate.

'Hang on,' she shouted. 'You'll need some help.' It was obvious she had not seen the previous high jinks.

'Oh, ha!' muttered Rachel, bitterly, not loud enough to be heard. 'Where were you when the balloon went up?'

As John Hamden's sister-in-law came trundling across, the necessity for owning so large a horse was evident at once. Though not very tall, she was extremely plump and was almost entirely out of breath by the time she reached Rachel.

'It was good of you to come and see Trojan,'

she puffed. 'Sorry I wasn't here. We missed the bus. Had to go to Chadwick and walk from there. He was too busy to drive us into Milchester, he said.' She indicated with her thumb the distant figure of her sister's husband. 'I'm Janet Fisher, I expect you realised. You got my message, I hope?'

'Message?'

'Saying Trojan was quidding his food and I thought his teeth wanted doing. I told John to tell you. I see you've brought your rasp.' It was still in her hand. In all that dizzying terrifying hanging on to Trojan's lofty head, she had clutched on tight to her tooth-rasp. The handle had made a great red mark across her palm.

So John Hamden had known all along what was wrong with the horse. The sod. Now he was probably having a good laugh at her expense, and would relish with the utmost pleasure the memory of her progress round the field.

Once in a confined space, and held firmly by his hefty owner, Trojan made no further fuss about having his teeth filed. Rachel was glad of that for one or two bruises were already beginning to make themselves felt in her body. She did not tell Janet Fisher of John Hamden's obstructiveness. There seemed little point in exacerbating the obvious dislike each had for the other, and neither did she confess to Malcolm Halliday the extreme stupidity of her own behaviour that day. She did, however, allow herself the luxury—just before she fell asleep after a long time settling her bruises comfortably in the bed—of planning exactly what she would do to John Hamden if he should spread abroad the story of her episode with Trojan the horse.

In contrast to this incident it was a real pleasure to Rachel to be called out some days later to the Ashton Stud to check over the weaned foals, and to examine Ashton Highlight, the stallion, who was off colour. She had often hoped to be sent there, but this was the first time.

Her road to the Stud took her past the field with the Jersey cow in it. Rachel stopped the car and went across to have a look over the fence. The cow was peacefully grazing: still looking poor, and with a coat that would have horrified Mrs Bellamy, but alive and chewing her cud. Rachel climbed over the fence and went to look at her more closely.

'What the hell are you doing? Get off my land!'

The man coming towards her, waving his arms, was presumably Bill, being furious again. Rachel wondered if he ever showed any other emotion. He was a man who looked as though he should be in one of the more important chairs in an office. His wellington boots and padded anorak sat on him like a clumsy diguise: even the weathering on his face seemed to have touched only the topmost layer of the skin. His anger was managerial irritation, not agricultural rage, and it had drawn down all the corners of a once-handsome face, spoiling the lines of it.

'I'm sorry,' Rachel said, 'I just came to look at your cow. I'm a friend of...your wife's.' It was not really true, but at least they were slightly acquainted. His fury seemed to abate a little.

'Are you the one that came when the stupid animal swallowed the clothes line?'

Rachel was surprised Anne Fowler had dared to tell him. 'That's right. The cow seems fine now.'

'Never better,' Bill said, his face relaxing. Rachel refrained from telling him that the cow could quite easily be a very great deal better, and remarked that she must be going.

'Oh, won't you come in? Tea or something? Anne always complains she gets no company.' His voice was friendlier now, as if he wished to atone for his snappish greeting.

'Thanks, but I have work to do,' Rachel said.

'Ah. A working woman, I see.'

Show me a woman that isn't, Rachel thought to herself, remembering the girl with the pigeons, and the bogged-down, tired-eyed mums she met in the town, with their shopping and push-chairs and tricycling toddlers; and the elderly dears that still cleaned and cooked as they always had, while their mates retired to slippers and pipe and dreams of past glory.

She said goodbye to Bill Fowler, went back to Jessica and set off again. It had been a wet night, and was overcast now. It was a muddy, glowering landscape. Only one tree stood out from the gloom: a huge larch, a great mature tree, still glowed bright orange, like the towering sparks of a November bonfire against the slate-grey sky. She drove towards it, where it stood at the gateway to which she had been directed, and a thin ray of sun escaped from the cloud, turning it bright gold for a second or so; then it darkened to orange again as she turned in the driveway of the Ashton Stud.

The drive was swept gravel and mown verges. It followed the line of a small stream, crystal clear and sandy-bedded, but in such a way that you felt the stream had been constrained to follow the road, and not the other way about. Some decorative ducks paddled in the chilly water, and reminded Rachel of those other ducks on that other, sunnier day. Dark, clipped hedges in fantastic shapes dotted a lawn that was quite unbelievably smooth, and of a green that glowed against the winter drabness of the further landscape. Only a handful of spent leaves lay scattered on it, and those were the late, last fallers. Someone obviously swept the turf like a carpet. The house was the seventeenth-century darling of some Cotswold wool-merchant, but one with as much sense as money. It was a delightful house. It was one that was photographed for all the guide-books. Architects and historians spoke of it with reverence. Tourists flocked to it on those rare days that it was open to them.

The merchant had been a horseman, too, and the yard was a dream of stone and timber and moss-grey slate, with clock-tower and dovecote and white doves wheeling from it. Something puritan in Rachel felt that it was all a little too perfect: that whoever lived here lived cushioned from real life: most of us sit on hard chairs, and few do it by choice. Would she wish it destroyed though, on the vandal principle that if I can't have it, you shan't? Never in the world: let someone have their perfect place. She drove into the stable-yard and found the head groom waiting for her. He was a little, plump man with very short legs. He was of Lady Bramwell's generation, probably almost of an age with her. Rachel could see a couple of lads in the background, however, wheeling barrows and carting muck, which she hoped meant that the old man was not expected to do the heavy work. It seemed that Cotswold air was conducive to lively old age. Would she, at coming up for ninety, still be delivering calves and vetting horses? The old man wheezed a little as he walked.

'Gassed me, like a bloody rabbit, in the first war,' he apologised as he trotted ahead of Rachel to take her to see the foals in the barn. There, in two big enclosures they waited for her: fillies to one side, colts to the other. Curious, playful, fearless thoroughbred young stock, cared for like fighting cocks. It stirred Rachel's heart to look at them. Whoever lived here loved horses, and knew about horses: no doubt about it. What was the owner's name? She glanced down at the card to remind herself. Helen Carrington, a widow, Malcolm had told her. 'Will Mrs Carrington be coming down to the yard, or do you want a written report on them?'

'Neither, miss. You just tells me if there's

116

ought wrong.' She checked over the youngsters, and found nothing wrong anywhere. Some of the colts were to be sold entire, and those to be kept would not be cut till they were yearlings, but some were to be gelded before they were sent away to new owners. She made a note of those and suggested a date.

'There are no flies now to plague them afterwards, and we're in for some sharp weather so there will be less mud. They're all injected for tetanus?' Harry Ellis, the groom, looked at her as if she were somehow lacking.

'Think I'm daft or summat? Course they are.'

He took her into his office and showed her his records. Every horse, every foal had detailed entries of its age, breeding, condition, feeding, attention from farrier, illnesses, accidents, treatments, routine injections, recorded in neat school roundhand with a dipped ink pen.

'You'd best go and look at Highlight now. The girl's put him in the isolation box. Only a bit of an old cold, I reckon, but you'd best make sure.'

He pointed to the isolation box, which lay at the back of the main block, but he made no move to go with her.

'Aren't you coming?'

'Well, all right, but only to the door. He don't like me. He don't like men at all. That girl looks after 'im but she's gone out with Mrs Carrington today.'

'What's he got against men?' Rachel asked.

'Sent up to a stud in Leicestershire he was,' Harry said. 'Not much more than a colt then: three year old: sweet tempered as a plaster saint when we sent him, but one of the grooms there got drunk and set about him with a pitchfork. When Mrs Carrington got to hear of it she had the horse back at once. It was a girl drove the lorry. She warned me, but I wouldn't listen. I walked up the ramp to bring him out and he got me by the shoulder. We've tried everything, but he doesn't forget.'

Highlight the stallion stood in the roomy box looking very sorry for himself. Yellow discharge trickled from his nose, causing him to snort from time to time in a rather gloomy way. The windows of the box were open, but he was well wrapped in rugs and bandages. A bucket outside the door smelt faintly of Friar's balsam. Rachel began to wonder why they had bothered to send for her. They had done most of her job already.

She was not one to be nervous of any animal just by reason of its masculinity, but Highlight

118

was very large, muscular and powerful, and the memory of Trojan was fresh in her mind, and in her bruises. She hesitated for a moment, and the groom encouraged her.

'You don't need to worry. He won't hurt you. The girl rides him out when he's well.' She went in, spoke softly, stroked the horse's bay-black skin. His ears were just the least bit cold, and she pulled them gently to comfort him. She looked him over, took his temperature, pulled back his rugs and sounded his chest. She felt his throat for signs of strangles. She went through all the routines, including asking a horrified Ellis if Highlight had been wormed lately.

'My word yes. I should just think so.' The old man was indignant.

'It's a cold,' she said. 'Just as you thought. I'll give him a course of antibiotics. That should fix him.'

'Balls,' said Harry Ellis.

'What?'

'Used to give 'em balls. Horse balls. When I was a lad there wasn't these anti this and thats, and these needles. Used to blow balls down 'em with a tube. If you was quick, and the horse didn't blow first.' He cackled from his safe place outside the door.

Rachel patted Highlight's neck and the

needle went in before he knew it. She completed the injection, adjusted the horse's rugs and came out. 'Bran mashes, boiled linseed, not too much corn,' she instructed, knowing she need not say it.

'I'll tell the girl,' Ellis said, 'when she comes back. She's taken Mrs Carrington to Broadway to look at a mare. They'll be back before evening stables, and then Mrs Carrington'll be down to make sure I feed them foals right.'

He laughed, not seeming the least put out at the thought of being told how to suck those particular eggs.

She sensed that Harry Ellis had a more than usual respect for his employer, which might explain why he had accepted Rachel's services as a vet without any adverse comment. She had certainly expected some when she first saw him: an old, professional horseman whose knowledge and skill could be seen in every aspect of the yard and the stock it contained. Yet there had not been as much as a raised eyebrow. She began to feel quite pleased with herself, quite cocky inside, until a less rewarding idea occurred to her.

'How have you managed before when Highlight has needed attention?' she asked. 'I assume he doesn't like male *vets*, either.'

'Ah,' said Harry Ellis. 'Ah well. Mrs Carrington comes down then, and she speaks to him. Speaks to old Highlight like a Dutch uncle, she does, and then he'll stand so quiet you could bring in the whole Brigade of Guards, and he wouldn't take no notice. Anyway, when I tells her it's a lady vet coming she says she's quite sure you'll manage.'

The was praise enough, Rachel felt, but she would have liked to meet this Mrs Carrington.

She took a final look round the yard, changed out of the boots she had put on, though they had not been necessary: everything was so swept and clean. It made a pleasant change from some of the places she had visited recently: inches deep in mud and muck, concrete filmed over with slime that took your feet from under you and assaulted your nose with a fearsome smell. Here was nothing but a pleasant air of good hay, well-groomed horses and sunlit stone.

On the way back down the drive, Rachel drew up for a moment to avoid the ducks rolling along like shore-going sailors from the stream to the inviting turf of the lawn. In the distance, across the expanse of green, she saw a girl of about eighteen in jeans and sweater, and beside her, a hand resting lightly on the girl's arm for guidance, a tall, splendid woman of middle age, whose eyes could see nothing of what was around her.

Rachel knew at once that this must be Mrs Carrington. She got out of the car and walked across to introduce herself.

'I didn't think to tell you she was blind,' Malcolm said, when Rachel was reporting the visit to him and noting in their own records the treatment being administered to the stallion. 'Mostly I forget she is. She can still judge a horse to a 'T', even without sight. Don't be sorry for her. She wouldn't thank you for it.'

'You didn't tell me about Highlight either,' she chided him. 'His idiosyncrasy about men.'

'I didn't, did I,' he said. 'But I knew Harry would enlighten you. Had it been females he was averse to, I would have warned you myself.'

Rachel was relieved to see that Malcolm looked better than he had done recently. He was completely reticent about his illness, except when it floored him entirely and he had to ask for help. Mrs Partridge was concerned for him too, and anxious because his appetite was failing and he sent back more than he ate, with courteous apologies expressed in his usual cool quiet voice. He was a man who carried his own frontiers with him: invisible, but un-crossable. People could not invade him.

It ran true to form, the week of the horses. She treated pulled tendons at the racing stable, inspected the ponies at the Riding Centre, vetted a hunter for Richard Harris, the new owner of Milchester Hall, who fancied himself as local squire and was determined to do the job properly. She couldn't help liking him, despite his nouveau richery. He knew what he did not know, and was prepared to be told, and to listen. That was refreshing. When she had vetted the big grey thoroughbred he had been sent on trial she was not surprised to hear it was Mrs Carrington who had recommended it.

'She told me he had a small splint, and to knock them down by fifty pounds on account of it,' Mr Harris said.

The splint on the grey's foreleg was so small that Rachel had nearly missed it. Otherwise the horse was fine, and just the right, wise sort that was needed. She chalked up several marks to Mrs Carrington.

It was the sort of week she had hardly dared to hope for: work she enjoyed and no nasty jobs that she would rather avoid, like giving enemas to constipated poodles, or testing wild-eyed herds of unhandled young cattle. She had

123

not seen a pig all week. Pigs were worst, as far as she was concerned. They had so little to grab hold of. There was little you could appeal to in a pig. They lived in their own world, and she felt they resented her intrusion in it. She had also once been badly bitten by one, and it made her nervous, which she dared not admit. She was lucky, really, that there was not much pig-work in the practice.

On the Saturday she saw Anne Fowler in the ironmongers, buying nails and staples and a roll of wire. She looked harassed and weary and her lack of decision about what she wanted was very obviously trying the patience of the young man at the counter, as he opened box after box for inspection. Rachel patiently waited her turn, and it was several minutes before the other woman looked in her direction and recognised her. 'Sorry, so sorry. I'm keeping you waiting. Oh dear, yes, those will do. I'll have some of those.'

The assistant began to wrap up the purchases with rapid relief, anxious that she should not change her mind again, and Anne Fowler turned to speak to Rachel.

'Thanks for looking at the cow again,' she said.

'That's OK,' Rachel assured her.

'And thanks for not letting on to Bill about

your being a vet.'

'I wouldn't dream of it.'

'I was wondering if you could come and have lunch with me, perhaps on your next day off. You do have days off, don't you?'

'Well, yes, it was a day off when I saw your cow.'

'Oh dear, of course. Well, if you'd have lunch, it would be a sort of thank you for that. Please say when you can come.'

Rachel did not really wish to accept the invitation. She had no particular desire to see more of Anne Fowler, with her faded county face and the voice that despite its tiredness carried still the upper-class stridency that set the teeth on edge. Yet there was something almost pleading about the invitation, as if Anne Fowler expected it to be rejected. Rachel imagined that she had lost many supposed friends when so much changed in her life.

'I'm off on Monday, if that would suit you?' she suggested.

'Oh, that would be splendid. Bill goes to Gloucester market on Monday. We'd have the place to ourselves.'

'Monday then. Thank you.'

'Do you like spinach?' Anne Fowlder asked, moving towards the doorway with her parcels and away from where Rachel stood, still waiting to make her own purchases.

'Yes, I do.'

'Good,' was the reply, and as she stepped into the street, a further remark, which Rachel did not clearly hear, appeared to be, 'that's just as well.'

It was spinach quiche, and it was excellent. Rachel thoroughly enjoyed it and ate far too much. Replete, and somnolent by reason of a large glassful of homemade wine, she began to think that self-sufficiency had at least some rewards.

'That was very good,' she told Anne Fowler.

'I did a Cordon Bleu course once,' her hostess said. 'We used to have dinner parties and so on. We all had to do better than the last woman; you know the sort of thing. Now I have to cook with what we've got: and what we've got is spinach and eggs, and spinach and milk and eggs, and spinach, of course. Spinach pancakes, spinach omelettes, poached eggs on spinach, spinach soufflé, you name it. Popeye wouldn't go one round with me. One of these days I'll afford a freezer and then we can keep more meat. As it is when we've got it we have lots. I salt some, but I'm not very expert and it doesn't always work, but the rest we have to sell.'

'Wouldn't your butcher salt it for you?'

'We don't use a butcher. Bill thinks it's...'

'Unnecessary expense?' Rachel said, wickedly.

'Yes, he does it himself. I have to help.'

'Do you mind?'

'It makes me sick. I go into the house and cry, and he gets so angry and says I have to be realistic.' She paused, her face set, as if it were frozen. Rachel could think of nothing to say.

'Bill used to be such a happy man,' Anne Fowler went on. 'He liked his job. He loved this house. It's my house, you know: my parents left it to me. It suited us both; our way of life. Bill worked for a firm in Bristol. Top executive he was. Very well thought of, and it wasn't just Bill who told me so. All his colleagues who came here and ate our meals and drank our wine said what an excellent chap: how they couldn't manage without him. Well, they axed him. Executed the executive. Ha!' It was an arid laugh: the sort the poor joke deserved.

'I'm very sorry,' Rachel said.

'We should have sold up: gone to London perhaps, and tried to start again, but somehow neither of us dared take the chance. Bill tried for dozens of jobs and didn't get them. Just the wrong age for all this whizz-kid stuff. He thought we could turn this place into some kind of living. It's just that. A living—of a kind—but it's killing everything we used to feel for each other.'

She sat with her shoulders slumped, staring at the plate in front of her. Rachel reached out to her and put a hand on Anne Fowler's shoulder, half-hoping, half dreading, that the gesture might open a flood of tears. However, none came and eventually Mrs Fowler got up, and began to clear away the meal, allowing Rachel to help when she asked to. Washing up, companionably, seemed to ease the tension a little. Afterwards they went outside.

'I'll show you round,' Anne Fowler said.

Rachel saw that just as Malcolm Halliday had been told, the old stable-yard had been converted to house an odd assortment of creatures. One loose-box contained cockerels for fattening, another turkey poults for the Christmas market, and yet another laying hens of various breeds and mixtures. In a weedy paddock beyond, some sheep grazed, and a heavily fenced enclosure held what looked, at a distance, like a Gloster pig. Only one stable held what it had been built to hold: a chestnut gelding of about fifteen hands, with the instantly recognisable features of the pure Arabian: dish face, wide brow and dark expressive eyes. He gave the Arab horse's distinctive, nostril-cracking snort to welcome them as they approached.

'This is Hassan,' Anne said. 'The only remnant of my former glory.' Her voice was warm with affection for the horse who licked delicately at her fingers and blew gently at her.

She brought him out. He stood with arched neck and tail flowing down from its bone like a waterfall: he was a horse who should have been all air and fire, but there was a weariness about him, as there was about his owner. Then Rachel saw why—and she had already wondered why—he had been allowed to remain when commonsense would have sold him. On his neck and sides were the pressure marks of harness: at the point of his shoulder a collar-gall where the hair would grow white.

'Bill says I can have him all the while he earns his keep,' Anne Fowler said, bitterly. 'I should sell the poor fellow, for his own sake, but I can't bring myself to do it.'

Rachel was careful to say nothing. They put the horse back in his stable, and walked on beyond the yard, looked at the sheep, which were nothing special, and arrived at the pig enclosure. It was a Gloster pig. She was a young sow, and under the roof of an open shed she was nesting. Rachel was used to commercial breeds of pig; Large Whites, Landrace.

The old sow whose gashed side she had sewn up was the only other of this spotted breed she had come across. Farrowing sows were housed on concrete, under lamps, confined in pens like some mediaeval Iron Maiden to keep them from crushing their young. This one, in a quarter-acre enclosure, had scooped out a hollow in the soft earth of her shelter, and was gathering straw in her mouth like a portly bird, and actually making a nest. Rachel, the pig-hater, watched entranced. 'Oh, my heavens,' Anne Fowler said. 'He thought she wasn't due till next week. She's going to farrow and he won't be back for ages.'

An even more uncomfortable thought than this seemed then to strike her.

'Look,' she said. 'She truly wasn't expected to do it today. I didn't ask you here on purpose or anything.'

'For heaven's sake!' Rachel protested. 'I'd never have imagined you had. Besides, she looks a very competent sort of pig. I imagine she'll cope very well, and if she doesn't I'll willingly help. As a friend, you understand.'

They watched discreetly, from a distance, as the pig lay thankfully down on the nest she had made, and in the course of the afternoon filled it with eight healthy bright pink, black-spotted utterly delightful offspring, who without the least trouble and in no danger from their recumbent Mama, ranged themselves at the milk-bar and began to suckle.

Rachel, with great tact, checked that all was well. It was, she thought, the most charming sight she had seen for a long time. There are pigs and pigs, she concluded.

CHAPTER 7

Sometimes, when the work demanded it, Malcolm and Rachel did the rounds as a team; when one of the larger herds was due for testing or when some other operation was to be carried out where assistance was essential. Rachel was rapidly learning how greatly owners varied in the amount of help they were either able or willing to give. Some seemed half afraid of their own beasts while others handled them with a skill that was a pleasure to watch: some took a genuine interest in the treatment that was being given, while with others their only concern was what it was all likely to cost and whether it would be worth it in the long run. Rather than risk reluctant or inefficient help, therefore, the two of them would arrange a session of such team jobs and set out together.

The countryside was becoming familiar to Rachel now: she had it mapped in her head, so that all the different areas to which she had been called since her arrival in Milchester now formed a pattern, a completed jigsaw puzzle, from the high bosomy fields beyond Nether Leybourne to the little valleys of the scarp. She was getting the feel of the land: could see the bones of it. It was far less cosy than she had always imagined the Cotswolds would be. She had seen little of it before, only the tourist villages with their tea-rooms and gift shops, the wide streets glittering with cars and thronged with camera-wielding, holiday-clad people. Now she saw it as working land; and not just as it was at present, worked to the tune of chattering machinery, efficient and high-yielding, but as it had been in the past; a harsh place where the plough struck stone continually, where the poor picked those stones off the bleak fields for a pittance and men learned the skill of building stout, sheep-proof walls with the stuff that lay all too abundantly to hand. She could imagine the strain and sweat of the heavy horses on the steep inclines that kept her own hand so often ready on the gear-lever. She saw behind the present refurbished stone cottages, from which now came the sounds of washing-machine and vacuum cleaner and tinny transistor music—the stone sheds in which too many had lived in the damp, with water from the yard pumps, a privy by the kitchen garden, and a long day's labour in the field to earn their right to be there at all. Yet when she spoke to Mrs Partridge about those times, it seemed that there was much to compensate for the harshness of it. Mrs Partridge was no romantic: she enjoyed her present comforts and had no illusions about the old times, yet, as she told Rachel, there were things that she missed, like the way her father would sit and play his flute in the evenings and they would all sit round in the small cramped room and listen, and watch the big scarred hands that had spent all day setting stone upon stone move precisely and delicately over the instrument, and coax such sweet sound from it.

'So pretty, my dear, it used to make me cry, and I'd look out the window so the others couldn't see. I was a proper daft little thing as a young girl. And I still miss 'im now, my old dad. 'E was a skilled man, and as well thought of in our village as anyone these days would be if they was famous on the television or whatever. We 'ad our own famous men in those days. Each village, each little town, 'ad its own. You'd remember 'em long after people today'd forget the name of some bloke on telly. You ask some of the old ones round 'ere to tell you about my dad, or about Tom Gregory that could shear sheep by hand faster than I could shell peas, or Joseph Ash the corn-dolly maker, or Steve Dodd who kept the best pulling pair of 'orses this side Oxford. They was real, not like these shadowy people nowadays that thinks so much of their selves. D'you know they was going to ask one to open our Red Cross fête last year: some woman it was: can't remember 'er name. Wanted paying for doing it, 'er did. I ask you. Told 'er no thank you very much they did, and asked 'is Lordship to do it instead. 'e was as pleased as Punch, and gave a dozen prizes for the tombola into the bargain.'

Remembering Mrs Partridge's face as she spoke of these things, Rachel chuckled to herself as she sat next to Malcolm in the Peugeot, on the way to a dental session at the Riding Centre. There were some animals due to be rasped, two newly-acquired ponies with wolf-teeth, and an old cob who has been kicked on the face by a playful companion, knocking one of his grinders askew.

'What's amusing you?' Malcolm asked.

'Mrs Partridge, telling me about the old days,' said Rachel, 'and being scandalised because some Personality wanted paying for opening a charity fête in Milchester last year.'

'Ah well,' said Malcolm. 'To Mrs Partridge, privilege has its duties and if you are privileged to appear on the magic box it's your duty to open things like fêtes. I don't expect she has thought to reckon up just how far such a person would have to travel, and how many flowery hats would have to be purchased, and how many times the words, 'I now declare this whatever-it-is open' would have to be said, if such a duty were undertaken on every request. Mrs Partridge is pleasantly uncomplicated. She has a clear eye for what ought, and what ought not to be: a niceness which a complex world has lost.'

Soon the two of them arrived at the Riding Centre. The session had been organised as a result of Rachel's earlier inspection of the animals there when she had decided that these particular jobs needed teamwork. Staff at the centre fluctuated wildly, for at the weekends and in school holidays the place was a-swarm with enthusiastic girls, all hopeful of earning a ride. On ordinary weekdays the only help came from the proprietor's aged gardener, who trundled barrows lugubriously from stable to muck-heap, cheered only by the thought that the vegetables would eventually benefit. Horses he loathed with a deep and impenetrable loathing which showed itself in every aspect of his body when one of them came near him. The proprietor herself was occupied during the weekdays with those few non-working mums in the area who had the time and the money to ride, so the patients had been left stabled ready for their treatment.

They began work. It was not difficult. The ponies were placid creatures resigned to the handling of innumerable different riders of widely varying degrees of ability and sensitivity. Had words been given them, they would have shrugged and said, 'Oh, what the hell, let's get it over with.'

As always, Malcolm did not assume that he would do all the work while Rachel assisted. They took it turn and turn about. Even when the second case of wolf-teeth, a younger and far more spirited animal, decided he was not happy at the prospect of being parted from them, even though they had made his mouth uncomfortable and his bit intolerable, Malcolm made no move to take over from her, but kept the horse restrained while she worked. She liked him very much for it: wished there were some way in which she could tell him so, yet knew inside herself it would be a mistake to try.

It was a long, tiring morning. The Topend cattle, their next job, were restless and obstreperous, moody because the cowman was ill and the relief milker chivvied them more than they liked. By one o'clock Rachel was parched, hungry and aching, and beginning to feel that it must show. It was an effort to be patient amongst butting heads, jostling shoulders, slapping tails and big splayed clumsy feet, to say nothing of the beasts' ability to squirt liquid dung with a range and power that would be the envy of a weaponry expert.

Malcolm said, 'We'll see Mr Gunter's pig and then we'll have lunch. Beer and a sandwich at The Fleece perhaps?'

That sounded exactly the right idea. If only the Gunter pig did not stand like a great gross shadow between the idea and the reality.

Of all the pigs Rachel disliked, this pig she hated most. Jimmy Gunter lavished upon it the affection his wife Amy rejected. Although its ultimate destination was the butcher, and although Jimmy Gunter would consume with relish the fat bacon and the huge hams that would result, until then the pig was the darling of his heart. He crooned to it, scrubbed its back with the yard broom, fed it hugely and tended its every whim. Modern pig husbandry produces a lean, clean animal, almost racy. This one was rolled in fat like an indulged baby, its eyes almost invisible behind fat cheeks and brow. It did not look unlike Amy Gunter, if one were being less than charitable.

These tiny eyes were the cause of its present trouble. A sharp awn from its deep barley-straw bed had got under the lid of one, causing great pain, irritation and bad temper, all of which the two vets had been sent for to relieve.

The Gunters' cottage was small and square, with its roof pulled down around its ears, giving it a snug and stalwart look. Its small garden lay round it neat as a pin with everything to attention.

Rachel felt uncomfortable twinges of embarrassment as they approached. She had not seen Amy Gunter since Vi Partridge's revelations. How would the fat old woman react to the sight of Rachel and Malcolm together? She would certainly have spread her malicious thoughts to her husband. Would he look at them both with a knowing leer? Rachel felt herself prickle with anticipatory anger even at the possibility of it. There was no sign of Amy, however, and indeed, at first, no sign of Jimmy either.

'I know where he'll be,' said Malcolm and strode away down the garden. Rachel followed.

The pig-sty, in the bottom left-hand corner, was white-washed cement, creosoted timber, with a roof constructed painstakingly of Stonesfield slates, rescued piecemeal from derelict barns and outhouses, and set up again in their proper courses, to keep the weather off Jimmy Gunter's pig. There, when Malcolm and Rachel arrived, was the pig, its fat bulk leaning against the slatted gate from the inside. There was Jimmy Gunter, thin and wiry as a stalk of old-man's beard, leaning against it from the outside.

'Ee's poorly,' said Jimmy, by way of greeting.

'So I see,' Malcolm replied. The pig's eye was surrounded by more than usually swollen flesh and was an angry pink.

'Will you fetch the old door, please?' Malcolm asked.

'Or-right,' said Jimmy, and trundled off, to return shortly clutching a solid half door with which to confine the pig in one corner of the sty.

His interest in Malcolm and Rachel was so obviously only in their ability to minister to the pig that Rachel relaxed and put her hackles down.

The pig saw them coming with the door and developed an agility scarcely believable in anything so lumbering and vast. Whichever corner they approached with the door, the pig was by some miracle in another. At last, however, they managed to pen it, and the door was pressed against it to keep it still. Through the stout timber Rachel could feel the heave and swell of infuriated porcine muscle. Not far from where her hands were it was gnashing its nasty teeth.

'We shall need as much weight as possible to keep the door in place,' said Malcolm.

'Shame my old woman ain't 'ere,' Jimmy remarked.

'Indeed it is,' said Malcolm, his face impassive. 'However, we must do our best, Mr Gunter, while Miss Bellamy dresses the eye.'

Rachel took a deep breath, which exhaled itself far more like a sigh of despair than she had intended. Of all the jobs. And on an empty stomach too. She recalled the delightful creature at the Fowlers, and the one that now faced her seemed all the more appalling by comparision. It was the essence, it seemed to her, of all that was nasty, unreasonable and unapproachable in the porcine species even in its best mood, whereas now it was decidedly annoyed. The pig glared evilly at Rachel but could not turn its neck to bring the teeth into play because of Malcolm's hold on the door. He looked perfectly calm. He did not look as though he wished the pig long dead and gone, as Rachel did. He looked as though taking a barley-awn out of a pig's eye was the idle work of a passing moment. But then his hands were on the friendly side of the door. She tried not to let her own hands shake as she inverted the eyelid and dropped in some lubricating and mildly anaesthetising fluid. She ignored the furious noises of the pig and the champing of its crocodile grinders. She searched for the little grassy spear that was the cause of the pain, and found it, without too much trouble. At her first attempts to remove it the animal lunged so hard to avoid her attentions that the two men staggered and almost fell. She glanced quickly to remind herself where the gate was in case she needed to beat a retreat. At the second attempt the awn came away clean and easy, and relief flowed through Rachel like wine. She put more drops in before the pig had time to think.

'Done,' she said, and they all left the sty.

'Thought 'e'd 'ave your 'and off, I did,' said Jimmy Gunter, his voice full of pride in his pig.

'It's just a matter of technique, Mr Gunter,' Rachel explained, smiling.

'A knack, you might say,' added Malcolm drily. 'Goodbye then, Mr Gunter. Give our regards to your wife.'

The old man looked at them and began to grin.

'In a pig's eye,' Jimmy Gunter cackled, and leaned over the railed gate to scratch his beloved's hairy back. As they climbed into the

Peugeot, Malcolm and Rachel could hear him singing and the pig grunting peacefully in reply.

The beer and sandwiches were as good and as welcome as Rachel knew they would be. The Fleece was a friendly pub, not done up for the summer trade, and unfashionably without piped music and one-armed bandits. They sat discussing the morning's cases and refreshing themselves for a precious half-hour before the afternoon calls. It was very pleasant. The pub was quiet and no-one bothered them. There was no sound but quiet conversation and the pull and rush of the beer-pump. A fat cat washed itself industriously in a patch of sunlight under the window, and a collie dog attended to its fleas on the flagstones at the entrance where the door was propped open to let in air and customers, for so far it had been a pleasantly sunny day for late autumn. Malcolm sipped slowly at his half of mild ale and ate a quarter round of cheese and tomato while Rachel devoured her own food with appetite. She saw, after a while, how far she was outpacing him.

'I'm being greedy,' she said, laughing, and licking the last crumbs from her fingers.

'After your last half hour's work you deserve a banquet,' said Malcolm. Then, with a small slow smile, 'Sausages, perhaps, and pork pie.'

When they set off again the day was beginning to cloud, the sunshine now only an occasional patch on a far hillside. Leaves danced down from the trees and pattered on the windscreen.

'Fickle weather. Just like a woman,' commented the stockman at the next farm they visited. 'Blow 'ot blow cold. Never knows where you are with it.'

The farm cats sensed the change and were leaping fluff-tailed up the timber doorposts of the barn, to pounce on each other with out-spread claws and ferocious growlings. By the time they were heading for home both Rachel and Malcolm were back in the warm jackets they had removed earlier, and a gusty wind, blowing in earnest, was making the trees creak and clatter their branches.

To make a short way back to Stapleton House they took the private road through Milchester Park. Richard Harris had no objection to the road being used by people he knew, and anyway Rachel hoped for a sight of the grey horse he had bought through Helen Carrington.

The park was only a hundred acres or so, small enough compared with His Lordship's, but Richard Harris had spent considerable sums on clearing and replanting, to repair the previous impoverished owner's unavoidable neglect. Secretly, Rachel thought she would have preferred it as Malcolm had described it to her, as it had once been: a quiet, tangled wilderness of overgrown shrubs and trees, with a dark lake at the heart of it. Now it was almost too ordered, too pretty, yet the man took such pleasure in it, and longed to hear it admired, and there was no doubt that it was as elegantly, carefully rural as Capability himself had originally planned. Vistas had been reopened, ragged clumps of trees restored to order, the parkland turf cleared of rampant docks and thistles. Green rides scythed through the beech and ash-woods and new plantations of young trees stood guarded by stout posts and netting against the fallow-deer that he had reinstated. Slowly, yard by yard, skilled men were restoring the perimeter wall to keep the deer from the surrounding fields. It would cost more than Rachel could hope to earn in a decade.

They drove past the lake, its waters dredged clear, the old sluices replaced, the stonework of the Gothic bridge repointed and gleaming. The wind blew fierce ripples along the surface, bobbing the coots about like corks in a bowl. There was something else in the water: a small black shape that was not a coot. Rachel looked again.

'Will you stop a moment, please?' she asked. Malcolm stopped the car. She jumped out; ran across the grass; began to wade into the water. She still had her boots on, but the water deepened rapidly, and soon it would brim over and spill down inside on to her feet. She tensed herself for the inevitable iciness. Then the object of her progress was swept a little nearer and she was able to grab it, to haul it towards her, and to carry it at arms' length, dripping water like a soaked sponge.

Malcolm was there at the edge to steady her.

'Look!' she said, 'just look.'

Malcolm, having seen what she held, said, 'I told you I didn't like people much.'

He took her find from her, went to the car and wrapped a travelling rug around the soggy bundle. It was a small black puppy, to whose hind legs was attached a length of rope.

'There was probably a stone on the other end, or an odd bit of iron: anything heavy would do. Poor little beast. I wonder how long it's been in the water.'

'Nearly long enough,' Rachel replied.

As they cradled the shivering pup and began to get back into the car, there was a sudden sound of hoof beats along the verge, and there was Richard Harris on his grey.

'Trouble?' he asked. 'I recognised the car. Anything wrong, or are you just having a look round?'

'We found this in your lake,' Rachel said. Harris looked.

'God?' he said. 'Poor little beggar. Someone try to drown him, did they?'

'It looks like it,' said Malcolm. 'You hadn't noticed anyone about?'

'No. I've been up at the trout hatchery. If I'd caught anyone doing this, they'd have regretted it, I assure you. What are you going to do with the poor little thing?'

'We are taking it back to the surgery,' Rachel answered, glancing at Malcolm to check that that was what had been intended. Then, looking briefly under the folds of the rug, amended, 'taking *her* back to the surgery.'

'Tell you what,' Richard Harris suggested. 'Drive up to the house. It won't take you out of your way much. I'll follow, and then you can have a good hot cup of tea while we dry the pup off. Whisky, if you prefer it.'

'Thank you,' said Malcolm.

Rachel demurred slightly. She knew Malcolm would want to get back, but the two men seemed agreed.

They drove to the house along an avenue of limes, which opened into a half-circle

147

around the building: a miniature of Palladian splendour, an oddity amongst the handsome grey houses that ornament the Cotswolds: something of a folly perhaps, but very attractive, like a rich child's doll's house. They walked to the door with the puppy and were admitted. Mrs Harris came down the curved staircase at the sound of voices and was immediately told the story of the half-drowned creature. She took it at once from Rachel's arms, saying that she would get it dry and warm at once and see if it would eat.

'Sarah, will you make some tea please?' they heard her call in the direction of the kitchen.

'We ought not to be long,' Malcolm said. 'There's surgery in an hour.'

'I won't hear of you going without some tea.' Richard Harris had arrived in the doorway. 'And that's final.'

A little later, while they were sipping tea and eating Madeira cake, Mrs Harris came back in with the puppy, amazingly cheerful and ready to play, its coat a rich brown now that it was dry.

'Young things are amazing,' Harris said. 'Bounce back in no time. Spaniel of a sort, I think. Nice little bitch.'

Malcolm continued to eat cake, and said nothing. The pup began to explore her surroundings, wagging her stumpy tail, trailing her ears on the floor.

'I like her too, Richard,' Mrs Harris said. 'Would you care to leave her with us, Mr Halliday, while you decide what to do with her?'

'Thank you,' said Malcolm. 'I should be grateful. We must get back now, but I'll telephone in a day or so.'

He almost bustled Rachel out of the house and into the car, with the briefest of farewells to the Harrises.

They drove towards Milchester in increasing rain, and a wind that was obviously set in for the night.

'Sorry to hurry you,' Malcolm said.

'Was there a reason?' Rachel asked. 'Apart from surgery, which doesn't start till six?'

'Harris had a dog when they moved there,' Malcolm explained, 'a beautiful labrador; as intelligent a dog as I've ever met. One of the lorries bringing stone for the park wall ran it over. He swore he'd never have a dog again.' They turned the last corner to Stapleton House, and drew up with rain hammering on the roof of the car.

'You think he may change his mind now?' Rachel enquired.

'I think he already has, don't you? And if

not, by the time I telephone in a day or so, that pup will have him wound round her paw.'

Even the short distance from car to door was enough to soak them in the downpour. Mrs Partridge came out of the kitchen as they took off their dripping coats and boots.

'My goodness,' she said. 'You 'ave got wet. There's plenty in the waiting-room I'm afraid, rain or no rain. You'd think they'd stay 'ome, weather like this. Oh well, there's a nice steak and kidney in the oven when you're ready, and a bit of Stilton for after. I'm off to see our 'Etty as soon as this lets up a bit. What weather! It's enough to drown you.'

CHAPTER 8

The last leaves blew away down the year, and sometimes, as she drove about on her rounds, Rachel would see the scattered multicolours of the hunt go flying across the drabness of the landscape. One day there was a meet next to the farm she was visiting, and there she saw Trojan, all posh and plaited: his owner, too, so transformed by her hunting finery that she was scarcely recognisable. Rachel drew Jessica to the side of the road to let everyone go clattering past and to watch the pied flood of hounds go by, all a-jostle, their jaws smiling, their ears cocked to the high exciting talk of the horn. It was a sight she had seen often enough as a child, and it reminded her sharply of home; of her father's comforting tales of the sly ways of foxes, and how as likely as not, if they found one at all, he'd outwit them all and come home safe. Rachel's mother, who kept a flock of Rhode Island chickens, had a more hard-hearted approach to the fate of foxes. Between them, Rachel got a balanced view of most things.

Her mind on Parkwood now, she determined she would go home at Christmas if Malcolm could spare her. She had involved herself so closely with her new life that she had spared hardly more than a passing thought for her mother: had not always answered the letters that came from home, giving her news, telling her anecdotes about the cows, regaling her with local gossip.

Once clear of the hunt, Rachel made good speed to finish her rounds, for the days were so short now that there seemed hardly a moment between morning's and evening's twilight. A surprising number of the smaller holdings were still without electricity, if not altogether, then at least in their outbuildings, and among the paraphernalia that cluttered Jessica's back seats, Rachel now carried a powerful battery lamp to make inspection of her patients easier. Only the previous day she had had to use the lamp in order to find her patient at all; a tiny black Aberdeen Angus calf, which had gone missing somewhere in a barn huge enough to house the entire herd. He had lain doggo with such success that she and his owner had taken a good half hour to come across him.

At Stapleton House the evening surgeries were all now held in artificial light, and the people who sat patiently waiting were swelled out with extra layers of clothing, which they always seemed to hope the length of their stay in the waiting-room would not justify removing, so that a most appalling fug of hot, damp people would be added to the usual smell of worried and not always continent animals that was characteristic of the place, scrubbed and disinfected though it always was. From time to time Rachel would peer through the little hatchway that looked out from the surgery, to suggest that someone might like a window open, but the idea was always greeted with horror, which she felt might rise to rebellion if they were pressed. So they sat and sweltered, and each, as his or her turn came, brought a fresh trail of mud and dampness into the surgery. Mrs Partridge waged constant war with footprints and pawprints and prayed for a good sharp frost to give her some respite.

She had equal problems in the house. Since the surgery had been made by an amalgamation of one-time sculleries and larders, and an extension had been built to create a waiting-room, there was now no back entrance to Stapleton House except through the waiting room itself, so the simplest way into the private quarters was through the front door. Just inside this, in the hall-way, Mrs Partridge had made a space for muddy boots, and she lined it each day with yesterday's newspapers. Malcolm, characteristically, was meticulous in placing all his muddy footwear there, and Rachel had soon learned to copy him, but Tom Adams would more often than not come striding through the house bringing half of Gloucestershire with him and a familiar voice in exasperated tones would be heard to say: 'Just take them boots off and leave 'em in the 'all.'

Rachel had found him, on one occasion, walking be-socked across the polished boards, his boots in his hand.

'When I get to Heaven,' he complained, 'and I'm there at the gates seeking entrance, you know what they'll say to me, don't you? "Come in if you must," they'll say, "but leave your boots in the hall." '

On most evenings Rachel and Malcolm worked together. They had established a working relationship that seemed satisfactory to both of them. He expected much of her, and for the most part she lived up to that. Sometimes, when something puzzled her, he would give an opinion. Sometimes when she used a method or a treatment she had learned at college, or from Colin Ross, he would watch with interest, question her, either approving or else suggesting an alternative. He rarely expressed criticism. If she made, in his opinion, some error, he merely looked at her with a mildly perplexed expression, as if it surprised him that she should do such a thing. Once, when they were particularly rushed, and she dressed a dog's wound clumsily so that it whined in discomfort, he quietly took over and completed the job himself. She had felt ridiculously resentful. She wanted him to shout at her, to tell her not to be a clumsy idiot, to lose that damned cool for a moment. His quietness shamed her. She swallowed the resentment and was more careful.

When one of them was due for an evening off, the other would take surgery alone. Now that she was more confident, Rachel found she enjoyed this. She was beginning to know the 'regulars' well: knew many of the dogs and cats by name, particularly those who seemed accident prone, and made frequent trips to the surgery. Just as some children can be relied upon to fall off walls, swallow pills, burn, cut or scald themselves however careful a watch is kept on them, so Rachel had particular patients that seemed to 'keep coming back like a song' with splinters in the paw, mites in the ear, insufficiently chewed up rubber balls in the stomach, fishbones in the throat. There had been a procession of such patients one evening, and Rachel was really pleased to see at last a new face, a delightful fox-terrier puppy, brought for his first injections against hardpad, distemper and leptospirosis by his owner. She was a woman of about sixty, dressed in tweedy clothes that had obviously been 'bought to last' when she was a great deal younger. Her equally old, good leather shoes were carefully polished. She was not so much neat as well-ordered: as if she had practised hard for a long time to keep herself tidy, but as a duty rather than a pleasure. She seemed a little nervous.

'I haven't been here before,' she said to Rachel. 'I'm Miss Pringle. I've never kept an animal until now, you see, but the kennels where I bought Simba said I should bring him to you for his injections. He came from Faracre Kennels: Mrs Jacobs.'

'I know Mrs Jacobs,' Rachel said. 'This is a nice puppy she has sold you. I like fox-terriers. I'm only sad there are so few about nowadays. What's his name?' Miss Pringle looked at Rachel shyly. She was a tall woman, gaunt and bony and very plain.

'When I was a little girl,' she explained, 'I had a book about a fox-terrier called Simba. It means 'lion', you know. I always said if I ever had a dog it would be a fox-terrier, smooth-haired, and I'd call it Simba. As you see, I had a long wait, but here he is.'

Rachel looked at the pleasure that showed in the ugly face with its surrounding scraped-back grey hair, and saw that the waiting had brought its reward.

Christmas approached, and Milchester shops put up their trees and lights. Unlike the larger towns whose plastic stars and Dayglo Wisemen had swung in every breeze since mid-October, Milchester believed in seasonal, private enterprise decorations which were far more to Rachel's taste. She still took a childish delight in all the harmless trivialities that are part of a foolish world's interpretation of Christmas.

Invitations to social functions began to fall on the doormat of Stapleton House, ranging from the carol concert at the primary school to the local hunt committee's annual sherry party, and Mrs Partridge rescued these copper-plated oblongs of card whenever she could from Malcolm Halliday, who tended to toss them at once into the fire. 'Miss Bellamy ought to go, even if you don't want to,' she chided him. 'Do 'er good. Time 'er 'ad some fun.'

Mrs Partridge seemed aware of something lacking in Rachel's life that Rachel was not herself conscious of. It did not seem right to Mrs Partridge that a young woman should spend so little time just enjoying herself. Malcolm protested mildly that in his experience any invitation accepted by a vet to any social occasion at all would call down upon that vet's head a flood of emergencies, usually in the middle of some delightful entertainment, or when dressed for a formal dinner or a fancy dress party. He recalled, with his normal serious voice and manner, a colleague of his younger days who had turned up to help at a difficult foaling still dressed as a banana.

The occasions that Rachel did eventually attend gave rise to no such lunatic situations, however, and indeed provided very little in the way of the sort of fun Mrs Partridge wished for her.

Small town gatherings, with the vicar much in evidence, are not given to levity or roisterousness, even at Christmas, and Rachel was of course out of the age-group that was asked to jollier parties, not so much because of her years as by reason of the supposed dignity of her profession. Mrs Partridge, privately, thought it was a shame. She needed to whoop it up a bit, did their Miss Bellamy. She wouldn't hear a word said against Mr Halliday, Mrs Partridge wouldn't, but he wasn't ideal company for a young woman and that was the truth, what with not getting on too well with people, and not feeling quite the ticket himself most of the time, poor man.

Admittedly, Rachel did sometimes meet, at one or another of these functions, some man to whom she warmed, for whom she felt the first electrical stirrings of attractions, but the pleasantness of the meeting was enough in itself and she wanted nothing more. She was far too busy for such things. What things? Well, certainly for what she had once heard described as 'sexual gymnastics'; and as for Romance, well, what of that? The high tower, the far off Prince, the shadows of ecstasy, all seemed highly unlikely in the midst of a busy and thoroughly down-to-earth professional life. The practical light of day reduced such things to nonsense. Romantic lovers have to die if they are not to succumb to reality, otherwise Juliet grows fat; Romeo loses his silver tongue. Six months living in a semi with Cleopatra and Antony would have loathed her. What was real love then? She had no pattern but that which had existed between her mother and her father, and that had been destroyed. Even if something so rare could be found again, who could ensure that it too would not be snatched away?

So although Rachel mildly enjoyed her outings, which Malcolm quietly tried to ensure she did not get called away from more than absolutely necessary, she did not scan the horizon for Mr Right, and Mrs Partridge despaired of her. She told Tom Adams as much when he came to take surgery for Malcolm while Rachel was on her Christmas visit to Parkwood Farm to see her mother. 'Nice young woman like that. Seems a shame she's got no one—no one special, if you know what I mean,' Mrs Partridge said to him.

'You shouldn't interfere, you old besom,' he told her, and picked her up and held her with her feet several inches above the floor, till she beat on his chest and told him to give over. He set her down then, and laughed till the plates shook on the dresser.

'Well, it is a shame, for all you say,' Mrs Partridge went on, when she could make herself heard. 'Some people's lives need a bit of steering, that's all: a bit of a push in the right direction.'

'And you're applying for your pilot's licence, is that it? Beware of rocks, my lovely Mrs P.'

'You can talk,' she said, her voice crisp. 'That silly piece you were walking out with nearly scuttled you good and proper. Yes, I know I'm not s'posed to mention it, but I'm old enough to be your ma nearly. I hope you've put all that be'ind you, and that's a fact.'

For a moment Mrs Partridge thought she had gone too far. Tom Adams swung round on her, his face darkening, and she waited, expecting an explosion of anger. Then he shrugged, his expression relaxing.

'Sunk without trace,' he said.

When Rachel arrived at Parkwood, it was with the oddest sensation of having travelled down an Alice like tunnel into her past. Everything looked so ridiculously unchanged: as if nothing had so much as breathed since she was last there. The season was different, of course, but it could have been any of the winters of her life: the cattle in the strawy yards, the dutch barns filled solid with last season's hay: Sam out on the tractor doing the final trimming of the field-hedges. Only one thing altered the landscape, made it different from the remembered winters of childhood: the great elms were all gone, whose tall figure-of-eight shapes had dominated the skyline. Even their dead skeletons were vanished now, felled and carted for firewood. The Dutch-elm disease had made for a bleaker, less hospitable landscape. Mary Bellamy had planted young ash and chestnut,

161

but these trees had a quarter century of growth in front of them to make the sort of size that would give that welcome greenness, that shade in high summer that the cattle loved: a lodging for nesting birds and sleeping owls, a citadel for insects of a thousand different kinds.

It was lovely to be home. She had not let herself realise how much she had missed it. Her mother spoiled her with small treats, breakfast in bed, a day out to Oxford and theatre in the evening: a last good play before the inevitable pantomime.

On the farm, she found herself looking at the cattle with a professional as well as a family eye. Yes, they were as good as she had remembered them. She could not, even if she had wished to, fault their condition and their splendid health. Her mother was a genius, there was no doubting it. With the land she had purchased over the last few years, the farm now stood at eighty acres: a fleabite of a holding against their big-business neighbours on either side, each of whom owned something like a thousand. Parkwood's land was particularly good-hearted though, and well watered, and the farmhouse was handsome in its plain mellow brick, under the shade of its blue cedar tree that Peter Bellamy's great great-grandfather had planted. The smell of that tree was part of Rachel's childhood too. Looking back, it was tempting to recall only sunny days and successes. The tree would remember her miseries too, like the day Grandfather died, and she had realised fully for the first time the fact of death, which is so much less acceptable than the 'facts of life'. These she had absorbed along with the rest of her knowledge of the farm, and found nothing remarkable in them. Death was far more remote. She had seen dead creatures often enough, but it was not the same as Grandfather gone for ever, his lovely gravelly voice no longer to flow, his long fingers lying still, with which he used to scratch the sides of his beard when he was thinking.

The tree had heard lesser troubles too: failed tests, school enmities, all the imagined injustices and tribulations of growing up. It had taken a good many kicks and hammerings from Rachel in a rage. When she had come home for her father's funeral, she had seen these past scars on it, and had felt that they were carved into herself.

For Christmas, Sam had gone up a ladder and filled the tree with lights. He was getting old now, and it alarmed Rachel to see him shinning about like an antediluvian monkey, an antiquated ship's boy, but she could not dissuade him, and he would not let her do it.

'That's my job that is. I knows where they goes.' And certainly he got them hooked up quickly enough, returning to the ground triumphant, if short of breath, to order Rachel to 'Switch 'em on then.'

The bulbs glowed out in half a dozen different colours, and Sam looked as pleased as if he had floodlit Westminster Abbey single-handed.

'It looks lovely, Sam,' Rachel said.

'Always does,' Sam answered. 'I knows where they goes, see. Makes all the difference.'

Parkwood Green, the village, was full of Christmas comings and goings, Rachel was greeted like a lost lamb returned, was asked how she was getting along, questioned about her new job. She saw many well-known faces, but some were missing, dead or moved away: the village population was changing. There were new people in several of the houses, and some of them were foreigners. One lot was from London, or so it was thought, another from some outlandish place up North. They'd bought The Grange after old Mrs Stackwell passed on, and these people only came down weekends. All week the place stood empty and they paid Dolly Marston a good wage to go in and keep it clean. It seemed a funny way to live, when you came to think about it, all to-and-fro like that.

For a few brief days Rachel became re-absorbed into her old life: shared with her mother all the old Christmas rituals: joined the long queue of communicants at the Midnight Eucharist. She had not missed going since she was confirmed at fourteen. It was tradition, rather than belief, that brought her to it, and yet it moved her to see the solemn progress of so many diverse people, from the chancel steps under the sturdy Norman arch, along the carpeted flagstones to the candlelit altar.

On Christmas Day Rachel went briefly—though she was not a great one for visiting graves—to see her father's headstone, in the lower corner of the churchyard, near the wall, where also a small tablet commemorated Miss Blanchard: just her name, her dates, and the words *'Miseris succurrere disco'*. That almost untranslatable piece of Latin was apt enough for the dear old battleaxe, Rachel thought. 'I teach compassionate care for the suffering,' had been her own translation of it. It had not only been towards animals that Battling Blanchard had extended her care, either. Rachel remembered a story about her taking some woman, a neighbour of hers, to the hospital to be admitted for a prolapse. There had been what Miss Blanchard later reported as 'an administrative cock-and-balls' and the woman had been told she must go home again, untreated, despite the fact that she was in considerable pain, and had a large, demanding and unsympathetic household awaiting her if she returned. Miss Blanchard, furious, had marched in and collared the specialist, told him all this, and added, enraged, that if the poor woman had been a cow, Miss Blanchard herself would have had her operated on and back out in the field eating grass by now.

Rachel had stood quietly for several minutes by these memorials. These two had been landmarks in her life. Then as the day began to darken, she went back to Parkwood, where her mother, the milking over, was waiting for her, with tea by the fire. She felt very content to live once again this old life she had known, yet something altered in Rachel over those days. As she walked among familiar places, talked to old friends, she found in herself a subtle feeling of change. She seemed, imperceptibly, to have stepped away from all these close and long-established things: even from her mother. When they spoke together, talking of Rachel's job, of Malcolm, of the assorted characters in and about Milchester, or discussed the cows, or did the daily, necessary things about the house and farm,

166

Rachel observed her mother closely: the greyer hair, the additional lines that betrayed her apparent unchangeableness. She was a handsome woman, even now, Rachel thought, and one I'd like, even if she weren't my mother. She remembered, ruefully, the battles, the obstinacy, the plain bloody-mindedness of the years of puberty, and was glad that was all over: that the affection had survived. It survived now, but although it was in no way diminished, that too was changed, as if their relationship, like a dance, now moved to a different pattern. Even in her new life she would be aware of everything here, but it would not draw her back so strongly, and in the knowledge of this it was difficult to leave when the time came. There had been so much to talk about, so much to catch up on, that a great deal had been left unsaid. She had not, even now, given her mother the full flavour of her new life. There were still a hundred stories to be told.

'Don't work too hard,' Mary Bellamy said, when Rachel was ready to leave, with Jessica's engine running in the sharp air. 'Write to me. Let me know how things are with you.'

Rachel nodded. Already her mind was racing ahead to Milchester; hoping Malcolm was feeling all right, that she hadn't left him too much to do.

'I shall miss you,' her mother said.

'I shall miss you,' said Rachel.

As she drove off in Jessica, Rachel watched in the rear-view mirror, her mother standing with one arm upraised, the other angled to shade her eyes against the winter sun.

Coming out of the shallow Parkwood valley was like stepping out of the water after a pleasant swim; refreshed, and with a desire to have a good shake and race off to get the blood moving.

Enclosed by the little yellow car she drove through the brisk, bright December day, and after a while she began to sing for the sheer pleasure of being herself. It was an exuberant Pollyanna mood, with nothing to discontent her.

The fields were humped and brown, just sugared with frost still where the sun had not risen high enough to warm them. Sheep dotted some of the pastureland, but most of the cattle were yarded now, to keep them well and fat, and to make sure their great splay feet did not damage the sward that would feed them in the spring. In one field she passed, a gang of woolly foals, weaned from their mothers, played their wild games, and made pretence of biting and kicking each other. Their manes

168

and tails were thick with burrs from where they had been browsing in the hedges. Rachel stopped the car and walked over to see them, and they came in a snorting, cavorting bunch to within a few feet of where she stood by the gate, like naughty children who have come bursting in on polite company. Only one would come to her: a little dun filly with a winter coat like a hearthrug, and brown glowing eyes fringed with lashes that would have been the envy of Hollywood.

Rachel, without particular motive, ran her hands over the foal and felt good firm flesh under the woolliness. So often a thick felting of hair could hide skeletal ribs as this time of the year. She was pleased the creatures were well, and cared for, despite their rough appearance. For their part they soon lost interest in her when they discovered she had brought nothing for them, and went thundering down the field again, their hoofs drumming on the hard ground.

Mrs Partridge met her at the door of Stapleton House when she arrived there, and hustled her into the kitchen for tea and gossip. Rachel had brought her a pottery cottage as a Christmas gift. She was known to have a great collection of them, and this one, all delicately painted with roses, pleased her very much. For Malcolm, Rachel had brought driving gloves, handmade by the wife of a saddler who lived not far from Parkwood.

'We've missed you,' Mrs Partridge said. ' 'e's looked like a lost dog over Christmas.'

Rachel looked at her with surprise.

' 'E doesn't say much, but I knows 'im well enough after all this time, and you've made a difference in 'im. There's more goes on inside than 'e lets on.'

'But he's been all right?' Rachel asked. 'Not ill or anything?'

'Oh, 'e's kept well enough, and that's a blessing, and we weren't too busy: only one emergency, and that was that stupid Jane Carter, stuffing 'er peke with turkey and not taking the bones out. Mr Adams saw to that. Gave 'er a right telling off, too. I 'eard him clear as day when I was cleaning the top bathroom. 'E took all the farm calls too, so Mr Aitch could 'ave a bit of a rest.'

'Oh goodness,' Rachel said. 'All that on top of his own work. I shouldn't have gone.'

'My stars, yes you should,' protested Mrs Partridge. 'It weren't no worse than before you come. 'E's always helped us out, Mr Adams 'as.'

'Mr Halliday's known him a long time, then?'

'Oh yes, from the time when Mr 'Alliday's mother and Lady Bramwell used to work together for the WRVS. Mr Adams is Lady Bramwell's nephew, you see. Did all them paintings 'er's got. Took me up there once and showed 'em to me, Mr Adams did when 'e was on 'is way taking me to our Maggie's house in Stroud. She was away, Lady Bramwell I mean, not our Maggie. Garn to the South of France on a walking tour, she 'ad. Wouldn't credit it would you, at 'er age?'

'Mr Adams painted those pictures?' Rachel was amazed.

'Every one. Don't take to 'em meself. Too bright. I likes a nice dark picture. Proper oils. Constable and that.'

Rachel decided that she would take more notice of Tom Adams next time they met. A man who could paint pictures like that deserved looking at. She wondered if he would show her more of them if she asked. Fancy his being that fierce old woman's nephew. Yet, when Rachel thought about it, there was something in the eyes that was common to both: a challenging intelligence, a wicked humour. She felt the same wariness in the presence of each of them: unease at their facility for outrageous comment or preposterous action. She wondered, practically, why Lady Bramwell did not have Tom Adams to heal her animals, as well as to decorate her walls. He was every bit as well qualified. Later, when she asked Malcolm this question, he explained. 'She believes everyone should do one job well and stick to it,' he said. 'She sees he's a brilliant painter, so she assumes he's not up to much as a vet. I've tried to tell her otherwise, but she's not a persuadable woman. She was known as HMS Implacable in her WRVS days, or so I was told. Tom's an excellent vet: a better diagnostician than me, and with a more modern approach, but Margaret Bramwell won't believe it. She approves of you, by the way. We had a long talk about you when I called last. She sees you as a standard bearer for the monstrous regiment, I think. Again, I thought it not worth my while to disillusion her.'

'Oh?' said Rachel.

Malcolm looked at her gravely. 'Despite your sex, my dear Rachel, I do not regard you as an ardent feminist. I have certainly seen no signs in you of a desire to prove that Women Are Best, and thank God for it. Some women are damned awful. So are a great many men. There is no battle between us. We work well together, and I am very glad you came.'

Even though no battle did exist between

them, he won a small unwitting victory over her, for she became quite flustered by the unusual warmth of his praise, stammered a reply, and hurried off on pretence of being needed in the kitchen.

Some weeks later, Rachel received an invitation to a private view of work by three local painters. One of them was Thomas Adams. She had mentioned to him, briefly, in the course of conversation, that she had seen and admired his work, and his reaction had been to raise one of his surprising, mobile eyebrows and say, 'Perceptive as well as beautiful. That's rare'—a remark which had left her feeling stranded for words, like a fish on a river-bank.

The invitation was a pleasant surprise and, chivvied by Mrs Partridge, she went along on the appropriate evening. In the Long Room over the museum, where the pictures had been hung, people stood in little groups, chatting and drinking wine, clutching their catalogues. Rachel moved among them. One or two spoke, a little loudly, of brushwork and focal points and chiaroscuro. Others appeared to be discussing each other, or the price of cheese, keeping their backs to the work on the walls. To have been invited was quite enough.

Rachel began her examination of the pictures. Against Tom Adams' work the other

paintings retreated and hid in their frames, and
she began to feel sorry for the other exhibitors.
They had put up pleasant, competent work,
and well worth looking at, if your eyes had
not already been dazzled by the colours and
forms of the Adams' landscapes, for they were
like kingfishers at a gathering of sparrows. She
felt a great longing to possess one, but the
prices were well beyond her, and anyway,
Stapleton House would have shaken with
astonishment to have any such thing on its
muted walls. She was pleased for Tom Adams'
sake, though to see that already one or two
frames were marked with the red spot that
denotes a sale.

'Is it up to your expectations?' He had come
up, soft-footed behind her, and made her
jump.

'Yes,' she said, a little breathless at being
so surprised in the midst of her thoughts.
'I like this one, of the beeches at the edge
of the hill, and that view down the escarpment.'

'I said you had a good eye. Those are far
and away the best which is probably why they
won't sell. I hope they won't. I like them too
much myself.'

She thought he might move away then to
speak to the many other people who were

hovering round but he didn't. Rachel felt that there was about to be a hole in their conversation and that she ought to fill it. She said awkwardly, 'I never imagined, when I first saw your paintings at Lady Bramwell's, that they were the work of a vet.'

He laughed. 'I nearly wasn't one,' he said. 'Halfway through university I wanted to chuck everything, live in Paris, do the whole Great Painter bit. Aunt Margaret was all set to fund me to do it. Then I grew up. Found myself enjoying the course. I serve two masters tolerably well, but Aunt Margaret was a long time forgiving me.'

Rachel looked at Tom Adams and considered him. His glance was away from her now, and he looked round the room at the people gathered in it. He was a large man, though not overpoweringly so. His beard, which was trimmed and neat, still had a wildness about it, like his expressive eyebrows. His voice, though it was not loud, was resonant and strong, without accent or affectation. His hands were large, square-fingered and very clean.

'You don't look like a painter,' she said, when his attention returned to her again.

'Oh, don't I now,' he said, and put his hands on her upper arms, quite gently, and turned her squarely towards him, looking her up and down with a serious expression.

'And neither do you look like a vet,' he remarked. She felt herself bristling, defensively, and her reply came out almost snappish.

'What do I look like, then?'

'You look...,' he said slowly, considering her: 'You look like everything a woman should be, done up in a small parcel. You look delightful. You are also an excellent vet, despite not looking like one, as Malcolm has made quite clear to me. Not that I couldn't see it well enough for myself.'

He still did not smile, but his tone was so light that she felt it impossible to take him seriously. Even so Rachel could not hold his gaze as he said this. She felt foolishly like some bashful child about whom the whole school has just been told something praiseworthy. She turned away from him. He was not to see her face flooding with colour like the heroine of some twopenny novel. 'Well,' she said, 'You paint a great deal better than you look.' She had not meant that. She knew what she meant, and the words had come out wrong, like an insult. She became entirely flustered, and murmuring, 'Goodbye,' she pushed her way through a gaggle of people and out of his sight, hearing as she did so voices making towards him with little murmurs of approval, stopping any possible pursuit of her with their demands for his attention.

CHAPTER 9

Winter deepened, and throughout January and February Rachel worked in appalling weather. The little yellow car put on snow-chains, and often followed the plough that came to clear the lanes. When she could drive no further towards some urgent case, she would wade through snow that was sometimes hip deep, clad in Mrs Partridge's nephew's fishing boots which were ideal wear in such conditions.

Lambs began to arrive. Ewes played their whole boxfuls of perinatal tricks. Barns and byres and stables were appallingly cold, and the northerly winds made draughts cut through them that turned fingers blue and made eyes sting and fill with water. A hand, placed ungloved on an iron gate, would stick to it and burn with cold, and ache for an hour afterwards. Between snows and frosts, when the wind veered, the mud was appalling, and could drag the boots off you between one side of a yard and the other. There were times when, numb with cold and damp to her bones, Rachel felt she would trade all her years of veterinary training for one peaceful afternoon by a roaring fire with a novel and a dish of buttered toast in a house with no telephone. The temptation did not last, but it was very real, and its voice was at its most wheedling when that dreadful bell cut through her sleep and the blackness of an icy night, to pitch her out on some emergency.

Sometimes, when Malcolm came in from such weather, he would look more dead than alive, but he stood his turn and did not complain. Occasionally though, when she returned from morning visits, she would find Tom Adams taking surgery.

'I've sent him to bed. He shouldn't be up at all,' Tom said on one such occasion.

'But what about your own practice?' she would ask, only to discover more often than not that it was Tom's day off, or it was a Wednesday when they had no surgery there. Sometimes, when she had taken breath and got warm again, she would go and assist him. He was very good. His diagnosis was excellent. She could not fault it, and found this un-justifiably irritating: and he would speak to her teasingly, and try to make her laugh when she wished to be serious, and this irritated her too. 'If they pushed that four-minute button I think you'd laugh,' she told him severely. He laughed again. 'You're out of date,' he said. 'I doubt we get that long now. Even so, can you think of anything more constructive to do with the time?' he asked. 'It's too long to say the Nunc Dimittis, and too short to make love. Laughing would do well enough.'

She wanted to box his ears.

She had little time to analyse her reactions to him: she was far too busy to discuss with herself why his ebullient and outgoing manner should seem...should seem what? Offensive, perhaps, after Malcolm's reticence. He cracked jokes with the children who brought their small creatures for treatment, was chatty and charming to the old men and women whose cats and dogs had taken the place their own children once filled. Whatever was, or was not, the matter, he sent them all away with something to rub on, to put in the food, to administer by some means or other. Very often this seemed quite unnecessary to Rachel and, eventually, her voice sounding considerably primmer than she had intended, she told him so. He looked at her, thoughtfully, as if weighing her criticism in the balance.

'That spaniel that just went out,' he said. 'Just what was the matter, would you say?'

'Nothing specific,' Rachel replied. 'She's just very old.'

'Got a cure for that, have you?' he asked, and when she made no reply, but busied herself tidying away the instruments, he said, 'Those chalk pills I prescribed will do her no harm, and her owner will feel better for giving her *something*. It's the same with kids, when their ponies are lame. You know, and I know, that nine times out of ten it's rest that brings about a cure, but the poor little so-and-so's that are missing out on their riding need something to keep their minds off the fact. Give 'em something to rub in three times a day: it reminds 'em they've got a lame pony there, and not one to go galloping about on.'

'Maybe,' Rachel replied, but a stupid inability to leave well alone drove her on to say, 'but I'm not sure its entirely ethical.'

There was a silence. Then, 'Good God!' he said in a great roar of sound. 'What will you think of next? Report me for malpractice, will you, for employing a few mild psychological tricks? You can be a very irritating young woman, Miss Bellamy, even without trying, and you seem to have been putting considerable effort into it since you came back to us.'

Rachel was so surprised that she shut her mouth and could think of nothing further to say. She felt it was almost certain that he would

181

think she was sulking, which she was not. No, she was not. However, there seemed no openings for any kind of conversation or comment, except on the work in hand.

The bad weather held: there was no respite. Soaked boots, snow-soaked garments steamed round the Aga in the Stapleton House kitchen every night, to make them fit for wear each morning.

On one particularly severe day, when squalls of snow kept blowing up and drifting the lanes solid as fast as the plough could clear them, Rachel struggled from early morning to get to outlying farms, mainly for lambing problems, coping not only with assorted veterinary dilemmas but equally with the gloom and depression of the farmers themselves as they recounted their losses, their searches after lost animals, the rapid depletion of their hay stocks. As she fought on from place to place, she felt, not surprisingly, increasingly weary, with every muscle aching with stepping through depths of snow, her mind numbed with the effects of cold. She had reached the point when she felt that enough was enough, and that it was just as well that she had finished the last call of the day, when someone came out from the farmhouse outside while she was packing her equipment into Jessica ready to head for Milchester, and said there was a telephone call for her. It was Mrs Partridge. Could Rachel call in to Ashton Stud on her way back to see a mare that was worrying Harry Ellis? The message was that the mare seemed colicky, and that Harry felt in his bones it was no ordinary colic, and Rachel trusted the experience in Harry's bones. He had been around horses for long enough to have an eye for a creature that 'just ain't right', though to anyone else it might look as well as usual, and he knew at once if a sick animal needed attention other than his own.

So, fighting against her body's desire for warmth, rest and food, she set off towards the stud. She found some chocolate in the glove-compartment and ate that. She put the heater on full and felt sensation come painfully back to feet and fingers. When she arrived at the drive of Ashton Stud it was impassable. She sighed, climbed out of Jessica and tramped away towards the stables. Snow had been cleared from in front of the loosebox doors in the yard, and the ground swept as far as possible, but muck and straw had frozen solid wherever they had fallen, and all the stand-pipes, despite their lagging, had drips of ice at their mouths. Harry was fussing like a houseproud woman caught on an off day, but

Rachel could read behind this minor irritation his concern for the mare, who was stamping and banging in her discomfort, making it quite clear how she felt. Harry apologised for sending for Rachel. 'That's all right, Harry,' she said. It was a mild enough colic compared with some Rachel had seen, but it was causing the mare to sweat and kick at her belly for all that. Rachel bent and listened at her flank for the usual orchestral noises of a horse's gut, and heard only the faintest murmur there. The mare's heart-rate was up, beating urgently against Rachel's ear through the stethoscope.

'She's got an impaction, I think,' Rachel said. 'I'll feel inside her.'

With the long glove on, Rachel made a rectal examination of the mare, Harry holding the head end, soothing, comforting, so she stood as quiet as her pain would allow. It was not long before Rachel's searching hand proved what she had expected; a great doughy mass, not obstructing the whole gut, but lying, as it were, up a blind alley, yet pressing painfully upon it, and on the developing foal.

'Well, the sooner we get rid of that, the better,' Rachel said. 'We'll tube her with Epsom Salts and liquid paraffin. It'll probably need doing daily for a week or so.'

Rachel had brought her stomach tube,

having been pretty certain she would need it. Harry brought clean buckets and the salts and liquid paraffin.

'Can't I ever catch you out?' Rachel teased him. 'You must have the best stocked medicine cupboard short of a vet's in the whole county.'

'Better safe than sorry,' Harry Ellis said. 'I've a few things in there you wouldn't approve of, I daresay. Still, I keeps me horses fit mostly.'

'Harry you're a genius. Now, stop fishing for compliments, and we'll get on with the job.'

They worked as swiftly as cold hands would allow, the mare standing quiet, as if aware that this extraordinary process would ease her. Harry kept up a constant flow of endearments, observations and mild curses, all delivered in the same soothing tone, so that there was no need for any other restraint. Harry would not have a twitch on his beloved horses. Under his spell, they never needed it.

When the job was done, Rachel left Harry to clear up, saying she must get home quickly, while there was still light. She walked swiftly away down the cleared pathway past the other boxes. She looked into the stallion box as she walked by. Then she stopped horrified. Highlight was cast against the wall and in a bad way.

Harry Ellis was the only one in the yard that day: the two lads and the girl had gone to Gloucester at the weekend and were stranded there because of the snow. There was no-one about otherwise but Mrs Carrington up at the house, with her elderly housekeeper.

Despite his thick bed, wheat straw banked to the sides of the box, Highlight had managed to get himself wedged, half on his back, half on his side, with his legs curled under him and jammed against the wall. His neck was snaked backwards, his ears low, his eyes glassy and fearful. Rachel judged he must have been like it for some time, for she and Ellis had been busy at some distance with the mare, and there was no-one else who might have come by to notice and give the alarm.

If he stayed for long like that he could damage himself internally. Eventually, he would die.

'Get some rope,' she called out, 'Highlight's cast.' But Harry Ellis, coming up behind her, had seen the horse lying there and had already been to fetch some. 'Here,' he said.

Rachel entered the box, speaking softly to the stallion. He rolled his eye at her, and his belly heaved and shuddered. The stonework was marked with the flailing of his hoofs where

186

he had tried, at first, to push himself back over. Rachel looped ropes over the fore and hind legs furthest beneath him. Had he been any less far over she could have rolled him on to his feet again without much effort, but as he lay she could not budge him. 'Harry!' she called. 'Is there no-one at all who could help?'

In reply he put his hand upon the door, as if to offer himself, but at that moment a large shape darkened the doorway.

'Need a hand?' a voice said. 'I saw that funny little car of yours from the top road. I wondered if you were stuck in this fiendish weather, so I came down to see.'

Rachel recognised the voice at once. 'It's Highlight that's stuck, Mr Adams,' she said.

'So I see. Well, if you'll call me Tom, I'll get him up for you,' he grinned.

'You wants to watch it,' Harry Ellis said. 'That horse doesn't...'

'It's all right, Harry,' Rachel interrupted. 'This gentleman knows what he's doing.' Weary though she was, there was a gleam in Rachel's eye that she was careful to hide from the two men. Tom took the rope that was looped about the stallion's hind leg.

'Keep the front rope steady and taut, I'll pull him over. Watch he doesn't thrash at you as he comes,' he said.

The ease with which he got the horse up would have been a pleasure to watch, had she been in a mood to take pleasure in it, but she was cold and tired, and she was angry because she had been unable to help the stallion, when for Tom it seemed no effort at all.

The black horse stood with his head down, and after taking several deep breaths he shook himself and snorted, as if it had been an everyday roll, and not almost his last. He seemed entirely docile, until Tom moved towards the door. Perhaps until that moment he had been unaware of a man's presence in his box. Rachel had never seen a horse so transformed. His eyes seemed to blaze out double their size, and his ears flattened themselves invisibly against his skull. The high, savage scream he let out into the cold air was terrible to hear, as he lunged at Tom with his teeth bared, his forelegs flailing.

In not telling Tom about Highlight's dislike of men, Rachel had meant only the most minor revenge. She had thought the stallion might nip at him or feint a kick. She had never imagined this terrifying hatred. All her idiotic desire to do him down evaporated. She ran between Tom and the stallion.

'Get out! Get out quick! He won't hurt me. It's you he's after.'

Harry Ellis had opened the box door. 'She's right, sir. Run for it!'

He did, but he dragged her with him, and they all tumbled in a heap in the snowy yard.

'I don't think he was in the mood to discriminate any further between the sexes,' Tom said at last. 'Thanks for the warning.'

Rachel listened acutely to the timber of his voice for the least tremor of sarcasm. There was none she could trace, but perhaps there was an intensifying of the gleam in his eye.

Harry Ellis did not betray her, and she was left to nurse a bruised conscience along with the sore wrist Tom had given her as he pulled her clear. They plodded through the snow to where Jessica was parked. The sun had broken through and sparkled off drifted walls and frost-heavy branches. All day the temperature had been well below freezing. If you had time to look, it was very beautiful. Colours that green earth would have absorbed gleamed back off the snow in brilliant reflections of blue and rose and gold. Everything was very still, very silent. Beside the faint creak of their boots in the powdery whiteness, the only sound was the running of the stream, carving blackly through its self-made tunnel of ice, its cold water steamimg amid the even colder snow. Rachel glanced at Tom as they walked. He

189

made no conversation, but looked about him, storing what he saw: these colours of a landscape turned Arctic. She felt it would be as well not to engage him in talk.

When they arrived at the car he got in with her, and they drove to where he had left his own vehicle.

'Thanks for the lift,' he said.

'Thank you for helping,' she replied. She felt very awkward in his company and was glad when he was back in his own car. She followed him along the two tracks of packed snow that kept the road just passable. It was not easy driving. Her arms ached, and her eyes were tired from concentrating on the snowy surface, but his lights ahead of her helped her see the shape of the road, until he took his own turn as they approached Milchester, stuck a gloved hand out of the window with thumb uppermost, and saluted her as he went.

She did not see him for some weeks after that. He had gone to Scotland, she was told, to give a series of lectures at Edinburgh University. Malcolm seemed to recover his health with the spring, and they coped well between them. Her experience widened. She did her first caesarian on a nice little dachsund bitch that had been waylaid by something large and shaggy. Her owners had brought her to surgery, wondering why she was so fat when her appetite was so small.

The variety of animals that came under Rachel's care was amazing, and if she had thought small-animal work was going to be all cats and dogs, she was proved entirely wrong. Mice, gerbils, toads, ferrets, an African grey parrot that kept muttering 'Get knotted', a miniature goat from the Children's Corner at the local stately home, all came to her for treatment. Even farm-work had its surprises. She answered a request for a visit to a farm out on the Cheltenham Road, and found herself faced with a llama, with toothache. It was an odd creature to find in a Cotswold pasture, but the farmer had several, and swore he was on to a good thing.

One day, early in the spring, she had an even greater surprise, and one that, as it turned out, she wished had never happened. Just as she finished surgery there was an urgent knocking on the door, and there, looking very grim, was Bill Fowler.

'Anne sent me. Can you come? It's the horse.' You could not argue with a face like that, or make any delay. As they walked towards the cars he said he had found the Arab gelding in the field, looking desperately ill, and had led it to the stable where it now was.

191

'Anne told me who you were then. Said if I didn't fetch you she'd leave me.' He looked shaken and apprehensive, as if someone were about to pull the world from under him.

'You go ahead,' Rachel told him. 'Let her know I'm coming.'

She checked that she had everything in the car she might possibly need, and set off to follow him at a dangerously fast and highly illegal speed. Whatever it was must be bad, for Anne Fowler to make such a threat. Rachel arrived at the house and drove round to the yard. Anne Fowler ran up to her, white, half-demented with worry. She ignored her husband, who had arrived immediately before the little yellow car, and seized hold of Rachel as if she were a lifeline.

'Please,' she said. 'Come and see. Please tell me you can do something for him.'

Rachel entered the box, and her heart sank. The beautiful Arab was a cruel, wooden caricature of himself; his legs straddled and stiff, his muscles in spasm, his neck and tail stretched out. The once expressive, mobile ears were pricked up in a ghastly alertness, and his nostrils were flared like a rocking-horse. She touched his rigid jaw under the chin, and saw the 'third eyelid' flicker across. She had seen tetanus before. This was a classic case: absolutely according to the book. And she was far too late. Somehow needing a moment's delay before telling Anne, Rachel asked if Hassan had had any injuries at all recently.

'No, none.'

'Yes,' Bill Fowler corrected her. 'He caught himself on his fetlock, on that bit of corrugated iron in the bottom fence. It was only a scratch.'

'Tis not as deep as a well, nor as wide as a church door, but t'will serve.' The words floated up to Rachel from the corner of her mind. She took a deep breath, and told them. She also told them that the symptoms were so severe that a cure was very unlikely, and that in her opinion, he should be put down at once, to save him pain. They both looked at her, in horrified and miserable silence, for a long while, before Bill said: 'Was there nothing we could have done before?'

'Yes,' Rachel said, her voice was angry, despite her effort to control it. 'You could have had him vaccinated,' she said. 'I suppose that was an unnecessary expense too?' It was wicked of her. She had no right to harass them when they were already so distressed. Yet she looked at the agonised creature in the stable and she could not help herself.

In a very small and very quiet voice, Anne Fowler said: 'Will you do it, please?'

Rachel's heart sank. Of all the things she had dreaded being asked, of all the jobs she had hoped to be spared for a while, this was her utmost dread: to have to shoot a horse. They could get the slaughterman, couldn't they? He could do it, and take the carcass away. No point making two jobs out of one. She started to suggest this, but already Anne Fowler was saying, 'Please. He knows you.'

The poor beast did not know anyone. All he knew was the pain of muscle in spasm and the terror that the disease brought with it. Rachel looked at him again and was aware she could not make him wait to be released from it.

'All right,' she said, her voice abrupt.

She sent the Fowlers away, almost shouting at them as they hesitated, hovering, as if offering help, though what kind of help they thought they could be was beyond Rachel.

'Go into the house, and stay there. Bill can telephone Milchester 318, they'll see to everything else.'

She knew Bill was acquainted with the number. Beasts of his had gone to the knacker's before, when his husbandry had gone awry.

As she walked to the car Rachel felt that peculiar unreality that surrounds such sudden appalling moments in life. She felt as if there were space between her and everything tangible around her. To open the car door, to grasp and lift the humane killer, all took positive effort, as if everything were just a little further away than where her eyes registered them. She walked as if she were in a black dream, back to the stable to where Hassan stood, his position unchanged, except that he flinched, violently, as the light from the opened door struck and terrified him.

She spoke to him very softly, but did not touch him, would not distress him further. In her mind she drew those invisible diagonals that the text books all showed: the exact position on Hassan's brow for the humane killer. It took the greatest effort of will to keep her hands steady, her eyes fixed on the place. Something welled up in her like a monstrous growth, and she felt she must choke.

When it was over, she turned towards the door and walked out, hardly remembering, afterwards, getting into the car, fastening her seat belt, moving off out of the yard and up the drive to the road. She became aware of herself only when she realised that she could scarcely see the road ahead of her, and when another vehicle, overtaking, tooted in irritation at her erratic course.

CHAPTER 10

For a while after that, nothing seemed to go right for Rachel. She found herself, as Colin Ross had warned her, making mistakes, errors of judgment, that must be caught quickly before they caused disaster. Her mind felt dull, all keenness of perception blunted. She was physically weary, dispirited, and full of those blues that long for spring warmth and sunshine, and the easing of the pressures of life. There was a spate of deaths among her patients: none of them avoidable, none of them—despite her frame of mind—in any way her fault, but she began to think they were.

She remembered, with particular anger against herself, the beautiful Labrador bitch who had lived at the newsagents in the High Street. Her owners, John and Pauline Martin, had been so proud of her: the first pedigree dog they had ever owned. They did not want her for breeding, just as a companion and a guard for the shop, though Rachel had doubted whether the bracken-coloured bitch would have made any sort of job of that; she was so ridiculously, ebulliently friendly. It was at Rachel's suggestion that the bitch had come to be spayed, for she had explained to the Martins that there might be problems with the town's stray dogs when Toba came in season.

Uplands Golden October. She had come into the surgery, waving her tail friendly and confident, not at all perturbed by the strange smell of the clinical room, the high scrubbed table, the trays of instruments. She made no fuss, and accepted all the preliminaries, trusting Rachel's voice and hands. She was the healthiest possible creature: deep bodied, heart steady and strong, good muscle tone, not too fat. The anaesthetic was no problem to her at all. The operation completed, Rachel had allowed her home, knowing that John and Pauline would nurse her devotedly. Yet within twenty-four hours she had haemorrhaged and died. Horrified, Rachel took the body back to the surgery and made a thorough examination. The ligatures on the ovarian arteries had not held. It was something that did happen: on rare occasions, but it did happen. So now when Rachel walked to the Martin's shop for the papers she could not bring herself to look at the corner from which Toba had so often risen to greet her.

Another, and continuing source of self blame

was the colt at Smailes' Barn. At Smailes' Barn lived Janet Andrews, who bred ponies in a small and catchpenny way. She had no spending-room, too few acres for the creatures she kept, and luck far worse than Job's. Rachel had been to castrate a colt foal for her: a poor, weedly little thing who would have done better to keep his masculinity a little longer, but Miss Andrews had a buyer for him if he was cut, so Rachel had done the job, and returned home satisfied that all was well. Next morning she was summoned by telephone to a house near Stroud, to which the foal had apparently been sent the moment Rachel had finished the operation, the conditions of sale having been fulfilled. A voice, near hysteria, announced that the foal was bleeding to death.

In a converted garage behind a house on the outskirts of the town, the foal, unweaned, uncomfortable and desperate for its mother, was whinnying high and shrill, and drumming its small hoofs against the wooden walls. A woman and a little girl were looking in through a wire-netted window. The woman saw Rachel coming, and ran up, incoherent with agitation, so that all Rachel was able to gather was that there was 'blood all down his legs'.

She too looked in through the window. The foal was wild-eyed frantic, terrified.

'Can you give me a hand with him?' Rachel knew, as she asked, what the reaction would be. 'Oh, I couldn't. Not with all that blood.' The woman stood wringing her hands. The child burst into tears and ran off to the house. A long frustating time later, after resorting to a noose of rope on the end of the clothes prop borrowed from a line of washing in the garden. Rachel was able to capture and corner the foal. The bleeding was not abnormal: only a little more than she would have expected from an animal subjected to travelling the day after castration. She reached towards her bag to find a sedative for the poor little creature, and at that moment it erupted in panic again, rearing right up against the wall, twisting its body, and falling heavily on its side. She was able to sedate it then, but as it rose and stepped away from her, one hind leg trailed, the toe of the hoof dragging on the concrete.

'Damn,' said Rachel. 'Luxated patella.'

It could have been worse. It could have been a broken leg after such a fall, instead of a slipped stifle. She left the garage and explained to the woman what had happened. The woman looked at Rachel as if she had committed some act of deliberate malpractice. 'It can happen quite easily,' Rachel said, hearing her voice sounding as if she sought to justify herself. 'A foal in poor condition can slip a stifle quite easily, and this one has been subjected to considerable distress.'

'Yes, he has, hasn't he' the woman said, still regarding Rachel with disfavour. 'What about all the bleeding?'

'Nothing at all,' Rachel said, her voice sharp. 'He's bound to bleed a little. Just wash his hind legs with warm water. Add a little salt if you like. The bleeding will stop in a day or so.' She was about to suggest treatment for the damaged hind leg, when the woman had grown angry, saying it was not her job to nurse the foal, that Rachel had no right to leave it until she had 'done something about it.' There had been an angry scene then, Rachel's temper having snapped entirely, and the woman had gone to the house to telephone for 'a proper vet'. This had turned out to be John Rudge from one of the Stroud partnerships. He had spoken to Rachel by telephone that evening, to commiserate with her and to assure her that her actions had been justified, but that could not blot out of Rachel's mind the memory of the wretched frightened foal. She could only hope its stay in the world might be a short one. Its future, if it remained where it was, seemed bleak enough. She learned, a short while later, that the meatman had taken it away.

Far more horrifying was the striking down of five of Matthew Sayer's cattle. There had been a freak thunderstorm: a mere half-dozen claps of thunder, but very close at hand, and terrifying to anyone outside at the time. Rachel had blessed the insulation of Jessica's tyres as she drove through the weird flickering of lightning from the purple cloud that hung overhead. Suddenly there was a terrible crack that seemed it must split the earth open. The top of a great tree in one of Sayer's fields burst into flame like a struck match, and five cows that huddled beneath it dropped, twitching horribly, to the ground. Rachel stopped the car. There was nothing she could do, she was sure, yet she felt obliged to get out to look at them. She had never wanted to do anything less in her whole life.

She had on her rubber boots and now, drawing Jessica into the gateway, she found a mackintosh and a pair of heavy-duty rubber gloves. After such a massive charge of electricity the cattle, and the ground on which they lay, would be capable of giving her a severe shock.

As she got out of the car the rain, which had so far fallen in slow, heavy drops, began to increase its pace, drumming down staccato on her waterproof coat, on the metal of the car, and with a softer pattering on the already wet grass. Thunder still muttered sulkily, but further off now.

Rachel walked cautiously across the field, as she might have done if there were mines laid. She knew she was safe against any residual shock, but she did not feel so. She felt the thumping of her pulse, and was ashamed of her cowardice.

When she reached the place where the cattle were lying, the scene was no less nasty than she had anticipated. They were all dead, all five, with bloody froth at their mouths. One still had its tongue wrapped round a mouthful of grass. There was an awful smell of singed hair and scorched flesh. The one that must have taken the worst of the shock was ripped open, with its guts showing. Its face was drawn and fixed into an expression of horror, as if it had seen hell's gates open. Rachel knew that this awful grimace was the effect of galvanic spasms and not necessarily a register of the acuteness of its death agony, but all the same she could not bring herself to look at it for long. It was a revolting sight, the dead cattle under the stricken tree, made all the more sickening because it was arbitrary, as if some deposed old god had chucked this thunderbolt on a sudden whim.

At least there was no doubt as to the cause of death. Sayer was a prudent man and well insured. She would call in and tell him now, and certify the cause of death for him, to satisfy the assessors. They were welcome to come and look for themselves if they wished. She felt she would not recommend it, unless their stomachs were unusually strong. On the way home, having called at the farm, that terrible stink of burnt hair came back to her, making her feel cold with nausea. Once back at Stapleton House, Mrs Partridge, seeing her green, pale face, had fussed round her with little snorts of disapproval and exasperated shakings of the head.

Rachel fretted about these incidents until even Malcolm mildly chided her, and it was only as she swung round on him, resenting his words, that she saw with sudden shock that he was now very, very ill. She had been hedged about with her own problems, had looked only into herself, but now she became sharply aware how his face had drawn down into its bones. His wrists were thin: she felt that if she held a candle behind him it would shine through.

Rachel was horrified both by this realisation and by her own lack of perception in not having been aware of his decline, but realising that it would do him no good to see how anxious she now felt for him, that any sudden concern might offend him, she left the house and took herself off for a long walk round the town. Mrs Partridge was out, visiting one of her numerous relations, but she would be back before long to answer the telephone. Rachel had considered removing the wretched instrument from its hook, to ensure Malcolm some peace until then, but she knew he would not wish it.

Huddled into her warmest coat she walked briskly about the streets of Milchester. If anyone greeted her she was unaware of it. She paced along as if on some important errand, yet she had no idea where she intended to go: the walking was for its own sake, and her eyes registered nothing of what surrounded her except that she was aware of objects to avoid, obstructions to circumvent, as if that part of her wits was under separate control.

Even in her thick coat, and walking at such speed, the March wind chilled her, and growing stronger, made her eyes water. She bowed her head to it and walked on. She turned some anonymous corner, head still bowed and bumped hard into Tom Adams coming the other way.

'Well, hello,' he said, and put his hands out to steady her. It was at this contact that she broke entirely. She walked into his arms, which in his surprise he closed around her, and she wept. She tried later to analyse why she had done so. Never in her right mind would she have behaved in such a way. Yet if all Milchester had been lined up to watch, it would have made no difference to her action then.

'It's all too much,' she sobbed. 'I can't. I can't.'

He did not enquire what it was that she could not, but took her by the arm and led her to the Black Cat Café, which was nearby, and filled her with tea, which she drank, and plied her with buns, which she could not eat. When he could see that she was a little more composed he said: 'You'd better come home with me and tell me all about it.'

He paid the bill, and took her by the arm again, as if she were an invalid, or blind. So far she had managed only half a dozen words more to him.

His flat was only a short walk from the Black Cat in one of Milchester's many back streets of stone houses. The flat stretched across the whole first floor of the building and looked down on to the quiet street and the garden of the house opposite, which was stepped back from the others behind lawns and trees.

The room into which he led her had large windows that showed this pleasant view, and which let in a golden, stone-reflected light. Out of the wind, the day looked more spring-like, and in the garden across the road there were fat daffodil buds and a few primroses. It was not cold in the room, but even so Tom went to the gas-fire and lit it, and sat her down in a large chair next to the warmth of it. Then he fetched another chair and sitting down opposite her, stretched his feet out to the flames. He did not prompt her to speak; only waited, without seeming to wait.

After a while, the whole quietness of the room began to calm her. It was a very plain, oblong room, high ceilinged, furnished only with chairs, bookshelves and a solid wooden table, four-square on stout turned legs. Light washed in from the street into every corner through those wide windows, whose sills were scattered with plants, open books, jars filled with pencils, brushes and pens. On the wall opposite where Rachel sat was the only painting that hung in the room: it was not of his own, the Stroud Canal. She recognised it: a stretch not far from a small-holding she had visited only a few days previously. The canal then had been an uninviting grey, very still under a grey sky. The picture showed it with boats, the water in shades of jewelled green, with bright sun sparkling light from the ripples. There were sluice-gates, their dank timbers echoed in their dark reflections, and a dragon-fly hung suspended over its own brilliant image. The tow-path was all hot, dusty summer; the canal its cool antithesis.

She looked, and at last something eased in her, so that she could tell him: about Hassan, about Malcolm, about her own wretchedness and self-doubt. Once she had begun she could not stop. She could hear herself telling him all these things, yet even as she did so, a nasty little voice in her head was suggesting to her that he would think her utterly stupid. Ridiculous. He found life such a joke. Perhaps this would amuse him too.

When at last she looked at him, he was not laughing. He leaned forward and took both her hands.

'Let's take one of your burdens at a time,' he said. 'About the horse. The job is done, and you must not distress yourself. You think it's a weakness in yourself, don't you, that you could hardly bring yourself to do it? Well, it's no weakness, neither in yourself, nor in your sex, dear Rachel, believe me. It's something all of us dread, because our proper job is to heal. They don't ask doctors to kill the people they can't cure; that's an aspect of the work that only we vets get lumbered with. You won't ever get used to it, but your skin will thicken a little. Give it time. Just remember: that horse was in hell, and you released him from it.'

Rachel tightened her hands on his, and nodded. 'Thanks,' she said. Then, after a pause: 'About Malcolm...' It was wrong, surely, to have put the other anxiety first? Yet she had needed to clear her mind, to be ready to accept whatever Tom could tell her. She felt he must surely know, and she dreaded what he might say.

The flames of the gas-fire flickered small tongues of blue and yellow around the elements, making them glow. They seemed to burn, and yet they were not destroyed.

'Malcolm?' Tom said. 'I knew he was worse. Like you, I had not realised quite how much worse.'

'What is wrong with him?' Her voice sounded almost pleading, as if he might hide from her what he knew.

He shook his head. 'He won't discuss it. Not with me, nor with Mrs Partridge. John Barton's his doctor. He knows, of course, but Malcolm won't have it spoken of. I've known Malcolm all my life. My parents were killed when I was in short trousers, and my days were divided then between school and various aunts. Margaret Bramwell rather took me over when the other aunts married or died or decided that a growing boy was a strain on the household. I used to be brought to Stapleton House when WVS committee meetings were held there. Malcolm felt sorry for me, I think: used to let me help clear up after surgery. Sometimes he'd let me watch him working, and I knew I wanted skill like that. My fingers itched for a scalpel with that same itch I get for charcoal and brushes. He amazed me: still does for that matter: his knowledge, his ability, and that terrifying, relentless energy. If you had seen him in the house, when his mother was alive, he seemed hardly more than a shadow, he was so quiet, so self-effacing. She did that to him: religious women have a deal to answer for. Everything positive in him, all his ability and energy, went into his work, and you could see it flow through him when he went through that surgery door.'

'He's still like that,' Rachel said. 'I have seen that change come over him.'

'Ah, but you've humanised him a little too, I think,' Tom said. 'Old Vi Partridge says you've done wonders.'

'If only I had,' said Rachel. 'If only he'd

tell me.'

'Look,' said Tom. 'I'll pull no punches with you. I suspected something was wrong when he told me he'd advertised for an assistant. After all, he'd always managed before, as long as I'd stand in for him in an emergency, and those were few and far between. When I was away in York for a couple of years helping out a college friend whose partner suddenly went off to Australia, he coped entirely alone: never thought of getting anyone else in. If he'd offered me a job working with him I'd have jumped at it, but Mrs Halliday was still alive then, and I'm sure he felt no one else should have to put up with her. He wrote to me when this other practice set up: suggested I might like to get involved with it: helped me in every way he could. By the time that dreadful woman died I was established with Alan & Co, and not long afterwards I became enmeshed in some problems of my own. A problem called Anthea in particular. Has our Violet regaled you with tales of Anthea?'

Rachel shook her head.

'No. Maybe she wouldn't,' Tom said, and grinned. 'She didn't like Anthea much. She saw Anthea crystal-clear from the start. I didn't. I thought Anthea was God's gift to mankind. She used to go on about my dedication to suffering, the healing power at my finger-tips. Stuff like that, I lapped it up, of course, being young and foolish. Then I took her out on my rounds one day. Time and again she'd begged to come. She wasn't too keen on some of the mucky farmyards we had to walk through, but she'd have survived that, I suppose. The last call we made was to a foal with a bloody great abscess on its neck. Never seen one quite so ripe and ready for lancing. She bent over to pat the poor little suffering creature just as the blade went in and a great spray of pus went all over her. She never felt the same about me again. She went off and married a doctor from Cheltenham. They've got two children, a Regency house and a private practice in Montpellier.'

'Lucky old Anthea,' said Rachel. There was a wicked edge to her voice. It pleased Tom. There's nothing like a little malicious amusement, he thought, to clear away misery. He found the memory of Anthea pretty amusing himself, now the distance was sufficient.

Aware that a degree of her normal resilience had returned, Tom felt he could risk telling Rachel what he suspected was wrong with Malcolm. He told her straight and direct, giving her no false comfort. She listened, and hoped, intensely, that he was wrong, though she doubted it.

Then, because the important things had all been spoken of, they sat quietly and talked, of small, trivial things, with no importance at all, and Rachel felt a gradual and pleasant sense of lightness, as if he had lifted her troubles from her like so many cumbersome parcels. The feeling was such that she lost, just for those few hours, the need to keep distance between them, and when, at the end of the afternoon he kissed her, it seemed entirely in the nature of things that he should do so. It was, in fact, both unsurprising and remarkably enjoyable.

It was only as she walked home through the darkening streets to help Malcolm with evening surgery that some of her old defensiveness began to creep back, like water through sand.

Twice that evening Malcolm complimented her on a job well done. Once was rare. She wondered, self-doubt stirring in her, if this was his way of commenting on the fact that she had given less than her best of late, yet she could, in truth, feel once again a proper precision of mind and hand, and could see in Malcolm's expression only a reasoned and honest approval.

Her skill returned to her, she worked very hard over the next weeks: to help Malcolm, certainly, but equally as a kind of atonement for her past inadequacy.

For reasons that she could not analyse, she found she was avoiding Tom. Looking back at their afternoon's companionship, knowing that it could have been watched without a blush by a spinster Sunday-school teacher of the most strait-laced kind, she had begun, even so, to wish that she had not had that chance meeting with him; had never made a hostage of him of her miseries and anxieties. They were part of her own life: part of herself; her own affair. She should have resolved them herself, not leaning on him as she had done. She braced herself so fiercely to the resolution of her own problems from now on that she began to feel the tension of it in her muscles, and at night she lay in her bed as if she were threaded through with piano wire.

Gradually, working all hours to take the pressure off Malcolm, watching him covertly, discreetly, for signs that he was overtaxing himself, she learned to live with those aspects of herself and her life that could not be changed: began to accept with less self-criticism and bitterness that she was not always going to be right, not always going to have an instant solution; and that these things did not diminish her, either in her profession, or in herself. It was not an easy lesson: balancing her inevitable, human fallibility against her wish, her strong wish, to succeed.

When Malcolm told her he had soon to go into hospital for exploratory surgery, she felt sadly unsurprised, and ungrateful for the new strength she had found within herself. She would need it.

He tried to make light of the operation he must undergo. 'I shall be Ozymandias,' he said, and there was a look on his thin face as if something at a great distance were amusing him. 'Let them look on my works and despair.'

She drove him to Gloucester Hospital and brought his small case of clothes home with her. Then she went and had tea in the kitchen with Mrs Partridge, and they both stared at the cloth and stirred their cups and for a long time they said nothing.

It was across this same table that Rachel had learned so much about Malcolm: had in the course of many conversations with Mrs Partridge and from what Tom had told her become, piecemeal, acquainted with Malcolm's history, his life at Stapleton House; for there, apart from his years of training, was where his life had been spent. It had been a narrow enough existence, in the world's eye, and explained with painful clarity the causes of so much of what Malcolm now was. In his childhood the house was a private dwelling, gloomy, over-furnished, tended by a staff of two women, a girl and a gardener, who were expected to be seen and not heard, and seen no more than was necessary at that. Mrs Partridge's cousin Etty had been the girl engaged to work there, and she had had many an angry confidence with her concerning the strictness and stuffiness of Charles Halliday, Malcolm's father. He was a severe man, his creed an odd kind of asceticism, which had not even a redeeming root in faith or belief of any kind. His severity of aspect and behaviour seemed to be for its own sake, his imposition of discipline for this same poor cause. 'You never saw that little lad smile if 'is Dad was in the room, our Etty used to say. Don't think me wicked, but when Charlie 'Alliday died it was the best thing that could 'ave 'appened for that child.' Mrs Partridge told Rachel. 'But then 'is mother got religion, as they say, and that were almost as bad.'

Mrs Halliday, her faith ridiculed and forbidden expression for years, became a devoted churchgoer and 'went very high', as Mrs Partridge put it. 'All candles and funny smells and bobbin' up and down.' She took Malcolm with her, of course, and now he was encouraged

215

with fervour to believe all those things that his father had so coldly denied. He became a quiet, devout little boy, listened attentively to the priest's instruction, was confirmed, would rise early every Sunday to serve at what was always referred to as 'Marse'.

Mrs Halliday, delighted by this, had him reserved in her mind for the Church. In this way she felt she could recompense God for all her years of enforced outward denial. It became an accepted fact that Malcolm would take Holy Orders. Only Malcolm having found a secret love, did not entirely accept it. Whenever he could escape from the house, from his mother's binding affection, he would find his way to barn, byre, kennel or shippon, and sit quietly in company with the animals there. He found, at last, an undemanding and rewarding companionship. He could touch these creatures and they would neither shrink from him, nor overwhelm him with their feelings. He felt affection flow from them which in no way threatened him.

All this Mrs Partridge had grown to realise through one particular incident at which she was present. Her Uncle Len, Etty's father, had a small-holding of six acres or so about a mile to the north of Milchester, and both girls were sitting on a warm stone bench near the house there one day when Malcolm came running, calling out to them, his usual quiet voice imperative.

'Quick! Come and help!'

His face was white, and they did not argue, but followed him along the track. Gradually they became aware of a terrible noise, a dreadful shrieking, sobbing noise. It sounded like a child, but if so, it must be most appallingly hurt. They broke into a run then, to catch up with Malcolm, who was already running. Then they saw the origin of the sound. Uncle Len's nanny-goat, Rosie, tethered to a post on a high bank overlooking the track, had leapt down for some reason off the bank, been checked by the length of her chain, and had fallen on to the chopped off stem of a hawthorn plant in the hedge that Uncle Len had been trimming. The stake had gone in under her elbow, and she was shrieking in pain like a child.

'I couldn't get her off. Not by myself,' Malcolm had said, heaving in breath as if his bellows had burst.

When Etty had looked closer at Rosie she had gone a very odd colour and had had to sit down, but Mrs Partridge, Vi Saunders as she was then ('not much good when it comes to blood, but someone 'ad to 'elp 'im') had assisted him in lifting the goat off the spiked stem, and had held her while he looked, apparently fascinated, at the gaping bloody hole. The spike had gone straight upward, behind the shoulder bone, and had not pierced the ribcage. The bleeding was nasty, but not disastrous. Even so, when between the two of them they had carried the goat home, they were slaughter-house colour, and Etty walked a good half-mile behind and would not look. By the time Uncle Len came back from Gloucester market, the goat's wound had been washed with carbolic soap and adequately sewn up with Etty's canvas thread and a needle they had held in a candle flame. Len had no money for vets and Rosie would normally have had to take her chance or be knocked on the head, but now here she was, sewn up neat as ninepence and already chewing her cud. Aware of Malcolm's severe upbringing and social status, Uncle Len repressed the words which would most naturally have come to him, when he heard the whole story. 'Well,' he said. 'Well b—bless me. I'd never 'ave thought it. Ought to be a doctor, that one.'

Perhaps it had been that remark that had planted the idea in Malcolm, perhaps it was already germinating, but it was not long after this that tensions began between Malcolm and his mother. As he grew older his church attendance wavered. She went without him. She grew disapproving, and her affection cooled as his faith shrank away. It seemed to Rachel that it might have occurred to Mrs Halliday to see the correlation of these two facts: in this symbiosis of faith and affection in a child who had been denied both—either the two are constant, or both die.

Eventually there was a resolution, of a kind, a reconciliation, of a kind. If he was determined to become a veterinary surgeon, as it appeared he most single-mindedly was, then he had better prepare himself for the necessary training, which was understood to be long and arduous. His father's estate would be sufficient for the fees, and to keep him throughout those years. However, she did wish to make it clear that she would expect him to practice his profession from his own home. He owed it to her, and to the community. Milchester must have the advantage of such skill as he possessed, if not as a pastor, then at least as a physician, of a kind.

This had seemed no particular hardship to Malcolm at the time. He liked Milchester, loved its surrounding countryside, had become involved, even then, with its farming community.

So he had done as she asked. The house had been altered to provide him with a surgery, and the rest of the household had continued much as before, with Mrs Halliday very much in control right up to the day of her death.

Of Malcolm's feelings on his return to this restrictive household after years of considerable independence, Mrs Partridge had no knowledge: could only guess, as Rachel did, how hard it must have been for him. He never mentioned old friends from those times, very rarely spoke of them. Those years were locked up securely, and if there were treasures hidden in them, he would not bring them into the light of day again.

Now the two women sat silent, thinking about him, and could find no words to say. The tea grew cold: the kitchen darkened: the first patients were brought to evening surgery.

Malcolm would be in for some time, the hospital said, for further observation, for more tests, and eventually, for the operating theatre. To cope on her own Rachel had to work so hard, even harder than she had done recently, and she had no time to think. She fell into bed tired as a dog, roused herself for night calls, climbed back between the sheets for a snatch of sleep before the next day's work. Malcolm had managed alone for years, she reasoned, and so could she.

She would not ask Tom for his help, and Mrs Partridge grew crosser and crosser with her.

In the end he came, invited or not.

'Why have you been avoiding me?' he asked Rachel.

'I haven't.' The sharpness of his question seemed to strip away all her new growth. She felt unsure again, and irritated that he should make her feel so.

'It seems like it to me.'

She paused. If she tried to explain it would sound so foolish. She tried. It did.

'You took advantage of me,' she said. 'I was feeling low, that was all. It could happen to anyone.'

His right eyebrow arched upwards and quivered like a startled bird. The corners of his mouth drew up, making a reciprocal arc. 'Took advantage of you, did I?'

This time, when she blushed, she could not hide it. 'I mean....' she said.

'You mean it was a case of instant rape on the hearth-rug? What a shame I didn't notice at the time, I might have enjoyed it!' His voice grew louder now, and a good deal angrier. 'For God's sake, Rachel, mayn't I kiss you without causing a major trauma? Mayn't I laugh at your idiocies? What *may* I do? I love you, damn it. Haven't you the wit to realise that? Use that intelligence for my sake that you use so well for everything else, and realise that you can be a beloved and desired female without losing anything else of what you are. Anyone would think I was some male equivalent of Delilah, brandishing the scissors. Why should I want to lessen what I love?'

She looked sharply at him. Was he serious, or was it just part of his blarney? From his expression she thought he did mean it, but pushed the thought from her. How dared he complicate a life that was already being pulled thread-thin in every direction. She told him he must go: that she had work to do.

'Then you'll need some help,' he said. 'And I intend you shall get it. If not for your sake, then for Malcolm's. He won't want you collapsing the moment he gets back.'

They met, over the next weeks. They worked together. They were stiff and polite and very formal. They went, separately, to visit Malcolm and to take him small gifts and books, and Rachel picked the last primroses for him. They were going the least bit papery, and would soon be supplanted by later flowers, but he was particularly fond of them.

'They were Disraeli's favourites, you know,'

he told Rachel. 'Queen Victoria sent him some on his death-bed.' His thoughts wandered a little. 'Queen Elizabeth the First refused to go to bed to die, did you know that? She stood till she could not stand, and then sat upright in her chair. A terrible woman. Ugly, you know. Wouldn't have mirrors.' He paused again, and brought all his attention to bear on Rachel. 'You should have mirrors, my dear Rachel. You are very beautiful, and you do not sufficiently see yourself.' He closed his eyes and appeared to sleep. That passionless grey face was so still. She stooped, and gently kissed it.

On her way out, Rachel saw the ward sister in her office, filling in forms. Diffidently, for the woman looked very occupied with this job, Rachel knocked and went in. She had seen the sister previously only at a distance, had not yet gathered up courage to speak to her about Malcolm's progress. The face that was raised from the papers in front of it was less severe than she had expected; younger, and more open.

'I'm Rachel Bellamy. I've just been to visit Malcolm Halliday. How is he?' Rachel asked.

Sister did not answer immediately, but paused as if to assess what kind of person this was.

'If I say he's as well as can be expected,

you'll think that's a stock answer,' she said. 'But it's the truth. He should have come in sooner. We shall do all we can.' She put a hand on Rachel's shoulder, and smiled. 'Come again soon,' she said. 'He hates this place. He tells me that you bring him news of the only things he cares about. He'd have all his patients brought in here at the drop of a hat, and run a bedside consulting room, I think.'

'I'll come tomorrow,' Rachel said.

Rachel had not seen the Fowlers since the day of Hassan's death. She could think of no particualr reason for going, and many excuses not to. Yet she did feel, uneasily, at the back of her mind, that she should perhaps have gone back sooner to comfort Anne Fowler. The horse was the one thing she cared for, and to lose him in such a way must have made her thoroughly wretched. Besides that, the poor woman had obviously begun to think of Rachel as a friend, and evidently she had few.

'I'm a heel,' Rachel told herself, and after her next visit to Malcolm, she went to see how things were with the Fowlers.

The spring had been slow coming. March was cold, with a late fall of snow at the end of it: big-flaked, mushy snow that weighed branches to the ground, snapped off the stalks of the budding daffodils, chilled the new lambs so that they drooped miserably, all the play gone out of them. Then April had come in even colder, with frosty mornings that slapped down the new shoots whenever they braved it above the surface of the soil. People, animals and plants craved for warmth, and shivered in the laggardly weather, so that when the sun did occasionally flit out and flirt with the landscape every creature seemed quite ridiculously grateful for it. Today there was no call for gratitude. Cattle huddled under hedges, birds sat fluffed up and refused to sing. Rachel was quite sure it was not going to be her day. She almost changed her mind about going, but that new determination that was growing in her kept the car's wheels pointed in the direction of the Fowler's house and would not allow retreat.

She found Bill digging in the vegetable patch. He dug like a man who has been digging for hours: the movements slow, mechanical, somehow spiritless. It was a spiteful sort of weather now, with a cold wind throwing handfuls of rain down from time to time, but he did not seem to notice. The spade bit, and turned, and swung, as if it propelled Bill, and not the other way about. She had to call to him twice before he heard her.

He stopped his digging and looked up.

'Am I glad to see you,' he said, in a voice that sounded as if it had little enough to be glad about.

'That's good,' said Rachel, cheerfully.

'Nothing's good,' he said. 'Not one damned thing. She's in the house. She won't speak to me. She's in such a state I'm afraid she'll do away with herself.'

Rachel could not quite believe this. If Anne Fowler were truly suicidal, her husband would hardly risk leaving her while he went out digging the garden, but it was obvious that Bill was genuinely worried.

'I can't get her to take any intereset in anything,' he said.

They walked together towards the kitchen door, with Rachel feeling, perhaps a little intolerantly, that a good many people had lost a great deal more than Anne Fowler and had weathered it with far greater courage. Both the Fowlers could do with a good smack, she began to think. Yet, when she saw the figure that sat hunched at the kitchen table, it looked so dejected that it was impossible not to stretch out a hand in sympathy. The face was dead white, and lines had deepened on it: the eyes were dark and blank. Here was someone who needed more help than a cheery pep-talk from a stupid so-called friend who hadn't the sense to realise that Anne Fowler's problem was greater than the loss of a horse, or even the loss of a known way of life. She sat down at the table with her, spoke to her gently, but after a while Rachel could see she was doing no good.

Bill Fowler was hovering in the doorway, waiting. They walked out of the house together.

'What am I to do?' he asked her. 'I can't bear to see her like this. That's why I was out in the garden. Having me near her just seems to make her worse.'

He looked pathetic, like a dog that has got lost in a crowd and has given up searching. Rachel, looking at him, felt irritable, and then, suddenly, just plain angry.

'For God's sake, Bill, what do you expect? She's put up with your Stone Age economy, your use, or misuse, of a place she loves for a whole lot of ill-thought-out rural ventures that haven't an icicle's chance in hell because when it boils down to it you've no real knowledge or skill and you won't be told. Well, I'm telling you now, and I hope you're listening. She would have rebelled against all this eventually, you know. The horse's death has hastened an inevitable end to an unbalanced relationship.'

Bill was looking at her with his mouth open. If she had thought he might grow angry in return, she was mistaken. He said, very miserably: 'You think it's all too late, then.'

'Yes,' she went on, relentlessly. 'So you'd better establish something better in its place, before she recovers enough to realise that there's nothing left between you. I'm not saying it's all your fault. She's been pretty damned stupid too, but she's paid dearly for it lately. The first thing you must do is to get her better in herself. She's very depressed and needs proper care.'

She paused, looking at Bill's face. He looked so miserable that her anger began to cool. There was so much in him to dislike, yet she began to feel just a little sorry for him.

'Get her to a doctor, Bill,' she advised. 'It's all gone too deep. She needs to talk to someone. Meanwhile, on a practical note, how far are you prepared to put yourself out to help her?' An idea had occurred to Rachel and she needed Bill's approval of it while he was still in this contrite frame of mind.

'As far as you like. Dear God, she's like a walking dead woman. I've been damned awful to her, I know, but I was up to here in my own problems, and my own silly dignities. It hit my pride for six, you know, losing my job like that: realising I was quite so quickly dispensible. So I took this place by the scruff of the neck and determined to shake a living out of it. Poor Anne, I think she's grown to hate me. I know she has.'

'Now you've realised that,' Rachel said, purposely making no concession to his admission, 'I think there's a practical way you may help to wean her back. Let her keep another horse.' He took a deep breath to protest. 'I know,' she said, 'I know there's no money to buy one. I'll try to get something on loan for her. As long as it has four legs and a tail, I think she can be persuaded to love it. Then she may learn to love you too.'

'Second string to a horse,' he said. 'Well, that's a new experience.' He shrugged, as if resigned to it.

'You would have to assure me, though,' Rachel went on, 'that you'd manage, somehow, to provide everything necessary for it. No extravagances, nothing exceptional, just good, basic, unstinted care.'

'You're on,' Bill said. 'If it'll help her, then do it, please. Find her a horse. The sooner, the better.'

'And you'll get her to a doctor?'

'Kicking and screaming if necessary.'

Rachel looked at him sharply.

'Trust me,' he said. 'I've been a fool, but at least I know it. I'll take care of her. I don't want to lose her.' Then, as Rachel turned to go, he said: 'What you said: I deserved it.' He looked at her, almost pleadingly, but she remarked, relentlessly: 'Yes, you did.'

Sometimes the answer to a problem comes so pat upon the posing of it that it would be easy enough to believe in angels.

It was only a matter of days after her visit to the Fowlers that Rachel answered the telephone to Mrs Carrington. Since the day of Highlight's accident she had been invited to visit the blind woman once or twice to take tea, to be presented with flowers and small gifts, to talk horses, to discuss life. Rachel found Mrs Carrington intelligent, knowledgeable and very likeable. She was delighted to hear her voice on the telephone.

'I need your help, my dear, if you can give it. The daughter of a dear friend of mine suddenly has the chance of an excellent job abroad for a year, which is not a problem in itself, but the girl, Marian, has a rather fine Connemara mare which is in foal to Highlight, and she has no-one to care for the animal while she is away. Now you may think that the answer is for me to take the mare on, but really, I have more stock than I should have anyway, and it's hardly fair on my staff to ask them to look after any more. The mare deserves the best attention. All her expenses would be paid, so that would be no problem. Just find me someone who would really care for her, and be prepared to look after the foal until Marian returns. If you can find just the right person, then Marian might even consider letting them have the foal when it is reared.'

Rachel was dancing about with the telephone in her hand. She would say nothing, though, until she was sure of Anne Fowler.

'Leave it with me, Mrs Carrington,' she said. 'I'm sure I shall be able to help.'

She was still feeling very pleased with herself when Tom came through from the surgery where they had been working when the telephone rang.

'Finished,' he announced. 'Waiting room's empty.' Then he looked hard at Rachel. 'I don't know what that call was about,' he said. 'But were you a cat, and had there been a canary hereabouts, I would think you'd most probably swallowed it.'

CHAPTER 11

Rachel was out driving in first light; cool pale light, with colour only just beginning to show in it. The sky had been black when the telephone rang, and she had swum up out of sleep to answer it. Still washed by waves of sleep, she had mumbled her name into the receiver. Then an answering voice shocked her with: 'My husband's going to murder me! Can you come at once?' God Rachel thought. What am I supposed to do about that? You need the police, she considered, not a vet. Surely it wasn't possible to dial Milchester 3481 in mistake for 999? She made a great effort to climb out of the wallowing waves as the voice continued: 'It's the ram. Only got him yesterday. He's collapsed, and if he dies my man'll kill me. Please come quick. Cotswold ram he is. Worth hundreds. Oh, I'm so vexed, I can't tell you. Nothing goes right when my man's not here.'

The the telephone clicked and went silent without Rachel having had time to utter another word. She became rapidly awake, and filled with exasperation, partly at having been so unnecessarily alarmed by the possibility of murder, but chiefly because the woman on the telephone, in her panic, had not identified herself. How on earth was Rachel to treat an unknown ram, with unknown symptoms, on an unknown farm? She groaned, and began to heave herself into her clothes, meanwhile belabouring an unwilling brain into thought. If it was a Cotswold ram, then there were only a handful of places it could be, though of course there was a chance this was not an established customer but just someone dialling the first vet they could think of in an emergency.

By the time she was fully dressed she had collected three possibilities: Valley Farm, near Stroud, Joe Clissold's at Sallerton, or Hawkshill Farm, up on the top road near the Fox and Hounds. Then she set aside Joe Clissold, because he was unmarried, a confirmed misogynist, and no woman would be telephoning from his house at this hour. It could be the Monkton's at Valley Farm except that she had heard Mrs Monkton's voice before and there was no trace of accent, whereas the voice she had just heard had the Gloucestershire burr. She'd go to Hawkshill and hope for the best that she was right.

Len Croft had a collection of rare breeds at Hawkshill; old breeds of cattle, sheep and pigs, which he kept, not purely out of interest or because showing them to the public in summer-time brought in a little extra income, but because he firmly believed they had a job to do in modern breeding, giving back their hardiness and vigour to the modern strains, which he regarded as a pretty soft lot and likely to die if you breathed on them. He kept splendid Gloucester cattle with great sweeping horns, Tamworth pigs, all bristled and gingery, goats of various breeds, a couple of heavy horses, some English game-fowl and a small flock of Cotswold sheep. These fringe-faced long-wools had been Gloucestershire's riches. They had made the merchants fat and prosperous in those high days when mills had clacked and clattered along every valley stream, and families of Weavers and Fullers and Clothiers had lived in Staple Road, Sheep Street, Flock Lane and Dyer Street, and had drunk their beer at the Woolpack and the Golden Fleece.

As she drove in the direction of the Fox and Hounds it seemed to Rachel increasingly likely that she was right. Mrs Partridge had mentioned that Len Croft had gone up North somewhere to sort out some problem among his mother's family there, a rare absence from Hawkshill, which he had left only on a handful of occasions in the thirty years he had owned it.

Jessica beetled along through the darkness, towards the first hint of day at the horizon. In the headlights a fox stopped on the road before them, eyes glaring suddenly green in the triangle of its face, before it vanished into the dew-soaked hedge. At the junction by the pub a deer came crashing past, frightened by the sudden eruption of sound from the engine.

When Hawkshill Farm became visible in the distance, its windows lit, Rachel, relieved, was convinced now she must have been right in her detective work. It was too early for the place to be awake under normal circumstances, even for milking, so here, almost certainly, lay her emergency.

Sarah Croft emerged from a lit out-building at the sound of Rachel's arrival. She looked as flustered and agitated as a hen in a high wind. She was an elderly country woman with a round, wrinkled face, whose normal cheerful lines were all down-turned with worry. She was still in her nightgown, with a man's coat pulled on round it, and a man's large boots on her feet.

'Oh, I *am* glad to see you,' she said. 'I'd put

that 'phone down and come back out afore I realised I hadn't said who I was. I went back in and rang again, but you'd gone, and I thought how's she going to know where to come when I never said. Still, you're here and that's a blessing. This way please: the ram's in here.'

She trotted away, hampered by her garb, towards the building she had just left, explaining as she did so that the livestock agents had sent the ram earlier than expected. He was due to arrive at Hawkshill the day after Len Croft's return, but for various reasons they wanted delivery of the ram taken a little sooner. Sarah Croft had been put out by this as she had more than enough to do with her man away, but they would have it that the ram must be sent, and they wouldn't take no for an answer. She hadn't thought much of the stockman who'd brought him either. A bit too ready to shout and prod at the poor creature; and he'd been driving at a fair old pace when Sarah saw the truck coming up the road.

'I didn't think the ram looked too good at bedtime, and I couldn't sleep much, thinking about him,' Sarah said. 'Then about three o'clock I woke up with a feeling. You know how you do. You wake and you say, "Something's not right." Well, I got up, and I came to look at him, and I found him like this.'

They were by now standing next to the pen in which the ram lay. He was flat on his belly with his legs spread spatchhock like a spaniel, and his head laid lugubriously on the floor. His breathing was rapid and he looked wretchedly distressed. Rachel climbed into the pen and examined him. After a while she said: 'I think we'll find it's a calcium deficiency; that, combined with the stress of the journey. I'll inject him now, and if I'm right, we should see a difference very soon.' She went swiftly to the car, leaving Sarah hovering anxiously around the sick animal.

A short while later he was responding to the treatment as if it were something magic.

'Well bless me! Well I never,' Sarah Croft kept saying, as she watched in amazement and relief. 'I never saw anything like it. He looks a different animal.'

Len Croft was such a careful and caring man that it was no surprise to Rachel that Sarah had not seen before the dramatic effect of mineral deficiency in sheep, and its equally dramatic cure. Certainly this ram would have no further problems of the kind while he remained at Hawkshill.

Rachel accepted a cup of tea from Sarah Croft before she began the drive home, and this boosted her energy for a while. She drove past still sleeping, curtained houses, with that sense of pleasant superiority that early rising brings with it. She opened the window and smelt the damp cool air. Once past the Fox and Hounds and on the main road home, however, even this fresh breeze could not stop her eyelids coming down. The car lurched, hedge-twigs rattled on the windows and Jessica waltzed a good thirty yards before Rachel could set her right again. There was only one thing to do. At the next lay-by she pulled in, closed her eyes and allowed herself to sleep.

Even while asleep, she seemed conscious of how delightful it was to be sleeping. She sank back down into those waves from which she had been so abruptly hauled in the night that was now past. She swam so pleasantly and idly, and there was no effort in it. Fish came past, darting and playing, their iridescent colours gleaming as they turned this way and that. One of them was less cunning in its turning and bumped her shoulder as it passed. But then another did the same, and another.

'Silly things,' she said. 'Look where you're going.' The bumping on her shoulder continued, and Rachel began to feel cross at this disturbance of her peace. 'Go away!' she said. 'Leave me alone.'

'Now come along, miss. Wake up.'

There was a gloved hand on her shoulder. A long serge-covered arm led from the gloved hand to the rest of the figure of a large policeman. He was peering in at her through the open window.

'Been to a party, have we?' He was sniffing the air inside Jessica like a hound questing.

'No, I have not,' said Rachel irritably. 'Have you seen many young women at parties in wellington boots and anoraks? I'm a vet. I've been out on an emergency call, and I felt so tired I was not driving well. I pulled in to have a catnap, that's all.'

The policeman continued to look at her, continued his suspicious sniffing. Really annoyed now, Rachel turned and took hold of her instrument bag.

'Look,' she said, opened it to display its contents, and took out the first tool that came to hand, which was an ecraseur.

'Ah,' she said. Then, as if he were conducting some kind of quiz, he pointed to the instrument in her hand and asked, 'What's that for?'

Rachel, with malicious pleasure, said, 'Castration.' At that moment a police car drew up behind Jessica, and another policeman got out. This was a known quantity, Mark Boswell, from the Milchester station.

'Good morning, Miss Bellamy,' he said cheerfully, recognising her at once.

'Come to arrest me, have you?' Rachel asked sweetly. 'Your colleague thinks I'm drunk in charge of a bag of veterinary tools.'

'I never said...' the first policeman protested. 'I found her here asleep. I thought...'

'Out on a case were you, miss?' asked Boswell.

'Yes, a ram at Hawkshill.'

'You do look tired. Move over, and I'll drive you home. Stokes, you can bring my car. Leave your bike here, and I'll bring you back for it.'

'Yessir,' said Stokes, looking decidedly grumpy.

'Never mind him,' Boswell assured Rachel. 'He's new.'

'I think he thinks I threatened him with an ecraseur,' said Rachel grinning.

'Poor chap,' Boswell declared, without the least trace of sympathy. 'That'll keep his legs crossed for a while. Come on, let's get you home.'

Rachel got a further hour's sleep before morning surgery. She did not mention her early activity to Vi Partridge, who announced she was glad to see Rachel had had a bit of a lie-in when it became obvious that the kitchen had not been used since the previous evening.

Surgery was fortunately not a very busy one, but by the time it was over, Rachel was longing for coffee and a biscuit and five minutes off her feet. Then she was sent for from Milchester market. When she had given Rachel the message, Mrs Partridge had sighed resignedly and put away one of the cups she had got ready.

'You get yourself something off one of them stalls. You've gone thin, you 'ave, and it don't suit you,' she said.

The town would be very busy, it being market day, and the complexities of the one-way system were such that Rachel felt it would be quicker to walk. She took her case and set off. She was well recognised now in Milchester, and the jostling people on the pavements, seeing emergency in her brisk and purposeful stride, made way for her like traffic at the approach of an ambulance, or the Red Sea at the voice of Moses. One or two, not quick enough in the crowd's opinion, were glared at by others till they hastened out of her path, so that she very quickly arrived at the market place.

Richard Bevan, the RSPCA man, saw her coming and moved to catch her attention. He

241

was on duty each market day to watch for any ill-treatment or mishandling of the animals that were brought in for sale. Usually it was only a case of preventing over-enthusiastic use of the stick, when cattle were obstinate, moving from lorry to pen, from pen to auction ring and up into the purchaser's lorry to go home. Only very occasionally did someone lay about them in real anger, or deliberate cruelty, though such cruelty did exist, to Bevan's disgust.

Sometimes beasts would arrive over-crowded and exhausted, having been brought long distances at speed, often by drivers with no experience of animals. In hot weather, sheep would pant exhausted and distressed, still unshorn, and sweating under their thick wool. Sometimes an ancient donkey or pony would appear with long marks about its quarters and flanks showing how its unwillingness to load had been overcome with a long whip.

Today's injury was not cruelty, but accident. A cow had somehow escaped from the pens and had run about causing havoc among the nearer market stalls, which were mainly iron-mongery, farm implements and general agricultural implements with which she had played percussion and drums for quite some while before she was caught again. Tin buckets

242

were scattered everywhere; one stall had collapsed altogether, its awning curtseying low to the ground and its boxes of nails, screws, hammers and files, saws and pliers and screwdrivers of any possible size lying at strange angles with their contents spilling from them. The cow's Waterloo had been a stack of garden implements. Having knocked these into a fullsize game of Spillikins, she had contrived to stand on the handle of a spade upon which the head of a pitch-fork was resting, and it had leaped up and torn a great rent in her udder, causing her to bellow her protest at the unfairness of the world, spoiling a poor woman's little pleasures.

She was still bellowing, mournfully, at five-second intervals, regular as an occulting lighthouse, when Richard Bevan took Rachel to see her. The cow was penned now, and there were plenty of willing helpers to hold her still while Rachel worked. The animal had been caught by trapping her in an alley way. Stall-holders, seeing the emergency, had unhinged the gates from some spare enclosures and had secured her, roping her horns so that she could do no damage. Rachel was relieved to see it. So often on these occasions it was a case of 'first catch your cow'.

Rachel administered a sedative by injection,

and waited for it to take effect. She felt like a dentist waiting for a patient to 'freeze'. Still at least she did not feel constrained to make conversation with the cow in the meantime. Slowly the bellowing subsided and after a good quarter of an hour the cow subsided too, first on to her haunches, and then with a grunt of expelled breath, on to her side, whereupon one of the cattlemen sat upon her neck to keep her still. Rachel gave a further injection, a local anaesthetic this time, and then she began to sew up the wound.

She became totally engrossed in the job, just as an interesting piece of work. Of course, somewhere in her brain, lookouts kept cave for sudden eruptions of movement from the cow, but her attention was concentrated on the small area of damage, for it was not a large wound, though bad enough to make the cow thoroughly uncomfortable, as she has been telling the world so clearly.

Rachel was so busy that she did not notice the crowd assembling round her. Only when she had finished, and stood up to stretch away the cramp in her legs, did she realise that she was entirely surrounded by on-lookers: some half stooped to get a better view, some craning over the shoulders of others, they had been watching every move she made. There were faces wrinkled with concentration, faces drawn up into expressions of queasy fascination, faces whose mouths were slack with amazement. These were not farmers and stockmen to whom such things were commonplace, but the men and women of the town, who had been scouring the stalls for bargains. Suddenly, here was Herriot in the flesh, and a female Herriot at that. Better than telly, this was.

'Ooh, I could feel it in meself when she put that needle in,' someone declared.

'I wouldn't fancy doing that to a cow,' said another.

'She can be glad it's not a bull, I should say,' commented an old man weighed down with shopping bags and trailing a disgruntled terriror on a lead. His wife, unencumbered, gave him a great dig in the ribs and said: 'She wouldn't be doin' that if it was a bull you daft ha'porth,' and cackled with laughter so loud that the crowd began to laugh too, so that the cow grew restless and swung her head.

'Come along now, ladies and gentlemen,' Bevan said. 'Move on now, we're all finished here.'

They began to disperse then, and as they did so Rachel saw Tom Adams walking towards her.

'Well now,' he said as he came near. 'If I'd

245

been a little sooner I'd have passed the hat round. You had quite an audience by the look of it.'

'I don't think the cow appreciated it,' Rachel said.

Tom bent down, and inspected the treated wound. 'Nicely done,' he said.

'Thank you.'

'You're all finished here, then?'

'Yes.'

'Well come and have coffee and a sandwich at that stall over there. My treat.'

Rachel glanced at her watch. The cow had taken up far more time than she had realised. Oddly, she didn't feel tired any more. The longing to get home as soon as she could and fall asleep again seemed to have evaporated. Perhaps she was just light-headed. She heard her own voice saying, 'All right,' and she was surprised at it. 'Dutch,' she added.

He sighed. 'Very well then. But when you invite me out for a meal, don't expect me to offer to go Dutch. I enjoy being treated.'

'All right then. You win. You can buy me a sandwich.'

'Your ladyship,' he said, bowing stiffly. 'Yours to command, ma'am.'

The ate their meal among all the bustle of the market. He was busy telling her about a complicated and interesting operation he had assisted Parker with the previous day. The owner of the coffee stall eavesdropped with open mouth and one of his patrons left his sausage-roll untouched. The meal over, Rachel thanked Tom and would have made her way home, but he put his hand on her arm and said: 'Don't go. I'm taking you out.' She began to explain, to tell him about her early start to the day, but he said: 'Don't tell me you're too busy. You've been too busy too long. I've come to a decision, and it's this. As I have been sending out signals to you for some while now, which you have totally ignored, I have now concluded that you are, telepathically speaking, a little hard of hearing. Adams, I have now said to myself, don't be subtle with that girl a moment longer. She can't help being exasperatingly slow to recognise a fine man when she sees one.'

'Oh,' said Rachel. Other words escaped her. 'So now I'm taking you out,' he continued. 'I've had your calls transferred to Alan Parker so you don't need to worry. Now, what are you wearing?'

He inspected her trousers and sweater and stout leather shoes. He looked at the jacket she was wearing, and seemed to find everything acceptable.

'It wouldn't do for a quick dash to Monte Carlo but it couldn't be better for what I have in mind,' he told her. 'You don't even smell of cow: or not much. Come on then.'

'Come on where?' Rachel asked. 'Anyway I ought at least to ring Mrs Partridge. She'll wonder where I am.' Rachel began to feel a little dizzy. The day was obviously catching up on her.

'She won't,' Tom said. 'I've told her.'

'Oh,' said Rachel. 'You had this all planned then?' She was still unsure whether to feel irritated by having her afternoon arranged for her. The fact that she did not feel that she minded too much must be the result of lack of sleep, she considered.

Tom was grinning at her. 'Yes,' he said. 'We could have set out earlier, if it had not been for that wretched cow.'

He took her arm and steered her through the crowds to where his car was parked, and handed her into the passenger seat.

'Are you sure you want to take me out?' she asked.

'Quite sure. Why shouldn't I?'

Rachel paused, looked at him, feeling a need to apologise, remembering, guiltily, the incident with the stallion.

'I haven't been very encouraging, have I?'

248

she said.

'I don't need any encouragement,' he grinned. 'We've prowled round each other at a distance long enough. We're colleagues. We may as well be friends, mayn't we?' He really seemed to want it. It made her realise how churlish she had been.

She put out her hand, and he shook it, very gravely, as if they had made a pact of some importance.

Then they drove out of Milchester into an afternoon that was turning fine, with palpable warmth in the air. The gardens of the outlying cottages smelt of sunshine and wallflowers.

'Where are we going?' Rachel asked.

'Mystery tour,' he replied. There was a sort of glee about him, like a small boy on an outing.

A mile or so out of town, Tom stopped the car by some high wooden gates in a stone wall. 'We're here,' he said.

Behind the gates was a small sunny yard, and there were stables, the pleasant, familiar smell of horses. There, in the two centre boxes, was a pair of amiable looking, sleepy-eyed cobs, tacked up and ready to ride.

'They belong to a friend of mine. I've borrowed them for the afternoon. They're as safe as the Bank of England, because I'm no David

Broome, so I hope you won't find them too dull for you.'

'We're going riding?' It was such a stupid question, but Rachel was too taken aback to think sensibly. Pleasure tingled through her: the fizzing, childish pleasure of a treat: and so it was, a rare treat, the prospect of riding through such countryside on such a day, and to know she was beyond the reach of the telephone.

Tom had procured for her a hat that fitted tolerably, and he stuck on to his own head an old green-stained bowler. This, combined with his black beard, gave him the look of a somewhat eccentric rabbi. Rachel regarded him and smiled, and recognised that she was going to like him. His refusal to dislike her for her recent extraordinary attitude to him made her ashamed. It was obvious he did not understand it. She scarcely understood it herself.

'Shall we go?' he asked.

She nodded, and he brought out the smaller cob, a bay mare, and helped her up.

'I hope I've got all this stuff on right,' he said. 'I told you, I'm no expert.' Then he clambered on to the larger grey. She was a good stout cob, but she looked none too big for him.

They clattered out of the yard and along the road.

'I haven't ridden since I left home,' Rachel said. 'There was not time at Christmas. Thank you for planning it all.' She was touched that he had given so much thought to this outing, that he had gone to so much trouble to please her.

'You're happy, then?'

'Yes,' she said. 'Yes, I am,' and was surprised to discover in what degree she was happy. Happy, content, relaxed. She had been too busy to be any of these things. And as they rode, and as they talked, a lovely sense of lightness, of freedom, came over her, as if she had emerged from a carapace. She could not wish to be anywhere else, or in any better company.

The hoof beats struck up lines of poetry in her head. Often, as a child, riding alone, she would say bits of verse to herself in time to the rhythm of Nero's paces, and the habit had stuck. Now there came into her mind the Chaucer poem about spring, and the restlessness that it brings, stirring people up with its growing green, its vigorous new life. The words came spaced and incomplete, and she said them aloud to see if the gaps would fill.

' "Then longen folk to goon on pilgrimages".'

The words of the rest of the passage floated elusively in her mind, some solitary, some clumped in phrases. She still had the flavour of it, but the exact ingredients were lost. She puzzled over them.

Her father had read Chaucer to her when she was a child resolving the difficult language for her, letting her hear the sense of it. He had been greedy for books, her father, and the farmhouse had spilled over with them. He had encouraged her always to read. 'It will make sure you are educated, not just processed,' he had told her. As she had been pulled across, inevitably, to 'the science side' at school, he had urged her not to narrow her mind. At college he had sent her a book of modern verse, on the flyleaf of which he had written: 'In the habitation of dragons...' and she had smiled, understanding the message.

The next words of the Chaucer poem continued to evade her. 'I know that one,' Tom said. 'We did it at school. Something about 'ferne halwes couth in sondry londes'. I always thought it meant ferny hollows. I thought ferny hollows would be splendid places to go on a pilgrimage. "Far-off shrines" didn't seem half so attractive.'

'We'll look for ferny hollows then, shall we?' Rachel laughed.

'Right. Come on then, pilgrim!'

They took a bridle path off to their left, which was still thick with last year's leaves, and overhung with branches like a tunnel. Then they emerged on to the headlands of fields, and struck out at a stately canter to where woods fringed the rounded edges of the horizon. They entered the woods, which were part of a huge estate: three thousand acres or so, and a great house at the heart of it.

'We won't call on his Lordship today,' Tom said. 'We'll stick to the outer rides, there's a particular place I want you to see.'

Rachel found all her old skill returning. Balanced to the movement of her horse, she was enjoying the rolling stride along the soft leafy track. Hoofbeats and leather and clinking bit-rings made a pleasant tune. The air smelt mossy, of a green and fruitful dampness that would make bracken shoot high and brambles spill over until in high summer the wide paths they now rode upon would be narrow jungle trails through shoulder-high insect haunted undergrowth; the delight of foxes in their summer lodging, a forest-within-a-forest for shrews and voles, beetles and snails, delicious morsels that would find a way down red throats, by way of sharp white teeth.

Into these woods ran an old narrow lane,

worn by centuries of feet and hooves, and at whose edges the beeches cling tight by their roots. Tom swung away from the perimeter track and led a way down this lane.

'Not far now,' he said. 'It's only a short distance out of our way. Come on.'

They rode on under the trees, until the lane quite suddenly came out into the open, into a bowl-shaped clearing that must have been made about fifteen years ago, for the beeches growing with it were all young, slim trees, and here and there the earth still showed where some huge old stump had been drawn and dragged away. Tom stopped his horse at the edge of the clearing, and Rachel came up beside him. The cobs snorted companionably at each other, glad to take breath after their exercise.

The sun shone between the grey-green trunks of the trees and spilled upon the floor of the woodland. It was still open, airy and light. High summer would enclose it and make it a more secret place, but for now the branches laced across the sky, with their leaves only just beginning to shake free. Everywhere bluebells reflected the colour above them, and in a clearing that was sky-colour from edge to edge, Rachel and Tom dismounted and gazed about them.

'It's so beautiful,' Rachel said. All her weariness had gone. She felt refreshed, peaceful and happy.

'It is,' said Tom.

They stood together, the reins trailing in their hands, the horses cropping delightedly on the fresh, bright grass at the clearing's edge.

'No one could look at this,' Tom said, 'and not see it is beautiful.' He stared in silence for a while, then shrugged, and said. 'But you can bet they'll go home, and buy some second-rate print of a third-rate painting called "The Bluebell Wood" and hang it up and think they have a fair respresentation of what they see here. Or they'll watch birds fly up off that lake down there, and go skeining across the sky, all free and glorious and beating their wings, and they'll go out and get themselves a set of plaster ducks and think them every bit as good.'

He turned and looked hard at her. Suddenly, unexpectedly, he said: 'That's what frightens you about love, isn't it? I really think that's so. You know what it is really, but everywhere around you you see it devalued, and misrepresented. I wish I could convince you that it can stay as real as all this is here. I'm not offering you plaster ducks. Do you believe that?' He spoke in that light, half-teasing voice again, yet his expression belied it.

'Plaster ducks, indeed,' Rachel said.

She had never thought in these terms: but now she considered what he said, she found he was uncomfortably right. As for his own feelings about her, she did not find them comfortable either. Yet there were little frissons of happiness in her, because of them, that she would not deny, nor call unpleasant.

She turned from him, not wishing him to come too close, but she was smiling. She gathered the reins and swung herself up onto the bay mare's saddle. 'I do believe you,' she said. 'There's not a plaster duck in sight.' Then she cantered off, leaving him struggling to mount, for the grey was anxious to be with her companion. Tom caught up with Rachel at the end of the lane, and she glanced back at him, half afraid that he might show annoyance, or worse still sulkiness, that she had not seemed to take him seriously, but there was nothing of either in his expression. Annoyance would have tarnished such a carefree day, and sulkiness in a man she loathed above anything. Had either of them been thinking in terms of battle he had won another victory. He had won a major victory, without a word spoken.

They rode at an ambling, easy pace all afternoon. They were in no hurry. Every path was an invitation, every new aspect worth stopping to see. They rode the hem of the woods until they met up with a stony track that led them from farm to isolated farm, over the high, clean springing fields. They saw sheep, butted and bullied by their strapping lambs: they skirted, with respect, a field containing a mountain-sized Charollais bull. Tractors chuntered here and there about their business, their drivers cabbed and invisible. Only at one farm did they see another person, a woman feeding hens in the yard; and they asked for water for themselves and the horses. She fetched buckets for the cobs, and brought Rachel and Tom great steaming mugs of tea.

'You're the vet, over by Milchester, aren't you?' she asked.

'We both are,' Tom said.

'Oh,' she replied. 'I'd heard there was a woman gone into the work. I'd never have thought you'd have been so young.'

'I'm not really,' Rachel told her. 'It's a long training, you know.'

'Well, I can give you a few years, my dear. I've been on this farm now for fifty years, from the day after my wedding.'

'You'll have seen some changes, then,' Rachel said.

'Yes, I have. And d'you know what, there's hardly been one that to my mind hasn't been for the better!' She waved them goodbye, and took the empty mugs and buckets, and disappeared inside the farmhouse.

They had been riding again through sheep-fields, this time along the edge of a small escarpment where the green meadow tumbled steeply down among briars and blackthorn bushes when Tom, whose horse was the nearer to this edge, pulled up quite suddenly and said: 'Ah well, no peace for the wicked. Look down there.'

Rachel rode nearer to the sheep-netting that edged the grassland, and looked where Tom was pointing. Halfway down the steep bank a sheep was entangled in a cluster of bushes. It had been there some time, to judge by the trampling in the soil around it, and the fact that it had given up bleating.

They did not discuss the matter, but dismounted at once, tied the horses to the fence and scrambled down the slippery, thorny, treacherous bank.

The sheep saw them coming and began to bleat again. She leapt, desperately, in her briary bonds and pulled them even tighter into her fleece. At last, Rachel was able to seize and hold her while Tom cut away with his pocket

258

knife to free her. She was ungrateful for his efforts and struggled and leaped in spite of Rachel's grip on her. It took a very long time and a great deal of patience before the ewe was disentangled and could be hauled up the slope and deposited over the sheet netting. Then she ran bleating to her companions, who showed very little interest in her reappearance, and when she saw they had no wish to hear of her adventures she shut up and began to graze.

Tom patched up the hole in the fence where wool-gouts showed the sheep had got through. Then he looked at his watch. 'Hell,' he said. 'We're going to be late if we don't hurry.'

They remounted and pushed on at their best speed until they came to tracks that were familiar to Rachel. They had ridden a good distance on their pilgrimage. Tom was no expert and she could imagine he'd be stiff tomorrow. He had given her such an afternoon. Already her mind had printed upon it those scenes that would stay with her: not of her choosing: they chose themselves. It was a choice that often seemed wayward: forgetting the dramatic moment, and fixing some tiny detail, some fleeting sight, like that of a broad hand gentling the head of a silly scared sheep on a sloping bank of briars.

They had been on known territory for a

while now, and time was getting short.

At the point where they had now arrived, the bridle-path reached a parish boundary. Nothing proclaimed this but an old tumble-down wall and a broken post with the remains of a gate-hasp dangling from it, but just at the entrance to this gateway the track split in two. The one that it was logical to follow, the direct route through Blackstock Woods, became a footpath only: the one that angled off to the right, and meandered several miles out of the direct way back to Milchester, continued as the bridlepath.

'If we've got to be back in time to take surgery, we'll have to go through the woods,' Tom said.

Blackstock Woods belonged to a man with a highly developed sense of property. Rachel had come across him before and did not relish meeting him, should he find them where they had no business to be; but Tom was right, of course. Surely no-one would be unreasonable enough to prevent two busy vets taking a com-monsense short cut, with an excuse as water-tight as theirs? Even so, she felt a ridiculous and quite disproportionate sense of guilt as they rode on under the trees.

So when a squat and instantly recognisable figure appeared before them as they rounded a bend in the track she found her heart thumping. Amy Gunter was ambling slowly through the woods poking into bushes with a stick, and muttering to herself. Rachel could have sworn her eyes lit up when she saw them.

'Not supposed to be in here, you ain't,' the old woman said, with no initial greeting at all. 'Not on them 'orses. Footpath only this is.'

She looked Rachel and Tom up and down with a kind of greedy triumph. For a moment the two of them stared back at her in silence. Rachel awkwardly fumbling for something to say. Amy Gunter beat her to it.

'What you and him doing in here anyway?' she said. That annoyed Rachel. She opened her mouth to make some haughty reply, when Tom said. 'I'll tell you what we're doing here, Mrs Gunter. We're going to ride into the middle of the wood, and then we're going to cut down some branches and build an enormous fire. And then Miss Bellamy and I shall make passionate love by the warmth of it. And after that we shall ride naked home to Milchester singing bawdy songs.'

He had drawn closer and closer to Amy as he said all this, and her jaw sagged further the nearer he got. Then, he leaned towards her from his saddle and announced in a loud and salacious voice, 'And if you don't go away now this minute and learn to mind your own business, *I shall tickle you with my beard,*' and he wagged that same beard at her with such a dreadful expression on his face that it was the undoing of Amy Gunter. She let out a small shriek, and trotted off away from them, all a-bristle like some fat hedgehog, glancing agitatedly over her shoulder from time to time.

They rode on. Rachel began to heave and shake with laughter that was nothing more or less than a fit of giggles. She spluttered and whooped, and the tears streamed down her face. It was intoxicating: a marvellous, childish, irresponsible delight.

'Oh you wicked man!' she hiccupped at him. 'You glorious, wicked man. I haven't seen anything so funny since heaven knows when.' There were tears in her eyes from laughing so much.

He reached across and took her hand, and a great grin lit up his face.

'She'll have it all over Milchester by first thing tomorrow that we've been up to no good, the pair of us. They'll all be whispering before long. "Have you heard about that Miss Bellamy and that Mr Adams? Can't wait to get his drawers on her washing line, that one can't." Of course, you'll have to marry me now. The scandal will be the ruin of you.'

'Don't be such an idiot,' she said, still laughing. 'Let's get home. We'll both be late for work.'

She set off at a fast pace, and he came thundering behind her. She felt light, airy, as if the day had just began.

'Slave driver!' he yelled, and the woods gave back the sound of their home-going hoofbeats.

CHAPTER 12

Helen Carrington telephoned to say that the mare she had told Rachel about was ready to be collected and taken to the Fowlers.

'I can't let you have transport though. I'm sorry. Harry Ellis has to go to the sales for me and he'll need my box. Can you get hold of Mr Smith to do it?'

'I'm sure I can,' Rachel said. 'I'll warn Bill Fowler, too. Thank you again for your help.'

'I hope it works out. If things aren't a success with the Fowlers, let me know, won't you, and I'll squeeze the mare in somehow. I'm sure you're right: I'm sure this will be excellent therapy for Mrs Fowler, but the mare mustn't suffer.'

'Of course.'

Rupert Smith, who ran the local horse-transport business, suggested amiably that as he had two-three ponies to deliver to Nether Leybourne he could pick up the mare on the return trip by going just a little out of his way.

'Save you a bob or so,' he said.

'I'd like to come with you, if it's possible,'

Rachel told him. 'I want to be able to hand the mare over myself.' Just in case the whole idea was a disaster: in case the sight of the mare should deepen Anne Fowler's hurt, instead of starting a healing process. Rachel was well aware that Tom Adams thought the whole thing could be a recipe for disaster, and meant far too much involvement for Rachel.

'You've got better things to do with your time. You can't afford to get too entangled. There must be a hundred and one animal owners with problems. You can't solve them all. You'll wear yourself out.' Even so, she wanted to try.

It was arranged that they should set out immediately after surgery. It would not take long, and Mrs Partridge was in to take messages. In the afternoon Tom had agreed to be on call while the two women visited Malcolm. He had seemed a little better, Rachel thought, when she had seen him last: his mind clear, his eyes less shadowed. She must tell him about the Hawkshill ram. She had bought some fruit to take him, and a copy of Youatt's *The Horse* that she had come across in a book-shop in Gloucester. She knew he wanted a copy, as much for its meticulous steel engravings as for its historic veterinary lore. She was delighted to have found it for him.

It was pleasant sitting up so high in the horse lorry, and reminded Rachel of her childhood outings to cattle-shows with her father, as she looked out from the wrap-around window of the cab, across the early summer landscape.

The trees were just in leaf: the beeches in that bright and vigorous green that fades in the high season. The fields were of a different but equally vivid green, where the crop was ready for the first cut of silage. In a distant meadow the machines were already out, gobbling up the lush stuff and spewing it into the high cages behind them. Under this greenness the fields were a surprising, pale sandy colour, where the roots had been cut off from the light by the rich growth above them.

Wherever they had not been dissuaded by sprays and fertilizers, wild flowers flourished, on headlands and in spare corners of fields where tractors would not waste their time going.

As they drove along the narrow lane, the lorry filled the way from bank to bank, and set the campions and Queen-Anne's-lace swaying and dancing as it rumbled along. They drew in by a house at Nether Leybourne, and three excited girls came dancing out to claim their ponies: hopping about with frustration at the slow descent of the ramp and Rupert

Smith's lack of haste to undo the inner doors.

'Hurry, Oh, please hurry. We've been waiting hours.'

'Well then. Another minute or so won't hurt you, will it,' he told them, and led out the ponies to be hugged and fussed over. 'Kids!' he said.

Beyond Nether Leybourne the lorry climbed steadily uphill towards Shipton Clive, down even narrower lanes between dry-stone walls. Once or twice they reversed for on-coming traffic.

'Won't do that when I'm loaded,' Rupert said. 'When I've got horses on, they goes backwards,'—he nodded in the direction of a passing van—'or God help 'em.'

'What if they won't?' Rachel turned and looked over towards him as he sat beside her in the cab, his eyes on the road, his hands steady on the wheel. Their conversation had been limited, partly because the lorry was so noisy that all voices must be *fortissimo:* only now as they paused for the passing traffic did the sound decrease to a steady pulsing: but mostly because Rupert Smith spoke only when he felt something wanted saying. Now he just raised his shoulders to the level of his ears in an eloquent shrug, and a great expressive grin broke up his solemn face. Rachel liked him.

He was a man who enjoyed his work, and knew his horses, though he had more the look of an amiable school-master about him than anything. He had a long bony face and long thin hands, and a slight academic stoop that reduced his lanky height. His eyes were intelligent, his voice quiet and accentless. He had a magical knack with beasts. Although properly in horse-transport, he was the carrier of all sorts of animals, to market, to sales from one farm to another, and cussed, cranky contrary creatures would move sweetly for him wherever he wished.

Rachel had come to the conclusion—not an original one, for it was widely held as a result of experience—that given any situation that involved a horse, a vehicle intended for the transporting of horses, and the necessity of persuading the former to enter the latter within a limited time, or for a particularly important occasion, then nine times out of ten there would be trouble. The horse—were it normally the most tractable—would instantly develop a dislike of the vehicle which might range in degree from obstinacy to hysteria, and its owner would eventually panic, or grow angry, and resort to all kinds of extraordinary devices by which to overcome this reluctance, none of which would have much effect. With

Rupert Smith, things were different. When Rupert suggested to a horse or pony that it might like to consider being loaded on to his lorry it walked up briskly and with no fuss at all. He just took it short by the head, murmured affectionately in its ear and up it went.

On one occasion Rachel overheard the words of this quiet incantation, this old soothing spell with its magical effect.

'Come up, you daft old bugger,' he lovingly crooned. 'We don't want to be here all day, do we?'

He always smelt—not unpleasantly—of what he called horse-oils which had been given him by a Romany horse-coper he'd met at a fair. The ingredients were secret, but Rachel's analytical nose traced aniseed, violet and peppermint in the mixture. Whatever it was, horses seemed entranced by it, and would snuffle and blow at Rupert like tobacco connoisseurs savouring a good Havana cigar.

When they arrived at their destination and the mare was brought out for them, she was no exception. She rubbed at him lovingly with her head as if she had known him all her life. She was very pretty: the colour of a newly baked biscuit, with a black mane and tail, and black legs to the knee as if she had long socks on. She was rounded out with her unborn foal.

Everything about her showed how well she was cared for: the gloss on her, her bright eyes, her confidence. Rachel quailed. If she had made the wrong decision: if Anne Fowler could not—or would not—care equally well for such a lovely creature...perhaps the whole thing had been a disastrous mistake. That would teach her to interfere, wouldn't it?

'Get along then, shall we?' said Rupert. There was nothing to delay them. The mare's owner had left for the airport that morning, taking her parents to wave her off and to drive the car back. It was a neighbour's daughter who handed the pony over to them, with all her papers and certificates, a detailed account of how she had been fed, the date of service, the date the foal should be expected.

'Her name's Belmont Honeydew,' the girl explained, 'known as Honey. Can you manage now? I'm late for a music lesson.'

'Thank you,' said Rachel. 'We'll manage.' With Honey aboard, they set off for the Fowlers, passing, on a fortunately slightly wider part of the lane, the girl they had just left, making wobbly progress on a bicycle. Strapped to her back like an odd-shaped rucksack was a cello in its canvas case.

'There's dedication for you,' shouted Rupert against the noise of the engine. 'Cycles to

Gloucester twice a week with that.'

'Is she good?'

'She is. National Youth Orchestra next year. Have to work hard for what they want, some of these rural kids: no popping down the road on a nice warm bus.'

Rachel remembered her own piano lessons. She had had to walk a mile for them, but at least she had not taken the piano with her. Anyway she had never really taken to it, and much preferred to listen rather than to perform. She waved to the girl as they passed, seeing in her that same kind of determined purpose that had pursued her throughout her own life, although along a different road.

Bill Fowler had said he wanted the pony to be a surprise: he would not warn Anne of its arrival. Rachel had doubts about this, but he was adamant. Honey's supplies of immediate food were with her in the lorry, so there was no worry there, but still there haunted Rachel the fear that this had not been one of her wiser ideas. Too late now: they were approaching the drive.

It seemed to Rachel that although the place looked as impoverished as ever, someone had been making some kind of effort with it. One or two leaning fence-posts had been set straight, and a broken gate-bar mended. The yard had been swept, and at the back door logs had been stacked, cut perhaps from the sprawled ancient apple-trees that had lain roots-in-air in the orchard, on Rachel's previous visits. Bill was obviously making an effort.

He emerged from one of the stables as the lorry stopped in the yard.

'She's in the house, hoovering,' he said. 'With luck she won't have heard you arrive. What's the pony like? D'you think this is going to work?'

He was so anxious, so eager; quite amazingly changed from his old irascibility. It would return, of course. If all went well, once he felt secure again, once his marriage had stopped turning sour, it would come back, but perhaps something of this new awareness would remain, to make it less acid and more palatable. Rupert brought Honey down the ramp and she stood looking placidly about her. The back door of the house opened, and there was Anne Fowler. She had lost even more weight, her unguarded expression was bleak as November. Rachel held her breath. Bill rubbed his hands up and down his trouser legs, like an actor who has forgotten his lines, and must occupy himself with stage business until prompted.

Rupert stepped towards Anne Fowler as she approached and pressed into her hand the end

272

of Honey's head-collar rope.

'This'll be rightly yours,' he said.

She stared at the pony, and they all waited. She stretched out her hand and laid it on Honey's neck, and you could have heard a strand of hay fall in that silence.

The bleakness was breaking: her face began to light, like a fire reluctant to catch on a damp day, when the flames lick up at last, and take hold, and dance upwards.

'For me?' she asked, her voice shaking.

'For you,' Bill said, and put his arm around her. For the first time in weeks he did not feel her muscles stiffen against him.

Rachel and Rupert left them to it. They unloaded hay and feed, and handed over the information they had been given about Belmont Honeydew and her care. Bill could explain the details.

Mrs Partridge was bustling about in the kitchen at Stapleton House when Rachel returned.

'That phone 'asn't stopped all morning,' she said. 'There's a raft of messages on that pad, and Topend want you out there as soon as you can. They think their bull's broke 'is tail. It 'urts 'im, anyway: won't look at the cows at all, 'e won't. I've put you some sandwiches and a flask. Mr Adams'll pop in on Mr

273

'Alliday, 'e says. 'E took that fruit you bought for 'im and that old book.'

Rachel had been so busy, she had hardly spared a thought for Malcolm since morning. How he must hate it, trapped in that hospital bed. All the minor indignities of being a patient seemed to distress him far more than the seriousness of his condition. She knew how they would intrude on him with their cheerful necessary ministrations, and how he would dislike it. She wished he could be here, and well, and going with her now to Topend, to inspect the bull's tail.

She read the messages on the pad: swiftly worked out an itinerary which would include the most urgent-seeming cases: asked Mrs Partridge to telephone replies to those who only needed advice. One or two known and proven panickers could wait. She could only stretch herself so far. She picked up her peripatetic meal and went to let Jessica out of her garage.

The sun was out, and Rachel drove off down the lanes. She set aside her thoughts of Malcolm and recalled instead that marvellous change in Anne Fowler's face that morning. It was going to work, Rachel was convinced of it. She swung Jessica left up the road to Topend. 'Watch out bull, I'm on my way,' she called out, and through the open window of the little car she could smell the first cut of hay sweetly wilting in the meadows, and the birds were all singing fit to burst in the hawthorns at the lane's edge.

Three days later Malcolm died. Quietly, and with his usual dislike of any kind of drama, he told Sister he would prefer not to be disturbed for a little as he was tired, and would like to sleep.

She left, respecting him, having learned in his first few days there never to jolly him, or to withhold any part of the truth from him. When she returned there was no need to take his wrist to feel for the pulse.

No need for the resuscitation trolley, and the brisk efforts to call an unwilling body back to life. She sent for the doctor, but only because procedure demanded it. Then she knelt, as it was her custom to do, and prayed briefly for him. A little later she telephoned Stapleton House.

Rachel felt desolate. She could scarcely believe in his death. His desperate illness had been a fact, visible and undeniable, and she had been saddened by it and was unhappy for him. Malcolm dead would not establish itself as a fact in her mind. The house was full of the echoes of his quiet presence. In every room she expected to see him, working or reading, or sitting quietly looking out into the garden at the birds that came to the food-table he had always furnished for them.

She made herself continue as usual with the work, though she came near to being over-whelmed when people spoke kindly and with sadness about Malcolm Halliday. Then she needed all her control not to break down and weep. As for Vi Partridge, she made no pre-tence, but stumped about the house red-eyed, polishing ferociously, making endless cups of tea for them both.

The Australian cousins, who had not seen Malcolm for years, post-scripted their letter expressing sorrow at losing him with a request that the house should be sold and the proceeds banked for them as soon as convenient, but Geoffrey Parr, Malcolm's solicitor, told Rachel that she must not worry. It would be six months at least before they could get posses-sion of the house. As for Rachel herself, Malcolm had left her all his books and in-struments, and a considerable sum of money. He had provided for Mrs Partridge too, and on hearing the news she sat down and wept afresh at such kindness from 'that dear, sad man'.

Well, whatever was to happen to the prac-tice eventually, Rachel decided that for the moment it must continue. It had become so evident to her, with the progress of Malcolm's illness, that as Tom's remarks had verified, he had taken her on after so many years alone so that the practice should not suffer as a result of a disease which he so clearly recognised as an overwhelming enemy. So except that on the morning of the funeral, surgery was closed as a mark of respect, she carried on with the work as usual. Tom was there, at the funeral, and a great many Milchester people, and many stories were recalled and recounted of Malcolm's skill, and his unsentimental com-passion for his patients: how 'all heaven in a rage' was never so effective as Malcolm's cool disapprobation if he found some creature misused. He had asked that there should be no flowers, but an old woman with an ancient dog came to the graveyard with a bunch brought from her garden. They had already begun to wilt with the time she had stood there holding them. She stood waiting, diffidently, afraid that she might not be welcomed to come further with the dog, but Tom saw her, and went and fetched her over, dog and all, and she laid the flowers on the fresh earth.

Everyone was asked back to Stapleton House. There was sherry, and sandwiches, and tea that cooled in its cups while the guests stood awkwardly, hesitating to be the first to drink; but eventually the strain of being sad became too much: conversations broke out, faces began, tentatively, to smile: life, doing its duty, went on.

Rachel wondered what Malcolm would have made of the gathering. It would certainly never had been called together in his lifetime. She wished he could have been aware of the affection people felt for him, although he had never invited it. There were the inevitable few who were there merely because they ought to be there, but there were others—his many colleagues, customers whose animals he had tended for two decades or more: Lady Bramwell, Janet Hodges from the Riding Centre, Humphrey Murton, whose llamas had so surprised Rachel, Helen Carrington, escorted by a brushed and gleaming Harry Ellis, who in Malcolm's honour had turned himself out with all the care he would give to a horse at a county show. John Barton, Malcolm's doctor, was there, the women from the local shop, Joe Harris the sadler, Mike Barnsby the blacksmith, at whose travelling forge Rachel had often warmed herself in the bitter months, and whose skill could often match a vet's in getting a horse's feet right. There were farmers from miles around, all sombre in their best suits, their feet cramped into good shoes, their hands scrubbed clean of muck and diesel-oil. The faces of all these showed clearly their respect for a man of such skill, whose compassion showed itself in making each sick creature's cure his total and absorbed ambition. On the rare occasions that he had failed, it had seemed to diminish him, physically, for a while. He had been a remarkable man. It had not taken his death to make Rachel aware of that, but it sharpened the awareness so that it hurt.

Tom was there, of course, but she found herself avoiding any close contact with him. She knew that his arm about her shoulders would crumple her altogether, so she concerned herself busily with all that must be done. He looked at her across the heads of the crowd in the room, but she would not meet his eye.

Surgeries in the next few weeks were, thank God, full and demanding, leaving little time for thought or for despondency. It was easy to make oneself busy being busy, Rachel found, and it was a kind of comfort, until slowly everything began to feel ordinary again. Out in the fields, the lambs she had delivered in the earlier months flourished and fattened and lost their charm. The Ashton Stud fields were gambolling grounds for a new generation of foals. Summer unfolded itself.

Rachel, doing her rounds, felt quite normal, quite everyday, but so subtly that she did not perceive it, the grief that she would not allow herself to show slid down into her bones, until she grew gradually leaden and spirit-less. She worked, but took less and less pleasure in it. Sometimes when she recalled the delights of that day on the hills with Tom Adams, they seemed to her to have taken place in a different world and in a different time. She would not see him, except when it could not be avoided. She did not wish him to be part of the narrowing existence that was all she felt capable of coping with. All that beautiful new strength of hers, all that growing assurance was gone, and she must find something with which to replace it, so over the weeks she developed an outer self who could be pleasant, polite, informative to the people whose animals were in her care. She could stand inside herself and listen to this person rattling on, being really quite impressive for something so hollow inside. No creature suffered a twinge more pain, received any less efficient treatment because of this hollow person's attentions. Yet there were some who were not fooled. When she called at the Ashton Stud, and Harry Ellis watched her with the mares, she said, 'What's up, then?'

'Nothing at all. It's just a routine check, Harry, you know that.'

'Not with the mares, I don't mean. What's up in yourself?'

Rachel looked at him ruefully. She had not thought it showed, had not thought of Harry as one so keenly perceptive of human emotion. Horses were what he knew about.

'It's obvious then, is it?' she said.

'It's not me that sees it. It's the mares. I've worked with blood-horses all my life. You can't fool a blood-horse. Look how she draws back from you. You've got her all of a twitch.'

He was right. She could see it now. They did draw back from her: would not give her that unquestioning confidence they once had. She was off their wavelength, and coming through distorted. She was a failure then, wasn't she? She felt one, anyway. She felt that anything she touched might turn wrong, like some terrible version of King Midas's predicament. She could not even bring herself to telephone her mother—and a visit to Parkwood, however fleeting was out of the question. She had had a long and compassionate letter from her, after the news of Malcolm's death, and this Rachel had read and reread until the words were all in her mind. She could recite it in her head. Yet she had still not answered it, and that bothered her too.

'You're feeling thoroughly sorry for yourself, aren't you?' Tom accused her when he cornered her after surgery at Stapleton House, giving her no chance to vanish quietly at his approach. His anger charged the air around him. She could not look at his face.

'Why don't you grow up, Rachel Bellamy? You're a big girl now: old enough to know that good men like Malcolm do die, and a great many the world could easily spare do not, or not as soon as we might like.'

'Oh, shut up!' she yelled at him. 'Shut up and go away.' And she went into the kitchen and put her head upon Mrs Partridge's skimpy bosom and cried, as she had not done since that day in the town with Tom. Mrs Partridge, her arms clasped around Rachel heard the kitchen door open, looked up over Rachel's head to where Tom stood hovering, and shook her head at him. Understanding her message, he went quietly away and Rachel never realised he was there.

There seemed to be something that would not leave Rachel alone over the next weeks: something that was determined not to let her regain her old quietness of mind. She had difficult cases, argumentative owners and plain bad luck to contend with. She began to feel, with some justification, that everything was going contrary with her, that she had slid back into a chasm, and even with the warnings she had had from Harry Ellis and Tom, she found it hard to fight against these defeatist feelings. She was bone-tired into the bargain, and would not accept help from Tom except when he practically forced it upon her. So when she was asked to go and see Old Toffer, what resilience she had left was almost exhausted, and the prospect of the visit daunted her more than anything she could remember experiencing before. Why me? she asked herself. Surely they could send one of the ministry vets. It was their wretched job, not hers.

CHAPTER 13

Old Toffer was a known eccentric: a strange, harmless old man who lived in a remote cottage in Blackstone Woods, and who wandered wherever the fancy urged him, looking about him, sometimes talking to himself; or else sitting still as a log, seeming neither to hear nor see. What his real name was, no-one seemed to remember, nor did anyone know the reason for his nickname, except perhaps that he spoke, when he did speak, in a cultured, quiet voice, quite unlike the braying of some of the country gentry, but declaring him to be some kind of toff, however fallen in estate. It was a pleasant romance, anyway, and excused his oddities in the eyes of the folk who were his neighbours. It also made the people in whose fields and woods he walked more tolerant of his trespass, but even if they had not been, there would have been little point in shouting at him. At those who tried, he only smiled mildly and continued whatever he was doing, deaf both to threats and reason. Land, he said, belonged to no-one. To work the land, one must be its servant and not its master. Mastery lay only in poisoning its roots and drowning it in concrete. They did not worry greatly about him. He was as likely to damage what they continued to regard as their property as they would be to murder their own children. So he walked undisturbed, and sometimes he would pick up handfuls of earth—his hollowed palms like cradles—and sing quietly to it, and caress it with his thumb. He was mad as a hatter, daft as a brush, fifty pence in the pound, yet children walked softly in his presence. They did not torment him, chant songs or throw stones, as they did to poor Bill Pratt, daft Billy Pratt, the slit-eyed, thick-lipped boy from Topend Farm, whom they picked on with more cruelty than any of their parents knew. Old Toffer was a different kettle of fish altogether. Had they met Merlin in the woods they could not have been more circum-spect.

Animals came to him, as they often will to the solitary, to saints, hermits, recluses: like Jerome with his cuddly, tabby-cat of a lion; Elijah, fed by ravens. Adders curled, un-disturbed and unprovoked, under the stones of his high-banked wall. A badger lived in his outhouse.

The badger was the trouble. The sett on the

north side of Blackstone Woods had been gassed by the ministry men. Dairy cattle grazed the meadows that fringed the wood, and tuberculosis reactors had been found among them, so what were they to do but kill off the badgers who were, after all, the obvious carriers. There were the usual protests, of course, and people waved banners, and some hysterical women cried, and tried to stop the men doing their work, but what other sensible course was there? The farmer must make his livelihood, and who would want milk from diseased cows? TB had been a major enemy and it was now in retreat. Nothing must give it an advantage again. All the same, it grieved Rachel to see such delightful and, in every other way, harmless creatures put to death. Malcolm had attended many of the meetings that had been held, quietly insisting that research should continue to find a better method of control: that the ministry should not remain satisfied with a policy of slaughter purely because it was the only one they had so far found effective. Now she must go and tell Old Toffer that there was proven TB among the dead Blackstone badgers, and that his own was almost certainly affected. His badger was no captive. She came and went as she saw fit but since, with Rachel's help, he had nursed the young sow when a big

286

old rose-thorn had imbedded itself in her pad and turned septic, she had chosen to live with him: in no way a pet: a friend.

They had rung up from Shire Hall to ask Rachel to go and see him.

'He knows you. He'll trust your judgement,' they said. You're scared of him, Rachel thought. He gives you the willies. Screaming women can't put you off, but Old Toffer can. Cowards. Nevertheless, for the old man's sake, she agreed, most reluctantly, to go, but even she felt nervous as she approached the door, and every single thing she had thought of to say to him seemed inadequate.

He came to the door and peered out to see who it was. His glasses were round his neck on a piece of string, and fumbling for them, he was able to recognise her and to smile his greeting.

'Ah, Miss Bellamy. Good-day to you.'

He had abundant grey hair, which was clean and fine, and surrounded his rather large head like a halo. His clothing, old and worn, clung to him, like the bark of a tree, yet his hands too were clean, though stained and marked with cuts and scratches. 'Will you come in?' he invited. His courtesy was so pleasant it nearly overset Rachel's purpose altogether. How could she say what she must do to this

287

splendid old man?

She walked into the cottage, which was little more than stone shed really, with one room down and one up, by way of a wide-stepped ladder. The walls of the lower room were unplastered stone; the floor, great earth-bedded flags, between which adventurous grass-shoots showed themselves here and there. The window was wide open to the air, and tendrils of wild clematis clung to it, and spilled down it like a green curtain. It was as if Old Toffer invited all outside to come in. Rachel wondered how he survived in winter. Then she saw that one whole wall was a huge open hearth, and there was timber enough at hand in the woods to warm him for a lifetime. Now a small fire of sticks burned there, with a blackened saucepan on it. He was smiling gently at her, as one might encourage a backward child to speak.

'How is Domina?' she asked. In view of her mission the question and its answer were both pointless. Her hands began to tremble. How the hell—her reason chided—how the hell can you expect to be a successful, professional woman when your emotions play the Fifth Column on you like this? Pull yourself together. Get on with it.

'It's about Domina,' she tried again.

'You seem distressed,' he said. 'She hasn't harmed you, surely?' He shook his head slowly, not able to entertain anything so unlikely, and indicated that Rachel should sit down in his chair, which was pulled up by the window that looked into the woods. She sat, and he pulled up an old box alongside and perched himself upon it, like a rusty old owl. All round them the woods were green with summer, blue in the depth of their shadows: so beautiful they seemed to draw her from her purpose. It would be so much easier to sit and gaze at the richness of Blackstone Wood and not say what one had come to say.

Old Toffer sat still. There was never any sense of haste to him. If she stayed there silent all day it would neither concern nor surprise him.

Rachel, at last, made the effort to speak. 'The badgers in the wood...,' she began.

'They killed them. I know,' he said softly.

'Domina was seen,' Rachel told him. 'You know she has a trail from your bank to the beech hedge where that badger-lavatory is, and their path goes down from there to the sett. She's often been in their company, there's no doubt about it, and she may well have the disease too.'

Old Toffer sat looking out of the window,

his gaze distant, his thoughts, apparently, as far away. The little noises of the room seemed very loud: the rustle of his cooking-fire, the creaking of the wicker-work chair, the clock ticking.

'She may well,' he said at last.

'I can do a test,' she told him, 'and be sure one way or the other.' Her voice was wretched. Even if the badger was not infected, Rachel knew Old Toffer would not agree to keep her penned up, which was the ministry's alternative to the sentence of death on her.

'That will be best. She is asleep now. I'll show you.'

Rachel and the old man went together out of the back door and walked over to a stone outhouse. Outside, cocooned in a pile of hay, the badger slept. She was so used to his presence, to his comings and goings in her life, that she was not disturbed by the opening of the door. She lay nose to tail. One paw, fringed with curved digging claws, was curled over her bull's-eye striped face. She snored softly, the breath stirring the long grey hairs that mantled the rest of her body. Old Toffer went creakily down on his haunches beside her, and Rachel did the same. Domina opened her black eyes, registered their presence, and accepted it. The old man stroked her head and spoke softly to her. He seemed to forget Rachel. She watched the scarred, scratched hands moving quietly over the badger's body, and saw the gentle absorbed affection that lit his eyes. The badger moved her paw to enclose his hand with it, imprisoning it so gently that the claws could not hurt him.

They stayed so for a long time, and Rachel could not bear to intrude on them; to remind Old Toffer of why she had come. She gazed at him, reading all the fine map-work of his face: the age-lines at the corners of his eyes; the long scar-like seam that ran the length of his cheek. As unobtrusively as she could, Rachel gently examined Domina, who made no protest, except to tighten, for a moment, her paw-hold on Old Toffer's hand.

'She looks well,' Rachel said. 'But I must make a faeces test. I'll tell you the result as soon as I can. I'm sorry.' There was a long silence.

When at last the old man spoke, it was softly, so as not to alarm the badger. 'Death is not so terrible, you know,' he said. 'Only, sometimes, the manner of it.' He turned to look at Rachel, but his hands continued to smooth the grey fur. 'If we were able to choose whether we should die or not,' he said, 'most of us would choose death in the end.'

The old man's voice trailed thinly away, and his eyes clouded, like a day that grows suddenly overcast. His mind seemed to absent itself, yet still the hands continued their movement. Rachel felt, as with a sleep-walker, that she should not call him back from wherever he was. At last, almost as if commenting upon himself, on his aberrant mind, he said quietly: 'Think of the Wandering Jew. He beats upon the earth with his staff. "Let me in, Mother," he says, but she will not. The children play out in the fields in the long summer evenings, and it is always too soon for them when they are called in. But if no-one ever called them home, they would be lost and afraid, don't you think?' He rose to his feet then, and she heard the old man's sudden quickness of breath, and saw the trembling of his hands and mouth, in spite of his efforts to control them.

'If you discover that she should die, now rather than later,' he said, 'then I must agree to it. It will be my grief, not hers.'

He continued to stand there, looking down at Domina, and he made no further move. Rachel felt herself not so much dismissed, as forgotten. She went quietly away, and walked back through the woods to where Jessica was parked, skirting the deserted sett whose ramified tunnels and deep underground chambers contained no life. There had been badgers in Blackstone Wood for generations. Now they were gone. Next spring would not see their bedding dragged out to air, and the cubs would not go rolling and tumbling in the loose earth at the tunnel's mouth when the summer evenings grew warm. Only Domina was left.

After a surgery packed to the doors with trivial ills and minor injuries, Rachel set up her equipment and made the test. It was positive. Now even Domina must go. It was stupid to feel heavy-hearted about it. Her death-warrant had been signed already. Old Toffer would never have agreed to keep her a prisoner.

Rachel was about to leave the surgery when the bell in the waiting-room rang, so sharply and so unexpectedly that it made her jump. She had already locked the hatch for the night, so she went to the surgery door. There stood Miss Pringle, all white and wild, her hair awry, and in her arms she clutched her good tweed coat all rolled into a bundle. Rachel brought her in and sat her down on a chair by the surgery table, taking the bundle from her as she trembled and shook.

It was Simba, of course. Rachel had known,

horribly, that it would be. The little dog was a mass of bloody fur. One foreleg was so badly broken that it seemed suspended only by a few threads of flesh. There was no point in wasting time with 'How did it happen?' Rachel doubted whether Miss Pringle could find the words anyway. She went and scrubbed her hands, and began to work.

The job took over, as it always did. They did not understand, the people who recoiled, even in their minds, from some of the sights that were part of her daily routine. If you could make a start on the process of healing it, then an injury became at once less horrific. Even now, grown in experience as she was, Rachel found it hard to stomach the violently dead: had to her shame turned sick on the motor-way when she had helped the traffic police to remove from the fast lane the corpse of a dog that had been smashed by a dozen sets of wheels; but all the while life remained, her mind fixed itself on the fight for it.

Then as she worked, she became aware of someone standing beside her, tall and still. Once or twice as she reached for an instru-ment, it was put into her hand. There was Miss Pringle, standing there staunchly, watch-ing. Her trembling had stopped, and her eyes, though still anxious, followed every move that Rachel made. Rachel could not stop to be amazed about it. Only when the leg was stitched and plastered, the blood gently sponged away, all the smaller injuries cleaned and dressed, and the usual protective injections given, did she turn and thank Miss Pringle for her help, but Miss Pringle did not want thanking.

'It was a privilege,' she said.

Rachel carried Simba into the recovery room. He was still unconscious, but his breathing was steady and his pulse strong. He was putting up a fight to earn him his name. 'Come into the kitchen, Miss Pringle. I'll make us some tea.'

They sat in the quiet of the kitchen, and Rachel learned that Miss Pringle had been walking with Simba along the quiet side streets that led to the Abbey grounds where she often took him for exercise. He was an obedient little dog, but still she kept him on his lead until they reached the open space. They had been within a few yards of it when a car came round the corner, roaring out of the junction fast and heedless, so that it mounted the pavement and hit the little dog in passing before it raced away out of sight. It could so easily have struck Miss Pringle too, but that fact did not seem to have occurred to her. It was a while before she could ask the inevitable question.

'Will Simba be all right?'

'If you mean will he live,' Rachel said, 'then the answer is "yes", I'm pretty sure of that. The leg is a bad injury. I've done all I can for the moment. He's a healthy, young dog, and with luck it should heal, but it may take a long time.'

Miss Pringle seemed relieved, even by this guarded prognosis, and began to relax a little and to sip at her tea.

'You know,' she said to Rachel. 'If it had not been Simba lying there on that table I might say that this evening has been one of the most rewarding in my life.' She said this with a brightness in the eye and a pinkness of cheek that took ten years off her, and softened the undeniable ugliness of her face. 'I wanted to be a nurse, you see. Always, from a little girl, that was all I could envisage for myself. But my father would not allow it. He made me train to be a secretary: said I was not to spend my life cleaning up after other people's misfortunes. In those days, my dear, fathers expected to be obeyed, and my father was a bully into the bargain.' She sighed, and stared ahead of her. Rachel waited for her to go on, sensing that these things had not been confided before: that they had been hidden in

296

Miss Pringle, carefully, so that they did not show.

'When my mother died—I was nearly thirty then—I had to sort out all her letters and papers. She had one of those lovely Victorian writing boxes, inlaid wood and mother-of-pearl, and velvet padded cubby-holes. I sprung a little drawer in it, and I am not sure what treasures I thought to find in it, but all it contained was a piece of card, and stuck to it a snippet of paper cut from a magazine. On it was written, "If you cannot have the man you love, learn to love the man you have." A trite enough exhortation, you may think, but it made me realise that my poor mother had not even had the comfort of once having really loved that bullying man, and that she had died still making the best of a bad job. And that is what I have done with the rest of my life. I have worked at a job I have loathed, try as I would, and the only nursing I have done was of my father in his final illness. Mind you, if you could learn all of nursing from books, then I expect I could run an entire hospital single-handed. The day after my father's funeral I went out and bought Simba. That was the first major decision I ever made, and I'm sixty years old, Miss Bellamy. Imagine that. What a stupid, useless life, don't you agree?'

Rachel reached over and took Miss Pringle's large, bony hand in hers.

'I don't agree, though I'm sure you must feel that it has been,' she said. 'What matters is that you have started making decisions now, and you're free to go on making them. You were a marvel tonight. I really admire you for it. Simba's going to need all your care: all your nursing skill. Now you won't let me down, will you?'

Miss Pringle took a fierce hold on Rachel's enclosing hand, and beamed.

'You can trust me,' she said.

A little later when they had visited Simba in the recovery room, seen him open for one rewarding second one puzzled brown eye, and seen the faint quiver of his tail when his name was called, Miss Pringle took her leave of Rachel.

'Thank you, my dear. May I come in the morning to see him?'

'Of course.'

'I became a little sorry for myself; forgive me. I can't help wishing that my life could have been more as yours is: my own choice: my own wish. I should be proud to have skill like yours.'

She walked away into the dusk, her heels clumping on the pavement. It occurred to

Rachel then that Miss Pringle might be cold without her coat, which lay forgotten and blood-stained in the corner of the surgery. She seized a spare raincoat of Malcolm's from the hallstand and would have run after her with it, but the tall striding figure had already vanished from sight, and the road was empty and quiet.

CHAPTER 14

Rachel arrived at the Fowlers feeling nervous, shaky, as if she had actually held her breath all the way instead of only feeling that she should do so. If the mare looked well, then much else would be well too. She wanted so much that this experiment should work. It had taken on an almost disproportionate importance in her mind.

She drove into the yard, and there was no-one about, except the various occupants of the looseboxes, who squawked, clucked or bleated their warning of her presence to the morning air. The door of the mare's loosbox was ajar, and Rachel went looking for her, out to the paddock at the back, across the orchard to the small field where the cow grazed, down towards the enclosure where the pig lay in a heap, surrounded by her now much larger offspring who were playing around her with surprising agility and sudden bursts of speed. Their small pleased squeals punctuated the slow minutes that she stood there, gazing round, waiting for Bill or Anne to appear, waiting to see Honey. At last she heard hoofs on the top road and an accompanying voice. At a carefully slow pace she walked towards these two sounds, and there was Anne Fowler leading Honey by her bridle and talking away to her nineteen to the dozen.

'Hello,' Rachel called, ridiculously relieved to see them.

'Don't worry,' Anne Fowler shouted back. 'I always talk to horses. They listen so appreciatively.' All three of them walked together, back towards the yard.

Honey looked magnificent. Her coat gleamed with, if possible, an even deeper burnish. She looked plump and content. The remains of a snatched tuft of lush grass hung from the side of her mouth. When they all came to a halt, she seemed to remember this prize, swept it inward with her soft lips and began to munch.

Rachel, feeling a twinge of shame that she had instinctively checked the pony's well-being before Anne Fowler's, turned her attention there and saw with relief distinct signs of improvement. Anne no longer looked as if she teetered on the world's edge. She was no less thin, but that drawn defeated look was gone. She was nowhere near as bonny nor as beautiful as the animal she led, but a start had certainly been made.

'Where's Bill?' Rachel asked.

'Gone to Gloucester,' Anne told her, and then with a sharp, deductive look at Rachel said: 'You don't need to worry, you know. I've stopped being stupid now. I'm quite safe left to my own devices.' The voice was mocking but there was no bitterness to it. 'Bill's gone to buy some cockerels. He's made some arrangement with a chap that runs the Golden Pheasant Hotel. We buy and fatten them, and then they buy them from us all dressed and ready. Bill says we can't lose on it. Maybe he's right. It's one of his less crazy ideas, anyway.'

They walked back to the yard and put Honey away in her stable. Rachel noticed that Hassan's box was still empty. In the bad days following his death, Anne had taken every blade of bedding out of it and had made a bonfire. Then she had scrubbed the place, floor and walls, till her knees were sore and her hands flayed pink. Bill had not dared to stop her: had not dared to say what she knew quite well in her right mind anyway: that the tetanus organism lurked in the soil, and not in any imagined dirt in the stable. He had left her to her impassioned, ritual cleaning, and had hoped she would cry, but she did not.

Now she said: 'He might as well put the new

birds in there. It's empty. I'll throw some straw down later,' and invited Rachel into the house for coffee.

There were still problems, of course. Nothing cures as easily as that. Everything about the house showed how lack of money—and very little hope of relieving that lack—was eating away at its fabric. The paint-work was more blotched and stained than ever: damp seeped in: window-frames were rotting. Daily it was becoming more depressing, more of a burden, as if someone, once loved, beautiful and endearing, had gradually turned into an increasingly unattractive invalid, in-curable and demanding. Even if Anne could shake off her own depression entirely, and resolve the difficulties of her relationship with Bill, this house could quite easily defeat them, yet Rachel knew that neither of them, for their several reasons, wished to leave it. One should not become so attached to something that was, after all, stone, timber and slate, yet Rachel was herself experiencing something of the sort, trying to make decisions about her own life. Leaving Stapleton House was unavoidable, and it saddened her, not only because it had been home to her for the past months, but more poignantly, because the house itself had so much in common with its former tenant.

Sombre, unornamented, it yet had about it a rightness of proportion, a fitness for purpose and a plain, enduring serenity.

Rachel had Geoffrey Parr's assurance that there was still no need for haste. He had been a close friend of Malcolm's as well as his adviser, and the importunity of the Australian cousins had turned him mulish. He was in no mood to make things easy for them: to let them make quick money out of a man for whom they had shown so little care. They could stew in their own peach juice for as long as his professional integrity would allow him to let them. So it was tempting to be Micawberish, to hope a solution would turn up: tempting to take refuge in immediate battles and ignore the whole pattern of campaign.

Alan Parker had asked her to join them as a fifth partner, and she was strongly tempted. She had begun to feel for Milchester, as for Stapleton House, that it was home now: the home of her adult, independent life. It began to contain her as Parkwood had done her childhood years. She would always love her old home, look forward to her snatched visits, to easy affectionate conversation with her mother, but she could not, and would not, go back to that life, any more than she would wish to be a child again.

In other ways, too, she had grown: was moving out and away from the depression that Malcolm's death had brought down on her. It was not, now, doubt of her own ability that made her hesitate about joining them she was delighted to have been asked, and the pleasure was in no way tinged with self-doubt. Whatever was healing her, it was working well. She smiled to herself, thinking how she would have reacted to the same proposal only a few months earlier. But Parker would not then have considered any such thing, even had she been available. She knew that when she first came to Milchester he had thought her an oddity, a bit of a joke really: had referred to her as 'that funny little woman of Halliday's', which had made Rachel fume.

She wanted to discuss this possibility with Tom, but he had been oddly evasive lately. On the rare occasions she had seen him he had been hurriedly on his way to or from something of great urgency. Once when despite her attempts at complete independence, she had been forced to beg a locum for a day, it had been Peter Wilmott who had come forward, and had subsequently rubbed Harry Ellis up the wrong way by snorting with derision at Harry's cow-muck treatment. Harry swore by applications of cow-muck for any heat in a horse's foot.

'Even if it works, which I doubt, it's pretty unhygienic, Mr Ellis.'

'Well, it does work, and costs nowt,' Harry had told him, sulkily, and had muttered as much to Rachel on her next visit. There had been quite a few hackles to smooth down after Peter Wilmott's day in her practice, and he was one of the prime causes of her doubts about joining a group of which he was a part. She had been worried, too, about the possibility of undertaking an even closer working relationship with Tom Adams, but if the past few weeks were anything to go by, she could forget that particular concern. Indeed she began to feel an odd sense of something lacking, as if some feature of a known and familiar scene had been removed, leaving her wondering exactly what. It wasn't just him: his not being there. It was something far less easily defined than that.

In spite of an undoubted improvement in Anne Fowler, Rachel's senses were still radar-alert for the least trouble from that source, so that when the telephone rang one morning in the following week and Bill Fowler's voice spoke, she felt a quick and apprehensive thumping of her pulse, and began at once to assemble in her mind possible solutions to any possible problem that might have arisen. These, as it turned out, were totally unnecessary: the problem was neither Anne's, Honey's nor, directly, Bill's. When Bill had arrived at the Golden Pheasant Hotel to let them know how many birds he had been able to buy on their behalf, he had found the manager, Harry Adler, so agitated and anxious that he could scarcely take in what Bill was trying to tell him. 'I'm sorry, Fowler,' he had said at last. 'Don't think me rude. I'm just at my wits' end about my wife's damned dog. She's up there crying her eyes out over it. I've ruined her birthday. Oh God! All this on top of the problems I've got in the kitchen. There's nothing for it, I suppose. I'll have to get a vet. Now where the hell have I put the yellow pages?'

Then Bill had offered to telephone Rachel, and now he explained that the Adlers' pomeranian puppy, ten weeks old, was very ill, probably dying. Could she come at once?

Rachel had some routine testing of cattle to do in that direction, so she decided to call in on the way: asked Mrs Partridge to phone the first farm on her list and say she might be a little late. It was Felgate Farm and its owner, Joe Mills, had been one of the most rigid in his opposition to her when she had first come to work for Malcolm. She had won him over gradually. She hoped it was by her ability, but she had also found him susceptible to charm, and had shamelessly set about charming him. Beneath his prejudice, he was a pleasant enough chap, but she was careful to observe all the courtesies with him. Now he could not greet her possibly late arrival with: 'Women! Never get anywhere on time.'

Mr Adler met Rachel at the door and almost dragged her from her feet in his hurry to take her to the sick puppy, which lay in an upstairs room in the private wing of the house. The room was full of scrunched wrapping paper and scattered with unheeded birthday cards and gifts, as if everything had stopped for the puppy's sake.

Inside a new, velvet-padded basket, someone had thrown down a dirty piece of wrung-out wet fur. The little creature's puppy-fluff, and what should have been a jaunty little bush of a tail, were wet and stinking. Its uppermost eye was dull and half-closed. It had looked at life and did not much like what it saw. The pup was hardly bothering to breathe.

'I would have washed him,' Mrs Adler apologised, 'but he's shaking with cold already. Please. Please help him if you can.'

The puppy's short history began to unfold as

Rachel got to work on him.

Mrs Adler had always wanted a pomeranian, and Henry Adler had been determined to find one for her birthday, but the local breeders could only offer labradors, spaniels, golden retrievers, the kind of dogs for which there was a ready market.

The Faracre Kennels had terriers of various varieties and nearer to Gloucester there were producers of poodles and dachsunds and even some more exotic breeds, but there had been no pomeranians anywhere. In desperation, and with Clare Adler's birthday getting nearer, he had telephoned a big commercial kennels that advertised itself as able to obtain almost any breed of puppy at short notice. They could find just what he wanted, they promised, though of course the price might be a little high. Henry had been so relieved that he had enquired no further, but drove up to collect the puppy the moment they told him one was available. The little creature was all ready for him in a wire-fronted basket when he arrived. Mr Adler was given coffee in the pleasant room in which he had parted with his money; a considerable amount, but well worth it, he was assured, for such a fine, well-bred pup. The pedigree and registration papers would be sent on as soon as possible: he would appreciate there was always some delay about these things, especially when the puppy had had to be found at such short notice. He had stayed only briefly, drove home delighed with his purchase, and had kept the pup secret from his wife for the couple of days that were left before her birthday. He bought food on the advice of the local pet-shop, where old Fanny Holder reigned supreme. She had all the things a ten-week-old pup should need.

'And mind you get him injected, now. They'll have given him one little jab at the kennels I expect, just to protect him in transit.'

'They didn't say.'

'Bound to have done: pedigree pup and all. You bring him in to see me when he's a bit older. My old auntie used to keep poms. Nice bright little dogs they are.'

The brightness had faded from this one, and not much more than a glimmer of life remained. Rachel very much doubted it was ten weeks old. It ought still to be with its mother, in a good warm fug of brothers and sisters, suckling the bitch's sweet nourishing milk.

'He didn't look too bad yesterday,' Henry said unhappily. 'He wasn't too keen on eating, but he had some warm milk, and he was moving around in his basket. Then when I went to bring him in to give to Clare, well, I was horrified. Foul at both ends as you see, and whimpering with cold. I should have given him a hot water bottle, but he seemed quite happy at bedtime: a bit quiet perhaps, for a young pup, but I never thought he was ill.'

'Young animals are like young children,' Rachel said. 'Illness can strike them down dramatically. Being too quiet is usually a bad sign in any very young creature.'

The two Adlers stood over her, looking so wretchedly unhappy that she tried hard to cheer them, even though she was full of doubts herself as to the likelihood of the pup's recovery. 'They can improve just as rapidly though. If we can control the diarrhoea and vomiting, keep him warm, keep fluids down him, we stand a chance of saving him. When I palpated the abdomen I could feel a thickening of the bowel there. It could be an obstruction, an intersusception of the bowel. It may be worms. In fact I think that is most likely: and that could be causing the vomiting. We'll dose him anyway, and then as soon as he can keep anything down he will need a course of vitamins and minerals to supplement a light sustaining diet. He is far too weak to be injected against distemper, and so on. We must treat him as if he were as immature a pup as he looks. Poor little fellow. He has a long hard fight ahead of him, and he will need a great deal of care and attention if he is to pull through.'

'If he's got any chance at all, that's a start, isn't it Clare?' Henry Adler said, putting his arm round his wife, who was hovering anxiously as Rachel made her examination.

'He must get better,' Mrs Adler said, 'he must.'

'Miss Bellamy's done all she can for now, dear.' Then, to Rachel, he said: 'Where will you be going when you leave here?'

Rachel glanced up at him. 'I have some calls to make at farms over towards Flintworth. Then I must go back to the surgery,' she said.

'You'll pass here, then. Call back. Look at him again on your return journey.'

Rachel hesitated. There was a strong chance the puppy would be dead by then. She could not bring herself to say so.

'All right. I've written down details of the treatment for you, and I'll leave you some worming tablets and a vitamin-mineral supplement. Don't expect miracles, please.'

It was an effort to keep her mind on Joe Mills' cows. Rachel dreaded the prospect of returning to the Golden Pheasant and finding the last spark gone out of that small heap of fur. Clare Adler had looked on the verge of hysteria. She looked too intense, too high-strung a woman to help with the running of a hotel. Her husband seemed almost too anxious to please her, as if he were trying to placate her. The puppy, lively and well, would have been tailor-made for the job, but its illness had brought her distress she could scarcely cope with. At best Clare Adler would not be the perfect dog-owner, she would be the sort to pamper and over-indulge, and would have to be watched so that she did not damage the dog with unsuitable food and too little exercise. Still Rachel would like to give her the chance with this one dog. If it lived at all, they could surmount the other problems as they arose.

As she worked, Rachel composed in her head vitriolic letters to the owners of the kennels from which the puppy had been purchased. For quick profit, it had been acquired from and despatched by some heartless breeder with an eye to the main chance. It was wanted in a hurry, so who was going to wait three weeks or so for it to be properly weaned? Despite the price, the pup could well be without a pedigree. There was a good chance it would be dead before the new owner began to worry about such things, and if by chance it did survive, well, they would be too fond of it, wouldn't they, to be bothered by the lack of a piece of paper. The survival of such places witnessed the fact that they had learned to ward off the kind of attack that Rachel planned, however. Somehow they continued to make a profit, to the detriment of good responsible kennels, and to the distress of the people who bought puppies from them.

Rachel was so boiled inside with frustration that she spoke quite sharply to Joe Mills, so that he looked at her in amazement. Watch it, she thought. The mask is slipping. She hauled up an unwilling smile and beamed it on him. 'Sorry, Mr Mills. Your heifer trod on my foot.'

'Clumsy female,' said Joe Mills, and Rachel did not like to enquire to whom he was referring.

Calling her back to the Golden Pheasant had been, in part, a ruse. The pup was, thank God, still alive when she was taken to see it, a great deal cleaner, and lying in a far more sensible bed of cardboard lined with easily disposable newspaper and old rag. When she had finished her examination, washed her hands, refused still to commit herself to saying what the pup's chances were, Henry Adler told her they would like to give her lunch in the hotel as an extra thank you for her help. Rachel did not really want it. She seldom ate much mid-day, and a sit-down meal would take up precious time, but she felt such a churl as she opened her mouth to refuse that she closed it again and smiled her acceptance.

'I'll telephone my surgery first, though,' she said, 'to make sure there's nothing urgent.'

Mrs Partridge answered. There had been no calls. 'You just enjoy yourself,' she said. 'I'll let you know if you're needed.'

Rachel felt able to relax then, and was shown to a table.

The food they brought her was delicious: the dining-room full. There was a pleasant, low murmur of conversation, the gentle sounds of civilised and appreciative eating. Rachel relaxed and began to enjoy herself. She smiled towards one or two faces she recognised. She could scarcely go anywhere now without someone realising that here was Miss Bellamy, the vet. She considered her short professional life and felt that, on the whole, she had not made too bad a start. Malcolm's death had plunged her in deeper than she had ever thought to be at this stage and so far, in spite of setbacks and disasters, she felt able to cope. There were still one or two who found it hard to accept her. Some had transferred to the Parker practice, once Malcolm was no longer there to rescue this strange female should she come to grief. This had annoyed Rachel and embarrassed Parker, but there was nothing to be done about it.

Her experience so far, both of animals and people, had been diverse and rewarding. The devil would have been hard put to find her idle—except at the moment, she grinned to herself, putting in another delicious mouthful of creamed chicken. She had grown to enjoy the work in surgery as much as being out and about on the farms, yet still she found that aspect most satisfying, and had discovered, to her amusement, that the women on the more isolated holdings greeted her as a friend and confidente: wooing her into their kitchens with tea and cake, bending her ear to their troubles, pouring out their problems, domestic, sexual, medical. She felt sometimes that she had done them as much good as the cow, sheep or whatever that she had come to treat in the first place. It paid off, though—had she thought of it in those terms—as they were her staunch allies. Woe betide the married farmer who did not carry out to the letter the treatment Rachel had advised. Moreover, news of her skill percolated steadily through the Women's Institute, the Young Wives' Club and the Mothers' Union, so that doubting husbands were left in doubt no longer that here was a woman who knew her onions.

The waiter brought her pudding: a lemon mousse like a tangy cloud. This is the life, she thought.

An elderly man, who had glanced up at her now and then from the next table where he sat with his wife, leant across and said: 'You're Miss Bellamy, aren't you?'

'Yes.' Rachel had not recognised the face: wondered if she ought to know him.

'My name's Ford. You treated my grandson's gerbil. He thinks you're the best vet in the country. Well, actually in the universe, he told me.'

'Oh dear,' Rachel laughed. 'I can't promise to live up to that reputation.'

Gerbils were tricky creatures. Her treatment, if she was being entirely honest, had been a little hit and miss, but it had worked, and young Simon Ford had taken his home, delighted.

This one had been moving about in its cage in the most curious fashion, twisting its small body with a corkscrew motion, as if trying to embed itself in the ground. Rachel had diagnosed cerebral haemorrhage, had administered cortisone, and then had wondered how on earth she was to immobilise such a tiny

317

creature. In the end she had put it in a small box, padded all about with cotton wool. It had done the trick, greatly to Rachel's relief, and Simon's grinning face, watching the little animal when it was able once again to sit up and comb its whiskers, had, been as rewarding an accolade as any Rachel could remember. This small success had come in the midst of one of her bad, despairing times, and had given a boost to her flagging morale. She felt very grateful to Simon Ford's gerbil.

'Are you enjoying your meal?' old Mr Ford asked.

'It's excellent,' she said.

'Yes,' Mr Ford sighed, 'it really is a shame.'

'Oh?' Rachel was puzzled. Why should such good food be a shame?

'They're losing their chef, didn't you know? All the regulars are horrified. He's been offered three times the salary in Germany. I can't think where they can possibly find anyone to replace him at short notice. I feel sorry for the Adlers: they've worked so hard to build this place up.'

Rachel made murmurings of sympathetic agreement, even as she continued to savour the delicious food. It would be a disaster losing such a chef. She had not eaten anything so good since... She considered for a moment, and

318

remembered when that was. And then an idea began to tickle the back of her mind like a far-off sneeze.

She was about to consider how she would take the idea to its next stage when she heard the telephone ring in the hall. She knew without being told that it was for her. She had had a whole hour and a half without being summoned, so it was inevitable that the waiter should be coming in her direction now, with an expression on his face that urged her to hurry.

As it turned out, she was too late. The cow to whose *accouchement* she hurried produced twin calves with considerable despatch about five minutes after her owner had telephoned, but Rachel checked her over and made sure the calves were in good fettle. They were curious, knobbly-legged creatures, looking at this new large world with dark, long-lashed eyes. They had found their mother's udder and suckled lustily, but when Rachel offered her fingers they sucked those too, with equal enthusiasm. They were delightful, and she allowed herself to enjoy, for a moment or so, this short lived confidence. The world would soon teach them to be a good deal warier.

From the farm where the calves were, the road brought Rachel into Milchester from the

other side. Tom's car stood outside the surgery. On an impulse, Rachel pulled Jessica up
into the space behind it and went in. It looked
as though she had tracked him down at last.

He was standing at the table, his back to her.
She found the view surprisingly pleasing.

'Hello,' she said.

'Just a moment.'

She had not realised he was working. Whatever the patient was, it must be pretty small.
She went closer and saw that it was a hare.
Tom did not look up, but by now he had registered her voice.

'Hello, Rachel.' He went on working. 'The
car in front of me sent her flying. I found her
in the ditch. I thought she'd fractured her
pelvis but it's OK. I'm checking for other
injuries.

The hare lay quiet, except for the rapid pant-
ing breaths that fluttered her whole body. Her
ears hung limp and cold. Her fur looked
second-hand and very much the worse for
wear.

'Wouldn't it be better...?' Rachel began.

'To knock her on the head?' Tom asked.
'You're right, of course. I was indulging
myself. Wanting to see if she could be put
together.'

They made the hare comfortable in a cage

and stood watching her for a moment.

'Hell,' said Tom. 'You're right, of course. It was just self-indulgence. Most of our so-called kindness to animals is, I suspect. Motive is all wrong, most of the time. I remember Malcolm talking to some woman about this wretched badger business. She was saying what a pity it was to kill such pretty creatures, and Malcolm gave her one of his classical looks; that sort of calm severity he had. I remember how he shook his head very gently and sighed. "What we must consider, madam," he said to her, "is whether or not the action being taken is a right one. The attractiveness of the animal concerned is not relevant."

'As he said to me afterwards, he could not imagine this particular lady, if the plague should break out suddenly in Milchester, carrying a banner proclaiming "Save the Rat". Well, we're all guilty, I suppose. I patched up the hare to prove I had the skill to do it. On the whole people keep animals to amuse themselves, or to be therapy for their troubles, or just to make a profit. We help them to do it. Perhaps that's a sort of self-indulgence too.' His tone was light, but Rachel could see he was serious.

'Still, I've lumbered myself now,' he went on. 'She's going to need a great deal of nursing if she's to recover.'

Rachel had been thinking, as she watched the hare, lying passive, patient, accepting whatever fate should come to her. 'Let Old Toffer look after her,' Rachel suggested.

'By God, you're right,' he said, his beard curling up at the corners with the width of his grin. 'What a bright girl you are, to be sure. The old man will take the best possible care of her. He's the exception, you see. You know the Ancient Mariner?'

'Well, not personally,' Rachel said, a little nonplussed at this apparent change of subject.

'When he killed that bird,' Tom explained, 'that albatross, it wasn't just a case for the Society for the Protection of Albatrosses, you know. He upset the whole balance of creation: set it on a new and darker course. Old Toffer is a restorer of balance: he lives in harmony with creatures: he doesn't exploit them. He's just the man to take on this hare.'

Rachel stared at Tom. The grin clouded. When he spoke his voice was irritable. 'What's wrong with you, woman? You think I'm daft, is that it? Well, you're probably right, but I've the sense to take your advice for all that.'

He picked up the cage and strode away with it, and Rachel continued to stare at the open door through which he had vanished, until the sound of his engine shook sense into her again.

What an odd business it all was, to be sure. Chance had put the hare into Tom's hands, rather than her dying in a ditch, or being picked up by some farmer who would have eaten her for his Sunday meal. Toffer would nurse her and get her right, and maybe she would live out her span, or maybe, slowed down by injury, she would be chopped by some dog out on the loose, shot at some field's edge by a boy with a brand-new air gun. Whatever you did, you could only prolong life, not save it for ever. Perhaps Old Toffer's philosophy was the most comforting after all, in a world whose harshness was never more than a furrow's depth below its pleasures.

CHAPTER 15

It was one of the best days of the summer so far on which Rachel went to take her idea to Anne Fowler. Ideas like pebbles under water, could often lose their brilliance when brought out into the air, and Rachel was anxious for this one: so much so that she scarcely saw the brightness of the day, hardly felt the warmth of the sunshine as she walked out to where Jessica was parked. Yet as she drove she became aware of the landscape that flourished around her, and opened her window to take in a good breath of summer air, and knew for sure as she did so that she did not want to leave these rounded hills with their beechen fringes, the steep narrow valleys full of the sound of hidden streams; the little grey villages where the houses sat on either side of a wide market-street, or huddled over a narrow one as if in conversation. She had been asked, time and again, in Milchester if she planned to stay. She liked to think she would be missed, but she hoped above all not to give them the chance to miss her.

The June riot of wild-flowers was almost over. The hay was in, except on some of the higher farms where the grass grew slower, or else the owners had not trusted the earlier good weather to hold. It would not be long before a slow subtle change began to work on the grain, turning the vivid and lusty green to bright gold, first in the barley fields, and to a paler dustier coinage in the wheat.

One or two other vehicles passed her as she drove. Mike Barnsby, the blacksmith, shouted to her from his tatty van as he went by in the other direction. He was busy at all hours now, keeping the local ponies well shod for gymkhanas and shows and pony club junketings of all kinds. He knew each pony by name and the state of its feet, and if a new one was brought in he could tell you what smith's shoes were on it, if it had come from somewhere within a good fifty-mile radius. To some of these brothers-by-trade he would give grudging recognition of their skill: of others he would say they couldn't nail a shoe on a barn door.

Now he pulled to a halt just past Rachel and called to her again. She saw him in her mirror and stopped too.

'They want you at the Milchester Show Saturday week,' Mike called as he walked towards Jessica. 'I told 'm if I saw you I'd give you fair warning.' Mike was on the Committee of the Milchester and District Agricultural Show.

'But Mr Parker's on duty there,' Rachel protested.

'No, no,' Mike said. 'They want you for a judge. Children's pets. Will you do it?' Rachel hesitated, trying to think whether she had any commitments that day.

'Go on,' Mike urged. 'You'll get your dinner free.'

'All right, I will,' said Rachel, 'barring emergencies.'

'Right. That'll please 'em. I'll tell them tonight, at committee. I'll let you get on now, and take myself to Topend Farm. They've got a new mare for that spoilt girl of theirs, so well-bred you need to pay to speak to it, but as for its feet, you can't put a nail in 'em without they split. Put up a notice big as a barn saying "no foot no 'orse" and they still wouldn't pay attention to it. Daft buggers, some of 'em.'

He grinned at her and stumped off back to his van, slammed the door several times to persuade it to hold shut, and rattled noisily away.

When Rachel arrived at the Fowlers and unveiled her idea, Anne Fowler nearly retreated into the woodwork.

326

'Me?' she said. 'Me ask to be chef at the Golden Pheasant? Oh, I couldn't. It's all very well doing the odd meal, but producing stuff to that standard every day is a very tall order.'

'I know,' said Rachel. 'That's why I hesitated to ask you. I just thought that the food I had with you was the only meal I could think of to compare with what they gave me, and I know you've had the training. It might only be a short-term thing, anyway. They may find a replacement, but they need someone to tide them over now. It isn't just hearsay. I checked discreetly, with some of the kitchen staff. The money would be good and, you never know, even if they got a new chef eventually, they might go on giving you work from time to time. It couldn't hurt to ask, could it?'

Anne paced about in her own kitchen, picking up utensils, putting them down again, opening and shutting cupboard doors. She went to the larder and stood just inside it, frowning and muttering quietly to herself. Then she came out and began to run her finger down the piles of best plates on a shelf over the sink. She had her lower lip caught between her teeth and was gently nibbling at it, abstractedly, apparently miles away from Rachel, who was waiting anxiously for some kind of coherent answer.

'I shan't go and see the Adlers,' Anne announced at last, and Rachel felt immediately deflated. So that was the end of that idea. What a shame.

'I shall invite them to dinner instead.'

'Yippee,' said Rachel, and the two of them did an undignified and most unprofessional dance around the kitchen, rattling the cups on their hooks by their prancing on the wooden floorboards.

'Watch out,' Anne said. 'We'll end up in the cellar, all among the Chateau Cobweb and the empty beer barrels. I'll try, really I will, and thank you for thinking of me. It would never have occurred to Bill, bless his cotton socks, though he's been eating my cooking all these years, and I don't suppose I'd ever have dreamed up the idea for myself. Now come on, come out to the yard and see your other prodigy.'

As they walked to the yard, Anne told Rachel how pleased the Adlers were with their puppy's progress. The little creature was improving daily, eating well, beginning to be mischievous.

'Clare Adler's over the moon about it. She's ordered an extra chicken a week, just for the dog!'

'Well, don't let her give it the bones,' Rachel

admonished. 'I thought she'd be the sort to over-indulge a dog. I'd better send her a tactful diet-sheet.' She sighed. Sensible dog-owners were like snow in June. Neglect at one extreme and pampering at the other were Rachel's usual experience. She wished there were more like Miss Pringle, determined to do it right. Her careful nursing of Simba was a pleasure to see: their relationship rewarding to each other. Rachel had called to see them at Miss Pringle's on a couple of occasions when she happened to be passing the house, and had found Simba bright-eyed, alert: patiently enduring his plaster, following on three legs every movement that his owner made.

'Don't worry,' Anne said, bringing Rachel back to the present problem. 'Clare will listen to you. In her estimation, you're only a little lower than the angels. Now, there's our maternity ward. I'll bring Honey out for you.'

It would only be a matter of weeks now before Honey foaled. It had been a last-minute decision to put her to Highlight, and she had gone to him late in the covering season. Most of the year's foals were already strong on their legs, and taking in sunshine and good grass out in the fields. This one would go young into its first winter and would need extra care. Judging by the condition of the mare, though, there would be no problems with the foal.

Anne led Honey about the yard so that Rachel could inspect her, and Anne's pride in every aspect of the mare shone out of her like a beacon that Rachel's obvious approval made burn all the brighter.

'She'll do then?'

'Yes. Congratulations. She looks splendid.'

'Listen. If I do get that job, if by any amazing chance I do, you wouldn't need to worry about her. She wouldn't suffer because of it. I haven't done all this alone, you know. Bill helps me too. I've never known him show the least interest before, but he can't do enough for Honey.'

Rachel knew quite well why, and was glad. There seemed hope for these two now, and her own interference had worked. It might have been disastrous. She had been lucky to get away with it. Everything had worked together for this particular good, and its achievement was a relief to Rachel: the letting go of that pent-up breath.

She waited to see Honey tucking in to her feed, and then said she must go. She had patients waiting, and then she must be back for surgery.

That evening Miss Pringle brought Simba, still in his plaster, of course, but getting about well, and with all his minor cuts healing fast. He had entirely recovered his high spirits too, and spent most of his time in the waiting-room harassing a large ginger cat whose owner, fortunately, had a soft spot for fox terriers himself.

'Such a pleasant man,' Miss Pringle informed Rachel. 'He spent his boyhood in India. We had quite a conversation, when Simba would let us.'

'Oh, that's Mr Frobisher,' Rachel said. 'Ginger's been fighting again, I expect.'

'So I gathered,' said Miss Pringle. 'Quite a seasoned warrior, judging by the state of his ears. Now Simba, stand still and behave.'

After surgery Rachel went out for a walk. The evening was warm and pleasant. A rosy sun reflected off the stone walls and houses among which she walked. She considered that it might be nice to have a dog herself. Then she laughed. Self-indulgence again. Perhaps Tom was right. Then she thought that it might be pleasant to be walking with Tom, and concluded that this could also be considered as self-indulgence. He certainly seemed to have foregone her company recently, except for their brief meeting over the hare. She hoped he had persuaded Old Toffer to take it. People she passed in the street smiled and greeted her.

Some stopped and gave her news of their animals, asked her how she was, whether she had decided yet what she would do about her future. Milchester was looking its best, as if urging her to stay: turning on all its charms of homogenous streets, the warm smell of geraniums from town gardens and window-boxes, the soaring, skyward-reaching golden shaft of its church tower that would go on glowing long after its fringing streets were full of evening shadows. She walked on, enchanted by it all: her legs carrying her a great deal further than she had originally intended. Now that she was so near Tom's flat, it seemed reasonable to call. She ought to find out if Old Toffer had taken the hare; and if so, how the creature was faring.

No-one answered Rachel's knocking, but when she turned the handle she found the door was unlocked. She touched the fabric of the stout armchair by the fireplace: stood looking about her at all the things that belonged to Tom. She walked about, picking up small items and replacing them, feeling a curious affection for them. Everything seemed to be waiting for him to come back, but he did not come, and the room grew cool. Rachel saw then that the door into the studio was slightly open. She went in to the smell of turps and linseed, the sight of canvases stacked by the wall, some just prepared for work, others with the tentative beginnings of landscape on them. There was an easel with its back to her.

She wanted to look, and was not sure he would want her to. Cautious as a cat in a pantry, she moved towards the easel so that she could see the canvas it supported.

There was a finished landscape on it. It was a picture of a bluebell wood. Pinned to the beam above were countless sketches from which the completed painting had taken shape. No wonder she had seen so little of him. It must have taken every spare moment he had. What a painting he had made. There was never a pictorial cliché in it. In the foreground the bright bell-flowers swung from their fleshy stalks, in the glowing colour and clear detail that was Tom's trade-mark. Further away, great trunks of old beech trees, scarred and wrinkled like elephant skin, sprung so vigorously from the ground that you could almost feel the growth in them. The air was tiger-striped with the light and shade of a spring morning just as the sun strengthens. At a far distance, shadow-shapes of deer stepped thin-legged and ready to run, on their way to drink from a shallow stream that ran beneath over-arching ferns, and everywhere hidden in the depths of colour, like a child's picture-puzzle, other creatures could be seen by those who would look for them: a great furred moth blended into the tree-bark, a weasel eased its few inches of wickedness among the flower stalks. A figure among the trees, watchful, she saw with surprise, and recognised as herself.

Rachel stared at the picture, and at this self that was contained in the picture; part of its design, washed with its colours, and felt for a moment that she was really there, with the haze of blue flowers all round her, the brilliant new green overhead. She went on staring for a long time. Then, 'Yes,' she said, aloud. And again 'Yes.' She was barely aware of what it was that she affirmed, but it was something undeniable.

A voice from behind the easel made her jump and go cold. There she was, where she shouldn't be, and talking to herself into the bargain: but it was only Mrs Appleby who 'did' for Tom. She knew Rachel well, and looked almost relieved to see her.

'Oh, it's you, miss,' Mrs Appleby said. 'You gave me a fair old turn, you did. I'd only just popped next door to feed their cat. Mr Adams asked if I would. He does it himself usually because they're both on nights next door and he's fond of that cat. He's had to go to Bir-

334

mingham, you see. Took some of his paintings to a gallery. I told him, you should take that one, I said.' Mrs Appleby indicated the painting on the easel. 'He wouldn't, though. "Got other plans for that," he says, and you can't budge him once he's made his mind up. Well, I'm glad it was you, dear. I thought it was burglars, and I'd have looked a proper fool, wouldn't I, when it was me left the door open? I shouldn't have been so long, I know, but it was so glad to see me, the poor creature, that I hadn't the heart to leave it without giving it the time of day. I'd have a cat meself, you know, except that my Jack's allergic to 'em. Comes out all lumps, he does; and cry? He can't stop himself. Tears run down his face as if the whole world had died.'

Rachel, quite swept away by this flood of talk, nodded and smiled until it abated at last, and said she really must go.

'Did you want to leave a message?'

'No, don't worry. I'll see him when he gets back.'

Rachel went out into the street, into an evening that had turned cool and blue. Street lights were lit and splashed brightness on to pavements. There was hardly anyone about, but the occasional couple arm in arm, and a gaggle of teenagers worshipping the motor-bikes that gleamed in the window of Halman's Garage. From the interiors of pubs came wafts of laughter and occasional bursts of song, and far away down the street, by the traffic lights, the last bus from somewhere chugged across on its way to the terminus. Rachel walked briskly, but without any real haste, hugging the evening to her. She watched her feet as they went, pat pat pat, carrying her along the pavement, back to Stapleton House, and she wondered what other roads they would tread, and where those roads might lead her. She considered, idly, how many pairs of wellington boots and good stout shoes she would wear out along the way, and whether her one pair of elegant high heels would outlast them all.

CHAPTER 16

On the morning of the Agricultural Show, Milchester woke to the teasing, rain-flirting weather that makes the outdoor events of an English summer such a strain on the nerves of their organisers. Everyone looked towards Stroud which, with a prevailing wind, seemed always to pass on its immediate conditions to Milchester. Grey clouds hung over it like a veil that was darker at its hem. The air was very cool. It would be a day for cardigans and plastic macs and wellies, it seemed.

Even so, from earliest light, stall-holders had been busy putting up their temporary emporia. Commerce was there, in the form of the local saddlery shop, fancy goods, garden equipment and DIY, but there were also traders-for-the-day, like the Guides with their bran-tub, the Round Table tombola, the WI with produce and home-made cakes and bread. These last were laid out under polythene sheeting to protect them from whatever the weather chose to do, but they would not need it long. There were women in Milchester who made cakes like a dream of delight, and the stall would be bare after the first half hour.

Early horse-boxes arrived, and Landrovers with trailers in every condition, from the old work-horses of the farm, held together with prayer and bale-twine, to the latest shining models with their trailers in matching livery. There was great clattering and calling of nervous little girls, fussing over their mounts, fretting over what might have been forgotten, cheeking their mothers, wheedling their fathers and, sorted out at last, thundering their way to the secretary's tent with their money burning in their pockets, to enter the bending, the egg-and-spoon, the chase-me-Charlie and all the other delights of the gymkhana.

One or two boys rode about the showground aloof, superior, thinking inwardly that riding would be a far better sport if it hadn't been taken over by females.

The field was coming alive now. Cattle arrived and went to their pens for a final wash-and-brush-up. Spectators strolled about, looking for the best vantage point. Once found, they would encamp themselves with ground-sheets and shooting sticks and picnic gear, establishing their territory for the day and, if necessary, loud in the defence of it. The first few dads vanished into the beer tent, from which some of them might not emerge again all day, except for necessary trips to the green canvas 'toilets' that had already sprung into place by the top hedge. People in the know made their visits early. By mid-day it would be pleasanter to find a private and concealing bush.

Show ponies arrived for the in-hand classes, rugged, bandaged and booted, and once revealed to the open air in all their splendour, seeming a different species from the ones the children were riding. Most of them would go into the ring for their class, and then vanish again into all their accoutrements to be whisked away to another show at another place.

By the time Rachel arrived, having first taken her morning surgery, there were cattle in the ring, and one or two known faces among the handlers. She would not be called on to judge the pets until early afternoon, so she was free for a while to watch and to enjoy herself. The heifers in the ring seemed to sense the importance of the occasion. Gleaming in their white parts, glossy in the black, their tail tassels brushed out like superior bell-pulls, they behaved like scruffy kids got up for a posh party: not entirely sure they were enjoying it, but thinking in the main that they probably were, and that it was worth giving a prance and skitter now and again to prove it.

More matronly cattle came next: milkers, with their udders all washed pink, and after them the calves, leaping and snorting on unaccustomed halters, some backing nervously from the advancing judges, some pushful and trying out their strength. Two of the first four, when the class had been judged, were calves that Rachel had delivered. She felt quite ridiculously pleased, as if she had won the rosettes herself.

She wandered away from the ring then, and browsed among the stalls: played tombola without success, bought some home-made sweets and some paperback detective stories: Simenon in French, which the stall-holder was pleased to unload on her for twenty pence the lot. She would have stayed longer, looking at the books, but saw out of the edge of her eye Amy Gunter at the produce stall, poking at some your marrows with her finger as if they had given her offence. Rachel fled, down the brief avenue of tents she went and saw, with pleasure, the tall thin form of Miss Pringle carrying Simba in her arms, and deep in conversation with the gentleman who owned the ginger cat. Rachel did not speak to them: they were too engrossed in each other's company.

She wandered on, idly, enjoying even on so

cool a day all the old familiar sights and smells, feeling all the threads of her memory plucked upon, and remembering in particular how her father had explained this very feeling to her, saying that we are everything that we once were; not just our at-the-moment selves; that every thought we have, everything we do, everything that happens to us, becomes part of our fabric, which is why memory, even of distant things, can come so sharp and clear, called up on the instant by an echo from the present.

She went to the secretary's tent and collected her badge: a red and gilt affair made of cardboard and a safety pin, with 'JUDGE' emblazoned grandly at its centre. She pinned it to her lapel, promised to be at the judging ring at two o'clock sharp, and was directed to the marquee where lunch was laid out for the officials of the show. On her way she met Alan Parker, labelled like herself, but his badge proclaimed he was the 'Official Veterinary Surgeon'.

'Have they found you any work yet?' Rachel asked him.

'One lame cow, one coughing pony,' he said. 'Oh, and I've sent one of your class home. Child with a little hairy dog. Full of fleas. Both of 'em by now, I expect!' He roared with laughter and slapped at his boot with his stick. He always dressed for the show in the full kit of breeches and boots and tweed jacket, though he never ever rode in it. He was strictly a ride-to-hunt man.

'Coming to lunch, are you?' he asked. Rachel said that she was. 'I'll tell you what we'll get,' he said. 'Every year it's the same. One half grapefruit, cut at eight o'clock this morning, and not sugared, so it will have formed a sort of seal across the top: one piece of ham, small, curling at edges: one piece of tongue, ditto: several lettuce leaves, limp: one half tomato, if John Harper's greenhouses are doing well: one quarter if they aren't: boiled beetroot with far too much of its own juice for everything else to swim in: one slice white bread, no longer anyone's Mother's Pride, and a glass of warm, flat beer.'

'Oh, dear,' Rachel grinned.

'Ah well, it's the thought that counts,' said Alan cheerfully, and he seized her by the elbow and propelled her towards the tent so firmly she felt as though she were being arrested.

He was right about the lunch, and Rachel began to think that this might be another job for Anne Fowler, but on second thoughts there would be bound to be those upon whose feet such a suggestion would tread, and Show

Committee warfare was not to be engaged in lightly.

'So they've got you judging the pets, then,' Alan was saying.

'That's right,' said Rachel modestly.

'Well, I told them she wouldn't come again, not after last year.'

'Oh? Who Wouldn't?'

'The Hon Mrs Fellowes, of course. Didn't you know? Have I put my foot right in it? My dear, I'm so sorry. The Hon Mrs F. had judged this group of classes for years. She's the President of the local Dumb Friends' League.'

'I've met her,' said Rachel stiffly. So she had been asked as a stand-in, had she? She remembered Mrs Fellowes all too well. All gush and sweetness, so that she made you feel you had struck treacle.

'What happened last year?' Rachel asked.

Alan grinned wickedly. 'Tommy Harper's polecat ferret happened,' he said. 'She'd held forth to the children for hours on the virtues of patience, love and understanding. She asked the children to bring their pets to her to be stroked, so that they could see how the dear creatures would react to her own kindly, sympathetic approach. She tried it on Tommy's ferret and it bit right through her thumb. She said something quite unrepeatable.'

'So she wouldn't come?'

'She was suddenly invited to the South of France.'

'So they asked me instead?'

'Yes. I do hope I haven't upset you, telling you all this. The committee obviously hoped that as a newcomer you wouldn't know their dark secrets.'

Rachel chewed the last unrewarding mouthful of her free meal. She smiled charmingly at Alan. 'I like ferrets,' she said, 'but I make sure they don't bite me.'

It was beginning to spatter with rain as they left the marquee, but the pet classes were to be held in a similar one, so Rachel would be out of the weather. She had rather hoped to find anonymous cages waiting her decision, as they do in fur-and-feather competitions. It is far easier to judge an animal coolly when it is not in the presence of its owner. Owners can influence a decision in a thousand subtle ways, and even the most resolute judge cannot help but be swayed if one owner is sweet, polite and reasonable, and the competing one an offensive know-all, if there's scarcely a whisker of difference between their two exhibits. Far easier to judge the pets as one might judge pots of jam, bunches of carrots, bottles of home-made wine. Put out your winning cards, and retreat before the multitude of unofficial judges descends to quarrel with your decision.

This anonymity was not for Rachel, however. Not only was every pet accompanied by its owner, but many of the owners were accompanied, at a distance, by one or both parents, aunts, uncles, older siblings and a multitude of other allies, more tenuous in their relationship, but rooting for a particular child, nevertheless. Rachel began to feel that however she made her judgement, she was laying herself, and her professional ability, open to all degrees of criticism from the supporters of those who did not win. She felt she would rather like to go home. However, she was announced almost at once, with great cheerfulness, by Mike Barnsby in his official capacity as a Show Organiser, and she entered the ring like a gladiator, to what she hoped was enthusiastic applause. There were old friends, of course, among the pets, though some were hardly recognisable, so spruced were they for the occasion. Who would have thought that little scruffy Monty, the mongrel, could be transformed with shampoo and trimming scissors into such a cloud of dazzling white fur? Monty's mother had obviously had a penchant for poodles, for she herself was a nondescript terrier. There were fat, glossy cats, bright-eyed rabbits, mice with their whiskers quivering into a blur of motion. There was a chameleon, its eyeballs swivelling independently, its tongue a marvel of speed and accuracy. There were the inevitable jokes from the sidelines about putting it on a tartan rug and watching it die of heart failure, which did not go down at all well with its small owner, who wavered on the edge of tears until Rachel spoke reassuringly to her.

Among such a heterogeneous collection of creatures, Paris himself would have made a poor choice but Rachel, remembering some of her own childhood's disappointments, had armed herself with all manner of unofficial prizes, with which to mollify those who did not achieve an official one. She divided the entries into groups, which at least made comparison easier to begin with. Then she picked the best in each group: not only best in itself, but in the care which had been devoted to it. Those who did not quite qualify, she gave a small prize, a few words of encouragement, and steered them back to their waiting families.

The rain was increasing outside. It rattled against the canvas, and a rising wind plucked at the walls of the marquee. It became very crowded as more people came in, ostensibly to watch the judging, more likely to get out of the wet. The smell of damp hair and mackintoshes filled the air. The children were growing fidgetty and Rachel knew she must make a decision soon. There were five rosettes, and finally she had five candidates. All that remained was to choose the order. Monty was one of the five with his owner, a small, unsmiling child, a girl of about ten. Rachel remembered she was called Marcia. Tommy Harper had not brought his ferret this time, rather to Rachel's disappointment. She had been secretly eager to show him that not all women were stupid when it came to ferrets. He had, however, brought a beautiful rosetted guinea-pig, tortoiseshell in colour and magnificent in size and condition. Rachel felt very drawn to that as a possible prize-winner.

A child she did not know, a Thelma Roberts, had a splendid grey cat draped about her neck like a fur wrap, and there was another feline, a charming fluffy black kitten, which had captivated all the non-partisan elements in the audience. Last of the five was Mark Ellis's old donkey. Mark was Harry Ellis's great-grandson, a real chip-off-the-old-block, and his donkey was turned out with such spit and polish she might have been a White City winner. She was groomed till her pepper-coloured coat had no hair out of place: her sparse mane had been washed and threaded with ribbons, and her ridiculous tail was decorated too. Her trim hoofs had been polished with blacking oil, and her head-collar was all gleaming leather and polished brass. Old though she was, the donkey's eyes were bright, and her huge ears turned, receptive as Jodrell Bank, to catch the sounds of everything round about. Mark, too, was polished and brushed, in breeches and jacket that looked as though they had seen a great deal of wear—perhaps they had once been Harry's—and the child's face was tense with a sort of terrible pride and anxiety all at once. Rachel looked at them both and was lost. Where else could she place the red ribbon but on that moke's great hairy forehead? So Flower, the donkey, got first prize, the guinea-pig second, the kitten—to great applause—third, the grey cat fourth and Monty fifth. Marcia did not smile even on receipt of her rosette, and Rachel hoped she was not disappointed.

'Well judged,' said a voice as Rachel turned to leave the ring, and there was Alan Parker again, inviting the audience to join him in applauding her. They obliged politely, although the fun was now over. After all no-one wanted to hurry away into the rain, and any excuse to stay in the dry was worth making the most of.

Outside the whole sky was now obstinately slate grey, with rain slanting from it, steady and cold. A few hardy spectators huddled under umbrellas, at which competitors' horses snorted and spooked as they trotted squelchily past, spattering everyone with sparks of mud. In the gymkhana ring the children galloped about regardless of the weather, while their mothers gloomily forecast colds and bronchitis, and sighed at the thought of so much mud to wash off, and all that filthy tack in the kitchen.

Those who had finished all they had come to do packed up and went home as soon as they could, to the sound of churning engines and wheels slithering on the mud, desperate for a grip, making more of a quagmire with every effort to get out. The tractor drivers came out of the beer tent, looked out their tow-ropes and awaited the grateful tips of those they rescued. The stalls came down and stall-holders stowed away their soggy canvas and their unsold goods. Trade had not been brisk, not since the rain began. By half past five, unusually early, the ground was almost deserted. The last of the jumping was cancell-ed, for the ring was awash, and a horse had

had a bad fall. Rachel felt sorry for the organisers, who must be grieving for their lost profits but still, there was always next year.

In the gateway, as she walked through on her way home, Rachel passed Mandy Partridge, perched high on one of the ponies from the Riding Centre. Mandy was soaked, from her hat to her boots, into which water steadily trickled from her sodden jodhpurs. The pony, too, was soaked, his mane plastered to his neck, his tail dripping. From his bridle hung the trophies of the day. Three soggy rosettes, already peeling away from their backing, drooped like storm-tossed flowers from the brow-band.'

'Hello, miss,' Mandy called out. 'I've had a smashing time.'

'I can see you have,' Rachel grinned. 'Congratulations.' She set off to walk home: it was no distance at all from the showground. But then a car drew up alongside, tooting urgently. It was Bill Fowler.

'It's all right, Bill. I can walk,' she said.

'I came to get you,' Bill replied, leaning across and pushing the passenger door open. 'Honey's foaling, and we're taking no chances. We want you there.'

He drove her to Stapleton House. She changed rapidly and collected everything she

might need to take out to his car. She held no
evening surgery on a Saturday, and Mrs Partridge would phone through any urgent calls.
She wondered how she would manage without
Mrs Partridge to lean on: it was to be hoped
her new employer would appreciate her.

Since Malcolm's death Mrs Partridge had
been so subdued that Rachel had not pressed
her to speak about the future: had not felt
disposed herself to dwell much on a time when
there would be no thin, bustling figure to make
delicious meals for her, to know to within a
minute when she would fancy a cup-of-some-
thing, to have a good fire going after surgery
on a winter's evening, or a chair set out ready
in the garden on a fine summer one. She had
been more than a provider of such services,
however: more than what some might consider
a luxury in a do-it-yourself world. She had
been a good friend to Rachel, and had provided a useful and necessary eye on Milchester's inner world: was a mine of information on the comings and goings of the town,
and knew most of what there was to know
about the owners of Rachel's patients. Colin
Ross had been right: knowing the quirks, and
the virtues, of the owner can be of the greatest
value in achieving the best possible care of
your patients. Taught by Mrs Partridge,

Rachel now knew most of the customers very well indeed.

Some days before the show, Rachel had been surprised to hear cheerful singing coming from the kitchen, and on looking in she had seen the familiar personage, or to be precise, her behind, protruding from the corner cupboard, which seemed to be attracting some very vigorous attention.

'You sound cheerful today,' Rachel had remarked. Mrs Partridge backed out of the cupboard and looked up, smiling.

'I've been offered a new job,' she announced. Rachel was very relieved and yet, at the instant of feeling so, sad that the end of their pleasant relationship was now certain.

'I shall miss you,' Rachel said.

'You don't need to fret. I shan't go till you're good and ready,' Mrs Partridge beamed, wiping dust from her face with the side of her forearm. 'But once you've gone I wouldn't want to stay in this 'ouse, so when I got this offer I was pleased as a dog with two tails. Other side of Milchester it is. Professional gentleman. Suit me down to the ground, it will.'

Certainly she looked more than pleased. She positively twinkled at Rachel as she scrambled to her feet and shut the cupboard door with a slam.

'I'm very glad for you,' Rachel said.

'That's all right then. I'll 'ope to see you as well settled. That's what I 'ope. Put the kettle on now, shall I?' And she stumped over to the sink, still humming to herself.

On this later afternoon of the show day when Rachel had appeared in haste to collect her equipment to go to the Fowlers, Mrs Partridge seemed agitated that she was in so much of a hurry.

'There's something been left for you. A parcel.'

'I can't wait now,' Rachel told her. 'I'll look at it when I come back. You've got the number, if anything really desperate crops up?'

'Yes, I know, Milchester 853.'

And Rachel had got back into Bill's car and been whisked off up the road in the direction of Honey and the expected foal.

In the deep straw of the box the mare was pacing, pacing and from time to time glancing surprisedly at her own flanks, puzzled by the discomfort that came and went and grew stronger at each coming. Anne was standing by the door, watching her. Rachel smiled a greeting and went in to check that all was well with Honey: then she emerged and asked for a cup of tea.

'What, now?' Anne Fowler said, in a tone of voice suggesting that Rachel proposed to leave a death-bed in order to whoop it up at an orgy.

'Yes, now,' Rachel laughed. 'With you peering at her like that, she won't get on with the job. Mares are shy creatures, and their instinct is to foal in secret, away from predators and other mares that might be jealous. I'm all for letting them foal out in the fields, in principle, but it makes it easier for us if she's in, and your paddocks aren't ideal as maternity wards.'

'Bill's working at it,' Anne said defensively. 'He's pulled out all the wire in the orchard and he's making a timber fence: it's only old wood, but it doesn't look bad.'

'Well then, Honey had better get on with producing a foal for you to put in it, hadn't she?'

They drank their tea in the kitchen, and Bill joined them, fidgeting nervously with his cup, and dropping every item he picked up, until Anne snapped at him to go away.

'For Heaven's sake, you two,' said Rachel, exasperated. 'Come out into the yard, and we'll look very quietly to see what's going on.'

Tactfully they glanced in, through the gap at the hinge-end of the open top door. There was sweat on Honey's neck and shoulders now,

354

and she stood with lowered head, concentrating hard upon her own problem that the prying humans were no longer of any interest or concern to her. Strong, grasping muscles were expelling this inner thing from her, pushing it towards the light. She sensed that relief would come when this was completed.

'I think we can go in now,' said Rachel. She did not usually encourage onlookers at a foaling, but these two had worked so hard and waited so patiently. 'You must be very still and quiet,' she added, and they crept in and sat like chidden children in the corner. After a few more minutes the mare folded at the knees and went down into the straw with a grunting, sighing sound. Contractions came more rapidly. Honey strained hard now, and raised her tail. Those fierce muscles brought two small hoofs into view, quite clearly visible inside the sac, the one slightly in advance of the other. The mare took a breath, and they retreated into the darkness, but only momentarily. At the next spasm the foal began to enter its new element, slowly, like a tentative swimmer, and then with a fluid rush, the whole creature slid on to the straw with only the hindmost parts of its legs still within its mother. Amazing, moving, it weaved about inside what looked more or less like a plastic bag. Rachel knelt and pulled away this clinging stuff from its nostrils, and it sneezed. It was a sound so ridiculous, so alive, from something that had existed for so long only inside the body of another. Here it was, a new creature, and instantly able to breathe, to sneeze, to raise its head and look at the world. Now it was free of the mare, except for the chord, and Rachel looked it over.

'It's a filly,' she said.

The Fowlers said nothing at all. Neither of them could find time to go on a search for words. They just stared at the foal and grinned like delighted idiots.

After a few minutes Honey moved to inspect this result of her labours, breaking the chord, making a final separation of their two physical selves, but at the moment of breaking, instinct reattached her to this small creature. She stretched her head towards it and began to clean the damp furry hide with her tongue.

Out in the yard, a bell rang.

'Phone,' said Bill. 'I'll get it.'

When he had left the stable, Anne stretched out her hand to the new foal, glancing first at Rachel, then at Honey, as if to make sure they both approved of this action. She could feel all the foal's young bones under the skin, the first beginnings of muscle.

'She's going to be dun, like her mother,' Anne said. 'You can see the golden colour, under all the dampness. She's a skinny looking bundle, isn't she, when you think what a bulge she made inside the mare?'

'She'll lose that crumpled look,' Rachel said, 'when she's had a feed. Food and warmth are what she needs now. Honey's dripping milk, so you'll have no problems, I'm sure. And make sure the foal gets rid of the meconium: it's a characteristic, black, sticky motion. I'll just wait on until she's suckled, and then I'll leave you to it and come again first thing.'

But Bill came in then to say she had been sent for to Platt's Farm.

'What's the trouble?' Rachel asked.

'One of his ewes. Prolapse. A bad one, he says.'

'That means he's tried half a dozen times to put the old girl back together with dirty hands and that disgusting old needle and thread he uses,' Rachel said. 'He doesn't deserve to thrive, but the devil looks after his own.'

She glanced round the box at Honey and the foal and the two Fowlers, both still looking as pleased as if the little creature were their own flesh and blood. She gave instructions, knowing they would be followed devotedly.

357

It was a scene to delight a vet's heart. Now she must leave it and go to rescue Sam Platt from the results of his own fecklessness and stupidity. It was a seedy decrepit farm, worked with alternate apathy and greedy industry, yet somehow Sam made a living out of it, and Rachel could never help but be irritated by the fact. Then she recalled the Fowlers had been scarcely any better when she first came across them, except that their efforts had been more honest and less successful. Still, look at them now. Sometimes you really could feel it was all worth while.

It was several hours before she was able to return to Stapleton House. Having put back the ewe's uterus in its proper place, making a thorough and pointedly hygienic job of it, under the nose of Sam Platt to whom she had given the task of holding the sheep up-ended while she accomplished this, she had then been found all sorts of other minor ills to look at 'while you're here'. He was hoping of course, that she would forget to set down on his bill some of these 'while your here' jobs, but she knew him well enough now, and kept strict mental count of every sheep over which she cast her eye. He had grumbled bitterly about his last bill. 'You wants paying for passing the time o' day with my ship,' he had accused, but he still went on trying to get free advice for all that.

She was glad when at last she could escape from the smelly kitchen in which he allowed her to wash her hands, snarled at as she did so by his thin, suspicious collie. She drove out of his yard and into the late evening air, and once well away from Platt's Farm she opened her window to smell the soaked earth of the roadside verges as she drove. It was a prosperous, near to harvest, smell, enriched by the day's rain, though the clouds were all swept away by now and the atmosphere velvety and warm.

She wondered if Tom were back from Birmingham. She'd ring in the morning. Tell him about the foal. As she came nearer home she wondered idly what they would call it. 'Paradise, perhaps,' Rachel laughed to herself. 'For she on Honeydew bath fed, and drunk the milk of Paradise.' No, that was altogether too fanciful. A good horse doesn't need a fancy name. Pleasantly occupied in pursuing possibilities, savouring them, and eventually rejecting them, she arrived home still searching. It was pointless anyway. It was up to Anne Fowler what the filly was called. She'd been given the job of naming it. Rachel climbed wearily out of the car, and walked the last few yards to the door of Stapleton House. It had been a long day, and she was hungry, and her body ached. Bath, supper and bed, and she could face tomorrow.

There was a folded piece of paper on the doormat. The words 'VERY URGENT' were scrawled across it.

CHAPTER 17

It was Bill Fowler's handwriting. 'Please come at once. Foal not well.'

Rachel went to the phone to let them know she was home, to ask what was wrong, to say that of course she would come, but as she stretched her hand to it, it rang out suddenly, startling her, making her heart thump.

'Rachel? It's Tom. I've just had the Fowlers on the telephone. They couldn't get hold of you and rang to ask if I'd come and look at their foal. I told them they should try to find you, but they sounded pretty desperate. Look, I was in the bath when they rang, and now you're back you'll want to sort them out for yourself, but I'll come too if you like. You've had a long day, from what I hear.'

There was a pause. Rachel was gathering her wits: already trying to line up in her mind all the possibilities : all the unforseen disasters that might have struck a foal that had seemed to have such a good grasp on life. These thoughts took only a moment, but Tom was already urging her to answer. Yes she would like him to come. She was tired, her wits were weary, and she felt afraid of what she would find, afraid she could not cope. 'I'll go at once,' she said. 'I'd be glad of your help, though.'

'I thought you'd never ask,' he said. 'See you later.' As she drove, she tried once more to envisage what might have happened. The first hours of a foal's life were a tremendous strain on its system as it adjusted from the inner existence of the womb to the demanding environment into which it was so precipitately thrust. It could be oxygen-starved during the process of birth, or have its frail bones crushed by its mother's contractions. The sudden cold of the outer world after its warm, foetal existence, the effort needed to move muscles of which few demands have yet been made, all these things must tax its newborn strength: yet this one had seemed quite remarkable in its vigorous bright-eyed approach to the world. Now what would she see? Convulsions, perhaps, or the aimless wandering of the 'silly' foal, who can neither suckle, nor recognise its own mother? If so, then she must help it, in its struggle to adapt to life, or it would die, no doubt about it.

Anne Fowler was in the stable, sitting in the straw with the foal's head cradled in her lap, while Bill attended the mare, who was looking anxiously at her offspring and whinneying softly.

'She was fine,' Anne Fowler said, and her voice was tight in her throat, she was so near to tears. 'She pranced about in the straw on her long legs, happy as a lark and quite unafraid of us. She was so strong, so perfect. Now look at her.' The little filly looked tired to death. Her breathing was rapid. Now and again she yawned for a deeper breath and shuddered with its exhalation.

'Did she suckle?' Rachel asked.

'Oh yes, for several minutes. Honey was so good about it: pushed her along with her nose until she found the right place.'

'And she suckled strongly?'

'Yes: just like the lambs do: wagging that silly little tail. You could see it going down her and, as you'd said, she really seemed to fill out by magic. We watched her for a while and then went indoors for a bite to eat.'

'I made her go in,' Bill interrupted. 'She's had nothing for hours.' They both looked downcast, as if this had been the whole cause of the matter.

'Then we came back,' Anne said, 'and found her straddled in a corner with her head drooped, as if she were desperate to lie down and had forgotten how to, and dog-tired, as she is now.'

There was no doubt the foal was very ill indeed. There was a long, still moment, in which Rachel's brain seemed made of wood. She knew several things that were not wrong with the poor creature, but at a time when diagnosis must be swift to be of any use, she could come up with nothing positive. A dismal sense of failure and helplessness pressed down on her. Soon they would ask her outright what was wrong, and she was going to have to say 'I don't know.' She prolonged her examination, and hoped for a miracle, a revelation, but she would have settled for even the smallest clue. There was the sound of an engine in the yard, of a car door slamming. In came Tom, and she could have cried with relief to have someone with whom she might justifiably share this burden. Perhaps she should be ashamed to feel so, but there was no denying it.

Tom spoke briefly to the Fowlers, and he must have sent them off on some errand, for they had vanished when Rachel looked up, without her having been aware of their departure.

'The filly's bad, Tom,' she said. 'I've never seen anything quite like it.'

He bent to look at the foal, asking her the questions she had already asked the Fowlers, and at each reply he nodded, as if ticking each fact off on a list. His examination was thorough. In completing it, he peered into the foal's mouth and the corners of her eyes.

It seemed a thousand years to Rachel before he spoke.

'No sign there yet, but I think she's haemolytic, all the same, don't you?' he said.

You rotten, marvellous fellow, Rachel thought to herself, you know darned well I had no idea at all what was wrong, and here you are, giving me a share in your diagnosis, to save my stupid pride.

'Jaundice,' she said. 'She's not showing yellow, though.'

'She will, or I'm a Dutchman. The white of these eyes will be canary coloured before long if she goes on like this. I've never seen a jaundiced foal: it doesn't happen often, thank God, but we're right. I'm sure of it.'

Now she knew what it was, she knew what they must do. They must take a blood sample, analyse it and see how bad the foal was. She did this at once. As Rachel drew away the syringe, Anne Fowler came back. Rachel looked at Tom, but he turned away, leaving her the explanation.

'The foal has jaundice,' Rachel said. 'The red cells in her blood are being attacked and destroyed.'

'Oh God,' Anne exlaimed. 'How has it happened? Will it kill her?'

'It's rather the same as the rhesus factor in babies,' said Rachel. 'The parents' blood groups are incompatible, and the mother develops antibodies that attack the red cells in the alien blood. Babies are affected in the womb, but it isn't quite the same with foals and it's much rarer. A mare might get away with carrying a foal with an incompatible blood-group and the foal might suffer no ill effects at all, but sometimes a few foal-cells leak through the placenta, stimulate the mare into producing antibodies and these are then stored in the first milk, the colostrum, pass through the foal's gut and attack the blood.'

Rachel glanced at Anne, and at Bill who had come back to join her, to see if this was making sense to them.

'Yes, yes,' said Bill. 'We see all that. So she was quite safe until she suckled?'

That was true. It was ironic, Rachel thought, that the first necessary, protective meal, the first in a new life intended to give the foal all its mother's immunities, should be what was killing this poor little filly; and kill her it would if they did not act at once. 'What do we do? Can we do anything?' Anne Fowler sounded as desperate as Rachel had felt as she fumbled for a diagnosis so few minutes ago, but Rachel's miseries were now swallowed up by a determination to save the foal, no matter what the effort.

'I've taken some blood for testing. Meanwhile she must have no more milk from her mother, I'll give antibiotics as a safeguard and Bill can go to see if Harry Ellis can find us a supply of mare's milk.'

'What about poor Honey? She's bursting,' Anne asked.

'Hand milk her. It'll make a treat for your pigs.'

'Shall we have to milk her every day? Wouldn't it be better to dry her off and find a foster mother?' Bill asked.

'Oh no, the mare's milk will be safe within thirty-six hours,' Rachel reassured them. 'After that the foal puts the barriers up, as it were, and the antibodies can't get in to attack the cells any more. What must concern us is the state of her blood at the moment. If too many red cells have been destroyed, it will mean a blood transfusion.'

'I'll take this sample home and come back with the results,' Tom said. 'Try not to worry. You spotted her quite quickly. You could easily have gone to bed thinking all was well, and by tomorrow she would have been in a very bad way indeed.'

'She looks bad enough anyway,' Anne said, miserably, and went back again to her cradling of the foal. When Tom had gone they were all very quiet. The only sound was the rustling of straw and the occasional fretful whimper from Honey as she nosed at her foal, hoping it would rise and suckle her, relieving the fullness of her udder.

Bill left too, to try Ashton Stud for some mare's milk, so Rachel and Anne were left with the foal. All about them in the yard, small creatures slept. Hens huddled into their feathers, calves dozed with drooping ears. Out in her enclosure the sow lay in a great heap and snored in her piggy dream. The mare's box was a cave of wakeful light: as if the light from the Tilley lamp and the careful watching would keep the foal alive. She seemed, perhaps, to breathe a little more quietly, but whenever she slept they were on tenterhooks that she might not waken again. They spoke little, because the watching did not call for speech, but they looked at one another now and again, each hoping the other seemed hopeful. The time went slowly by, measured by the foal's rapid breathing and the anxious pulses of the two women. Every sound called them to attention, and their ears were alert for the noise of a car approaching. Each minute might be the one to bring news, good or bad: the moment they would look back on afterwards as the turning point, the pivot on which the whole night's happenings swung. At last they heard the noise they had promised themselves for what seemed so long.

Tom, who had the shorter journey, was first to return. They could scarcely wait for him to come in, to give them their answer.

'I think we'll get away with it,' he said. 'The damage is not too great. I've brought a muzzle to put on her so that she can't suckle from her mother, and we'll get some safe milk into her as soon as possible. If she goes downhill, then I've some blood available for her, but maybe we shan't need it. Bill's just come back by the way. I saw his lights as I turned the car. I hope he's been successful.'

Bill arrived then, bringing the milk, which he had put in a bottle with a calf-teat and stood to warm in a pan of water.

'All done according to Spock,' he said, trying to be cheerful.

The foal took little interest at first. She still felt too tired to bother much about what went on around her. But slowly, drop by drop, they persuaded the milk into her: not much, but enough to give her a little energy.

'No need to muzzle her until she's more mobile,' Tom said. 'Until she can stand she can't get at her mother's udder. We'll put it on later: it will save her worrying about it until it's necessary.'

Rachel saw that Anne was swaying as she bent over the foal. 'Take her to bed, Bill. She's worn out. We'll watch here.'

She had not meant to say 'we'; had not meant to assume that Tom would stay, even after he had done so much already, but the word was out now, and he made no comment.

'Are you sure?' Bill asked.

'Yes. Be off with you. If there's anything to report, I'll wake you. I promise.'

When they had gone, Tom said, 'If you do this sort of thing for all your patients, you'll be in your grave in a few years, do you know that?'

'I know. But this one's special,' Rachel answered, looking at the foal, who had made a poor attempt at getting up, failed and thought better of it. She went and took up Anne's position with the filly's head cradled in her lap.

Tom sat on a straw-bale nearby, and together they watched the foal. The night moved on slowly round them as they remained quietly in the sphere of light from the Tilley lamp. There was little to do now but watch. The life in the little filly seemed more vigorous, but it must be given no chance to flag again. The mare shifted her weight from leg to leg, rustling the straw. Her head and neck were low, her ears at a backward angle. Every line of her showed she was still weary after labour, yet she would not lie down, but kept a wary watch out of the corner of her eye at this new life that she had produced and that caused so much high drama in so short a time. She felt that these two in the stable with them threatened no real danger, though their strange actions from time to time had set her maternal alarms clanging, and she would not trust them entirely. Tom spoke softly to her, reassuring and eventually she allowed her eyes to close and dozed, standing, her senses so close to waking that the least thing out of the ordinary would arouse her again. Her ancient instinct kept her on her feet, though she had no endless plains, no vast herd of companions, nowhere to run from her fears, no one to share them but these curious human creatures.

'Are you cold?' Tom asked Rachel.

'A little.'

He moved closer, so that she could feel the warmth of him.

'Thanks.'

'Anytime. It keeps me warm too.'

'I meant, thanks for helping me with the foal.'

'You would have managed. I was only another pair of hands.'

'No.' Rachel fell silent, stared at her feet and then at her own hands clasped about the foal. She unclasped them and reached across to him.

'You were more than that,' she said.

Tom got up and began to check the foal. He was very thorough, and it was several moments before he was satisfied.

'I'm setting up my own practice,' he said, over his shoulder. 'Did I tell you?'

'No, you didn't.' It was cold suddenly in the stable, without his warmth beside her, and she shivered, drawing her jacket close around her.

'I'm buying a house, the far side of Milchester, near the Stroud road. It's not a bad house: nothing much to look at, but solid and with excellent rooms for a surgery and so on.'

'In Milchester,' she repeated.

'Yes. Had you thought of staying in Milchester?'

'Well, I...'

Tom turned from the foal and moved towards her. Something in his voice made her own trail into silence, with her mouth still

372

forming the 'I'.

'A brass plate,' Tom was saying. 'A good big brass plate for the gatepost, don't you think? "Rachel Adams MRCVS" engraved on it, and Thomas Adams, ditto, underneath. Strictly alphabetical order, you notice. How does that seem to you?'

Her mouth remained open. Gently, he closed it for her.

'Well?' he asked.

'You are an idiot,' she said. 'You are a beloved idiot.' She looked at him across the recumbent shape of the foal, glad he was sharing this battle, thankful he had come when he did. He was waiting for her answer, his expression very different from the light tone of his voice. She was aware of a terrible power to hurt him now, if she wished it. But she did not wish it. 'Yes to your brass plate,' she said, and put her hands out towards him.

'And yes to me?' he said, catching and holding them.

'And yes to you.' Her voice was low, but he heard the words and his face lit.

A short time later he said, 'I have a confession to make.'

'So soon?'

'I proposed to Mrs Partridge as well. Not marriage, of course: strictly housekeeping.' He looked a little sheepish.

'The wretched woman,' Rachel laughed. 'So that's why she was so smug about her new job. What would you have done if I'd said no: married Mrs P?'

'She'd have more sense than to have me.'

Outside the stable window the stars were fading in a summer velvet sky. The house beyond the stable-yard was lightless and still. Soon it would be daybreak, dewfall, dawn chorus and all the other beginnings of a summer day, with night creatures turning for home, cattle ambling in to be milked, farmhouse kitchens coming awake, dogs thrown out to air, the first bruising footsteps across the shimmering grass.

The two sat close together and kept their watch. After a while Tom smiled to himself and said, 'Now that we are so respectably engaged, I suppose we might have thrown etiquette to the wind and spent the rest of the night in glorious sin, but you know of course what would have happened?'

'What?' asked Rachel.

'Why, the telephone would have rung in the house, and out would have come one of the Fowlers to summon us to it.' He picked up an imaginary telephone and held it to his ear.

'Is that you then, General Billington-Smythe?' he enquired. 'You have three hundred and seventy-five Ayrshire heifers down with the galloping lergy you say? Have no fear, I shall come at once and bring my new partner with me. What's that, General? Oh yes: very well qualified indeed. I'd say she's the best there is.'

'Fool. I love you,' said Rachel, laughing. Somehow it seemed safe to laugh now. Their voices had roused Honey from her sleep, and she stretched herself and took a mouthful of hay. The foal stirred, and she turned towards it, calling in a soft, maternal chuckle. Rachel and Tom watched, as the little filly raised her head. Rachel moved her arms to help. 'No,' said Tom. 'Let her try it alone first.' Slowly, slowly, the foal gathered her strength, brought up her big-kneed, spindly forelegs under her chin to make the effort to rise. They watched, their breath pent in them, as she rose, tottered and sat again on her haunches. Then, after only a short rest, she set herself again to over-come the problem of her unruly legs. This time—Rachel thought—this time I really think she'll do it. The foal was suspended over all four limbs, now swaying like some strange piece of space machinery, but her joints were supporting her, and this time indeed, she did not fall.

Outside in the yard, a pale light began to show the outlines of roof and wall. Somewhere in a far corner of the orchard, the first bird of the day found a voice.

With only an hour's sleep between the long night and the morning's surgery Rachel felt as though she walked in concrete boots in a vast room full of echoes. Everything she did was done with huge effort, like moving in an atmosphere of a different planet. She could spare no energy to think of the incidents of the previous day, to remember its despairs and elations, and the commitment of herself that she made to Tom. She wanted to savour her happiness but her mind was tired and resolutely sombre.

Then, when she pressed the buzzer for the last patient, in came Miss Pringle, with Simba. Today the plaster on his leg was due to be removed and they would see, at last, to what extent he had mended.

Concentrating on this, Rachel began to feel more herself again: the desire to drift back to sleep began to fade. This was important; for Simba, of course, for Miss Pringle, whose good friend he was—perhaps the first good friend in her whole long life—and for Rachel, who wanted her skill to have justified itself. She wanted to have made a good job of this one. Please God.

The plaster came away. Miss Pringle was holding her breath, and her long fingers were clutched tight around Simba's lead. 'Well,' she said, as Rachel began her examination. The word came out like a sigh, barely audible.

The leg was clean. The little dog could bear his weight on it. The bones had knitted.

'It's fine,' Rachel said. Simba, pleased to be free from the encumbering plaster, gave a sharp bark. 'Thank you, Miss Bellamy. I can't tell you how grateful I am,' said Miss Pringle.

She continued to look at Rachel, as if there was something further to be said. On her face was the smallest shadow of anxiety. Rachel waited encouragingly for any questions she might have. There was a lengthy pause.

'Miss Bellamy,' said Miss Pringle at last, hesitating, her old shy self again for a moment. 'Miss Bellamy, in your professional opinion, could a dog and a cat learn—if they have had no previous experience, I mean—could they learn do you think, to live happily together?'

Rachel was aware this was important. She spoke carefully, giving consideration to her reply. 'Given time and patience, I'm sure they could,' she said. 'Animals are very adaptable, you know.'

Miss Pringle picked Simba up from the table, smiling. Her nice plain face went deepest pink and blossomed like a rose.